GILBERT MORRIS
AND BOBBY FUNDERBURK

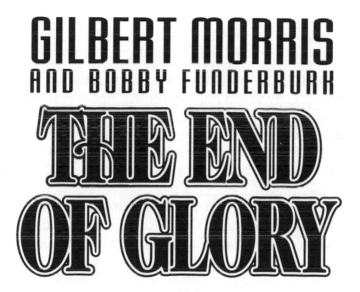

THE END OF GLORY

WORD PUBLISHING
Dallas•London•Vancouver•Melbourne

Library of Congress Cataloging-in-Publication Data

Morris, Gilbert.
    The end of glory / Gilbert Morris and Bobby Funderburk.
        p.   cm. — (The Price of liberty series : #4)
    ISBN 0–8499–3825–2
    I. Funderburk, Bobby, 1942– . II. Title. III. Series: Morris, Gilbert. Price of Liberty ; 4.
    PS3563.08742E5   1993
    813'.54—dc20   93–24236
                                                              CIP

Printed in the United States of America

3 4 5 6 7 8 9 LB 9 8 7 6 5 4 3 2 1

To Mike, Linda, Shawn, and Kelli

CONTENTS

Part 1

LEAH

1

NEW GIRL AT LIBERTY HIGH

*T*he paths through the schoolyard had healed over the summer months. When the doors had closed in May, the spring rains had brought forth a startling emerald color, and the hard-packed dirt paths that the feet of students had cut into the carpet-like turf had slowly closed.

All summer long the yard had been desolate, visited only by wandering bands of restless youngsters. The equipment for the younger children appeared lonely—the swings hanging motionless in the sweltering, breathless heat, and the seesaws pointing toward the sky.

All this changed on September 8, the first day of the new school year in 1938. By seven o'clock the sere blades of grass were being pounded flat by the screaming hordes destined for the elementary school. The chains of the swings clacked loudly, and the seesaws pounded the dirt, sending puffs of dust into the air. A large black-and-white dog fled from behind the trash cans, shocked out of his peaceful retirement by the shrill yelps of small boys rousting him out. He bared his fangs in a halfhearted way, but when this failed to deter the yelling Apache-like boys, he tucked his tail between his legs and left the scene.

All this took place around the one-story building dominating the southwest area of the grounds and set off by a chain-link fence from the three-story red-brick building that was the junior high and high school. The woven-steel fence served as a sort of social barrier for the young people of Liberty, a demarcation line stronger than the steel itself. Those on one side were children, but when they crossed to the other area, it was a rite of passage marking their first step into the strange, mysterious, and frightening world of adult-hood.

Three fifteen-year-old boys stood watching the elementary children at play. The trio were posed on the threshold of another age, for they were sophomores. No longer in junior high school! One of them, a tall robust boy with thick blond hair, cast a contemptuous gaze on the small groups of junior highers and said, "Look at 'em, you guys!" He spat on the ground with disdain and shook his head. "Can't believe that just last year we were in junior high!"

One of his companions, Jack Clampett, a thin boy with a sallow complexion, looked toward the group and nodded. "Yeah, they look like babies, don't they, Keith?"

The third member of the group, Taylor Spain, was a good-looking boy with an acne problem. He leaned back against the red bricks of the wall, grinned, and said, "Well, we've moved up one floor, but we're a long way from being seniors." He nodded at a group of older youths, adding, "There's the big dogs—the seniors."

Keith Demerie gave Taylor a look of disgust. "They put their pants on one leg at a time, don't they? I ain't waitin' two years before I make a dent in this place."

Jack nodded—as he usually did whenever Keith made a pronouncement. Keith was the son of Tyson Demerie, a state senator and a power in the state, while Jack's father, Ring Clampett, was the night marshal of Liberty. "Me neither, Keith," he nodded. He spat as Keith had done, but the spittle didn't clear his lips; instead it dribbled down onto his chin.

"Better get your mama to wipe your face before you take over, Jack," Taylor laughed. "You won't impress anybody dribbling like an idiot."

Keith joined in with Spain, then said, "Let's go down and take a look at what comes in on the country buses. Might be some stuff in the way of good old country girls."

Jack wiped his face with his sleeve, then nodded with a lascivious grin. "Hey, them country girls are pretty hot cookies."

"How would you know?" Keith scoffed. "You struck out with Lily Marr—first time that ever happened with her." He led the way to the parking lot where several yellow buses were unloading their cargo. The three boys stood loose-jointed as the students filed by, snickering and making crude comments on the girls.

Finally Taylor said, "Well, there's the last bus. I ain't seen nothing good yet." He grinned, adding, "Ol' Jack here, he'd run like a rabbit if a girl ever looked straight at him!"

Clampett scowled but scorned to answer. He studied the girls that filed by, then shook his head. "Nothing here! Looks like at least *one* of these country girls would be something a guy could go for!"

Keith shrugged his heavy shoulders and started to turn, but then he paused. His eyes narrowed as he watched a girl step off the bus, then his thick lips curved into a smile. "Hey, Jack," he said, "There's a chick that's about your speed."

Clampett was leaving, but when he turned and threw a quick glance at the girl, he frowned and answered sharply, "Aw, c'mon, Keith! She looks like an old woman!"

"Never judge a book by its cover, Jack," Demerie grinned. "I'll bet she's got a body under that ugly dress that'd make your eyes pop."

The girl was tall and slim. The hem of her gray dress came within six inches of the tops of her worn black shoes. The dress was ill-fitting and had seen long wear, and it managed to make even the girl's slim figure look awkward. She had an oval face, somewhat thin, and her best features were her gray-blue eyes, large and shaded by very heavy black lashes. They were beautiful eyes, but none of the boys could see them, because she dropped her gaze and moved nervously along the sidewalk after sweeping the school with one brief, frightened glance.

"Give her a thrill, Jack," Keith grinned. "She don't look like much, but you can bring her along—teach her a few things."

"Yeah, I can do that!" A lewd grin appeared on Clampett's thin lips, and he winked at his two friends. As the girl passed within a few feet of him, he stepped forward and grabbed her arm, saying, "Hey, Sweetie, I'm Jack Clampett. What's your name, Honey?"

The girl flinched, lifted her frightened eyes, and tried to pull away. "Please—" she whispered, "let me go!"

"Aw, come on, Honey, this is your lucky day. I'm gonna show you the ropes around here." Clampett's sallow face showed pleasure as the girl tried to break away. He glanced at Keith and Taylor, then said, "Come on over behind the stands. I'll let you have a puff or two on a Lucky Strike."

A sharp fist suddenly struck Clampett in the back, and a voice said, "Turn her loose, Jack!"

Startled, Clampett released the girl's arm and whirled to find a boy his own age and a girl somewhat younger standing with their eyes fixed on him. "Mind your own business!" he snarled. "And keep your hands off me, Rachel, you hear? If you wasn't a girl, I'd bust you."

Rachel Shaw was thirteen, two years younger than Clampett, and her hazel eyes were sharp with anger. "Tom's not a girl. You can fight it out with him, Jack."

Tom Shaw was fifteen and tall for his age. At his sister's words, he grinned and stepped closer to Clampett. "Yeah, let's see you hang on to my arm and take me behind the stands, Jack." Reaching out with a long arm, he pushed Clampett on the chest lightly. "Now, let's see you bust *me!*"

Jack swallowed hard, glancing toward his two friends and seeing that they weren't about to get involved. He scowled and muttered, "Better watch yourself, Shaw!" then walked stiff-legged back to where Keith and Taylor were standing. "C'mon," he said shortly.

"You sure showed Shaw not to mess with you," Taylor grinned. "He's so scared he won't sleep for a week."

"Aw, he's a big blow-hard," Jack shot back. He turned to see the Shaws walking along with the girl in the long dress. Clampett muttered, "I'll make that girl have a smoke with me; you'll see!"

"Bet you don't," Taylor remarked. "She's from the Farm. Don't none of them smoke or drink or do anything else."

Keith glanced back at the girl. "Yeah, that's right. That's the way they all dress. See some of 'em in town on Saturday sometimes. What kind of nuts are they, Taylor? They don't have cars— still drive wagons."

"It's a religious thing," Taylor shrugged. "My dad says they don't believe in modern things. Not even tractors. Farm all that land over by the river with mules and horses. Make their own clothes. Never been any of them in school because they don't believe in sending their kids to public schools. Afraid they'll be 'corrupted' my dad said."

Clampett said angrily, "Well, I'm just the one to do the corrupting!"

Keith laughed at the smaller boy. "Better do it when Tom

Shaw's not around, Jack." A thought came to him, and his brows raised. "Now if she was just a little better looking, I might just educate her myself."

"Better be careful, you two," Taylor warned. "Those people at the Farm might be backward about cars, but they've got guns. When I was out hunting squirrels with my brother last month, we ran into a couple of men from there. They were carrying rifles and their sacks were full." He blinked at the memory, then added, "They looked pretty rough, with those big beards. Better not fool with their women, Jack. You might wind up like one of those rabbits!"

As soon as the three boys walked away, Rachel Shaw turned to the girl and said, "Don't pay any attention to him. He's just a show-off." She smiled, then saw the frightened look in the girl's eyes. Quickly she added, "My name's Rachel Shaw and this is my brother Tom. You're new here, aren't you?"

"Yes." The girl spoke so faintly that the two scarcely heard her, and she dropped her eyes as they stared at her.

She's so nervous! Maybe I can help her, Rachel thought swiftly, then said brightly, "What's your name?"

"Leah Daniel."

"What grade you in?"

"The tenth."

"I'm just in the eighth!" Rachel said. "I'll bet you have lots of classes with my brother, Tom, though—" a loud buzzer sounded, and she glanced toward the red three-storied building. "There's the bell—we'd better get inside." Seeing the girl's helpless look, she smiled. "We'll go to the auditorium first, then we go to counselors and get our schedules. Come on, we'll sit together."

Leah nodded quickly, and her eyes showed relief. "Thank you, Rachel. I—I'm a little scared."

"Nothing to be scared of," Tom Shaw spoke up. "You'll be bored to death in this place, just like the rest of us."

"Don't pay any attention to him," Rachel sniffed. "You'll like it at Liberty. Come on—"

Leah walked quickly along, relieved that she didn't have to enter the big building alone. She had been inside only once, two weeks earlier, but there had been no students and almost no faculty. Her father had brought her to meet with Alvin Ditweiler, the principal. As she was jostled by the stream of students all crowding through the front doors, Leah remembered how frightened she'd been as she'd gone along the silent, dark halls to his office. Her father had been angry, and the memory of the meeting came to her sharply, especially the exchange between her father and Mr. Ditweiler . . .

"You understand," her father had said almost harshly, *"it's against my will to put Leah in public school."*

"I know you folks believe in educating your children at home," Principal Ditweiler had answered, *"but the law says that you can only do that with small children. You just don't have the background to teach high school subjects."*

"We have the ability to teach them to stay away from the Devil's ways!"

"Well, there's no point in discussing that, Mr. Daniel. You'll agree that you're not equipped to teach chemistry or foreign languages?"

"We don't hold with new-fangled inventions—and English is good enough for us."

"Well, that's as it may be, but the law says that Leah has to attend school here, so let's make the best of it . . .

As Leah moved down the hall, bewildered and frightened by the crowds and the noise, she longed to run away, to go back to the Farm where she'd spent her whole life. But she'd gone over that with her parents many times and knew there was no hope.

"There's some seats," Rachel said and led the way down the aisle. Leah followed her and stumbled over the feet of some students who were already seated. When Rachel stopped and plopped down, Leah looked down at the remaining seat with bewilderment. "There's no seat here," she said.

Rachel looked at the seat with surprise, then back up at her new friend. "Sure there is," she smiled. Reaching out she pulled the curved wooden seat down into place and laughed at the expression on Leah's face. "You've never seen seats like these before?"

"No," Rachel admitted, easing herself down carefully.

"They're like the seats in a picture show."

"I've never been to a picture show."

"Really?" Rachel stared at the girl, then shrugged. "Neither have I. But you and I are about the only ones here who haven't."

16

She cocked her head and inspected Leah carefully. "My pa's a Pentecostal preacher. We don't believe in picture shows."

"My folks don't either," Leah said quickly. A smile touched her lips for the first time, and she added, "I guess you and I have something in common."

"Are you Pentecostal?" Rachel asked.

"I—don't know," Leah confessed. "I don't even know what that is."

"Why, it's a church," Rachel answered. "Like Baptist or Methodist—except we don't believe in sinful things like picture shows or wearing makeup or jewelry or dancing."

Leah studied a thought, then shrugged. "We don't do those things at the Farm," she said. "Maybe I am Pentecostal." She had a sudden hope that she *was* Pentecostal so that she would be *like* someone at Liberty High. She'd been warned harshly by the Reverend Cletus Sandifer, the leader of the Farm, that all the students at Liberty were full of the Devil and would lead her astray if she didn't keep her guard up!

She wanted to ask more about being "Pentecostal" when a man stepped to the podium and held up his hand for quiet. Leah didn't see how he could talk loud enough for everyone to hear in such a large room, and she gave a start when he did speak—his voice boomed like thunder! She'd never heard a loudspeaker and was fascinated by it.

"All right—settle down!" The man waited until the loud talking settled to a tiny hum. "We'll all stand and pledge allegiance to the flag and sing the national anthem, and then Mr. Sloan, our superintendent, will lead us in a prayer."

Leah stood with the others—after figuring out how to lift the seat of her chair—but she didn't know any of the words to the song they sang. *I'll have to ask Rachel to teach me the words,* she thought. She felt relieved that there was someone she could ask questions without being ashamed, and she knew from the kind light in Rachel's eyes that she could trust her.

A tall, portly man with a balding head came to the front of the stage and said, "Let us pray." He prayed in a high-pitched, rather strange tone, and after he said "amen," he spoke differently. Leah was to learn that Superintendent T. P. Sloan considered his ordinary speaking voice too common to address the Almighty—though his praying voice was rather whiny and unpleasant.

"I'm sure you're all happy to be back in school—" he began, stopping and waiting for the groans that swept the room to die down. "And I'm certain that this will be the *finest* year that Liberty High School has ever known!" Another faint groan went around the room, and the girl sitting on Leah's left muttered, "That's what he said the *last* two years!"

Sloan seemed to never look at the students directly. He stared instead at a spot in the ceiling to Leah's left. She grew puzzled when his eyes remained fixed on that particular spot as he droned on about rules and schedules. Finally she swiveled her head to look. There was nothing there but the motes that swarmed in the bar of pale sunlight that fell through a high window. *He must be talking to those little specks of dust,* Leah mused. She was accustomed to the direct gaze of the Reverend Cletus Sandifer, whose eyes were black and as threatening as a brace of cocked pistols. Leah was rather relieved that Superintendent Sloan was much less threatening than the spiritual leader of the Farm, and she relaxed as she tried to keep his instructions straight.

When he finished, however, dismissing them to their counselors, she discovered with a start of fright that she hadn't the foggiest idea of what he had said.

Seeing her friend's confusion, Rachel said quickly, "He's a dreadful bore, isn't he? Nobody understands a word of what he says. All we have to do is go to our counselors and get our schedules. Let's see . . . Daniel? Mr. Gifford takes the A's through the F's. Come on, I'll take you to his room."

"I—I'd be lost if it weren't for you, Rachel!"

The younger girl smiled, and it struck Leah as a really nice smile. "Oh, in two days you'll know this place inside out, Leah. Come on."

The pair joined the jostling crowd leaving the auditorium. "All your teachers and classrooms are on the top floor," she informed Leah. "The junior high has the first two floors." Mounting a wide stairway, they dodged the other students, most of whom were talking, yelling, and laughing, until Rachel stopped in front of room 304. "This is Mr. Gifford's classroom." She hesitated, then said, "Tell you what, let me go in and introduce you." She saw the relief in Leah's eyes and knew that the girl was petrified with fright.

"He's a nice man," she said encouragingly. "Be glad you don't have an old dragon like I do for a counselor!"

Leah followed Rachel into the room and found a man standing at the window. He turned and smiled at the two, saying in a pleasant baritone voice, "My first customers of the day. Step right up."

"This is Leah Daniel, Mr. Gifford," Rachel said quickly, adding, "She lives at the Farm—and this is her first day in public school."

"Is that right?" Leslie Gifford responded. He was very thin and no more than medium height. His hair was very long, touching his ears and his shirt collar. But it was his eyes she liked most. They were the color of old pecan shells and dominated his face. It was not the peculiar color that encouraged Leah, but the kindness she saw there. "Well, now, that's fine," he said quickly. "Why don't you sit down and we'll make out a good schedule for you."

"I'll see you later, Leah," Rachel said and left the room quickly.

Gifford moved away from the window toward a table laid out with folders, and Leah was shocked to see that he was crippled. He dragged his right leg as he moved, and she saw that his left arm was smaller than his right. She saw that he noticed her stare, and her face grew red as she dropped her eyes.

But Gifford apparently was accustomed to this and said only as he sat down, "Now, you take that seat, and we'll see what we have."

Leah sat down and waited silently while Gifford selected a manila folder, took out a single sheet of paper, and studied it. She looked out the window, noted a flock of sparrows scuffling on the ground outside, then looked down at her hands.

"Well, this won't be too difficult," Gifford said. He looked up and asked, "You've never been to public school, Leah?"

"No, sir."

"Well, you must have had some fine teachers. Your basic scores in math and English are very high."

"It was only my mother and Mr. Dale," Leah said.

"Is Mr. Dale a teacher?"

"Oh, no, he's a carpenter."

"Well, he and your mother certainly did a fine job," Gifford smiled. "I wish my other students had scores as high. Now, let's see what we can do . . ."

Gifford spoke very quietly but went into great detail. He ignored the other children filing in and taking seats, giving his full attention to the girl with the enormous eyes. *Poor kid is scared out of her wits*, he thought. *She'll have a hard time in this place. These kids don't have much mercy on people who are different.* He looked down at his withered arm and his sensitive mouth tightened suddenly. But he quickly put his feelings away and said, "That's about it, Leah. We're on a half-day schedule today. Just go to the rooms I've listed when the bells ring."

"Thank you, Mr. Gifford."

He nodded, then leaned forward speaking in a confidential whisper. "Your last class is in here, my sophomore English class. We'll both be worn out by then, so we can take a break. Okay?"

Leah smiled and rose from her seat. His kindness had encouraged her, and she left the room with some degree of confidence. She had no idea what to do until the counseling was over, so for the next hour she kept to herself. Finally the bell rang and she went at once to room 324, where she managed to take a back seat while Mrs. Ora Peabody, the history teacher, spent the twenty minutes telling them how they would have to work hard to keep up with her class. She made an assignment after the bell rang, and Leah had to hurry to her next class.

As the morning wore on, Leah spoke to no one. Finally the next-to-last period ended, much to her relief. She went at once to room 304, where Gifford greeted her warmly. "Made it this far? Fine! Take that seat by the window, Leah. You'll probably like watching the birds better than diagramming sentences."

She took the seat at once, and the room began to fill up. Shock ran through her when Jack Clampett and the two boys who'd been with him came in. Clampett saw her instantly and, with a grin, took the seat behind her. She started when she felt his hand touch her back. Leah leaned as far forward as possible, but she could not escape his fingers running up and down her back.

"We've still got a date behind the stands, Sweetie!"

She said nothing and was relieved when Mr. Gifford came to stand in front of her desk. "Keep your hands to yourself, Jack," he said sharply. "If you can't handle that, I can see to it that you visit with the principal. He'll be able to teach you better manners."

Turning away from Clampett he began to welcome his students. Unlike Mrs. Peabody, he didn't threaten them with failure if they didn't come up to his standard. Instead, he read them a paragraph from Thoreau's *Walden*. It was about a sort of duck, a "loon," and Leah was fascinated by it.

Closing the book, Gifford said, "The man who wrote that has been dead a long time. But people all over the world are still enjoying his words."

Keith Demerie said, "Why? It's just about a duck, Mr. Gifford. I don't see nothing so great about that. Anybody can write about a duck!"

"You think so? Well, that'll be easy to prove." A light of humor touched Gifford's brown eyes. "Your first assignment is to write about a duck."

A groan went up from the class, and Taylor Spain whispered, "I wish you'd keep your mouth shut, Keith!"

Demerie would not back down. "Nothing hard about ducks." He suddenly caught Leah's eyes and demanded, "You people got ducks out at the Farm?"

Leah felt every eye on her and wished she could drop into a large hole. Finally, she whispered, "Yes, we have ducks."

"I'll bet you do," Keith grinned. "I'd like to come out and see what all you got out there. Be like going back to the Dark Ages!"

Gifford said sharply, "Keith, watch your mouth! We'll see just how enlightened you are when I read your paper to the class."

Demerie's face reddened, and he cast a baleful look toward the teacher, then toward Leah, but he said no more.

After the last bell rang, Leah got up slowly. She knew somehow that Demerie and Clampett would be waiting for her—and she was right. They were lurking just outside the door, both of them grinning. "Hey, what about we walk you to the bus, Leah?" Clampett grinned.

She shook her head and started down the hall, but the two at once put themselves on each side of her. Both of them took her arms and walked her down the hall and down the stairs. They kept up a running commentary on what a good time she could expect, but some of their remarks were beyond her.

When they stepped outside and started toward the bus, Leah tried to free herself but couldn't. Tears welled in her eyes, and

Clampett saw them. "Hey, don't cry, Sweetie—I'm gonna take care of you!"

But they were brought up short when Tom and Rachel Shaw appeared, both of them standing squarely in the middle of the sidewalk.

Demerie couldn't stand a challenge. He had been stung by Gifford's challenge and was ready for trouble. "Get out of the way, Shaw, or I'll stomp you!"

"Aw, he's a preacher's kid, Keith," Jack laughed. "He'll have to turn the other cheek if you whomp him!"

Tom shook his head. "Wouldn't count on it," he remarked. His eyes were bright, and he stood with his feet planted and his fists clenched.

Keith stared at him. Tom was taller but not as husky. Besides, there were two of them to handle him. "Get out of the road, Shaw," he said threateningly and loosened his grip on Leah to move forward. It gave him a thrill to think of pounding the preacher's kid— but he stopped when another boy came to stand with Shaw.

Ben Logan faced Demerie. "Little trouble here, Tom?" he asked, not taking his eyes off Keith.

"Nothing but a couple of guys who think they're tough because they can manhandle a girl."

Demerie's temper flared. "We'll just take care of you too, Logan!"

"Fly right at it," Ben said cheerfully. He was tall and wiry and hard as nails from working in the woods with his father. The idea of a fight didn't seem to trouble him, and from the gleam in his gray eyes, Keith and Jack considered that he just might welcome it.

Demerie was posed and ready for trouble, but Clampett was staring at the two in front of him. "Come on, Keith," he muttered nervously. "She ain't worth it."

When his friend walked away, Demerie blinked. The odds didn't look very good, so he said stiffly, "You two are gonna get hurt if you don't watch out!"

As Keith walked away with Jack, Tom said, "Too bad, Ben. I think we could have improved their looks."

Rachel said glowingly, "Ben, this is Leah Daniel."

Leah said, "I—I'm glad you came."

"Ben would have stomped them both!" Rachel said, her eyes worshiping Logan. "Wouldn't you, Ben?"

"We'll never know," he smiled. "We're going to the store to get an R.C. and a Moon Pie. Come along with us."

"I—I better get on the bus," Leah said. She turned to Rachel and noticed the younger girl's eyes fixed on Ben Logan. She wanted to say a great deal, but could only murmur, "Rachel, thanks—" and then ran to get on the bus.

Ben stared after her. "Sure does wear ugly clothes, doesn't she?"

"She's scared to death, Ben," Rachel said defensively. "You and Tom are going to have to keep those two from making her miserable."

Tom nodded. "Always a pleasure to whip a pair like that." Then he added, "Let's get that Moon Pie, Ben!"

2

MAGWICH

Mr. Chips greeted Leah as she left the house and started across the backyard to the henhouse. His sharp black eyes were almost hidden by his shaggy fur, and it was this expression that had led Leah to give him this name. She loved James Hilton's novel, *Goodbye Mr. Chips,* and the undersized, starving stray that appeared one day at the Farm reminded her of the aging Oxford professor. She had adopted him on the spot, dubbing him Mr. Chips, and had fought a determined battle against the advice of almost everyone to keep him.

Stopping to stroke his rough fur, she whispered, "I love you, Mr. Chips!" His rough tongue lapped at her hand, and she laughed quietly. "Come on, let's see if those old hens have done their duty."

A few pale stars gleamed, the last harbingers of the day, as Leah crossed the yard, but the dim glow in the east showed in a thin line across the low-lying hills. She entered the henhouse and moved down the line of wooden boxes, carefully reaching under the fat, fluffy hens who clucked with alarm. The eggs were warm, and she placed them carefully in the basket she had woven from white oak strips. The acrid but rich smell of the place made her nose burn, and she sneezed once in a staccato fashion. Mr. Chips looked up in alarm. *Wuff?* Then he sat down and panted while Leah finished collecting the eggs.

Leaving the henhouse, Leah took the eggs to the kitchen, washed them carefully, and placed them in the ice box. She looked under the box and muttered, "Oh, fuzz!" The pan that caught the water from the melted ice was full; she had forgotten to empty it. Dragging it out, she took it to the back porch, sloshing some on the floor, and threw the water out into the yard. Macbeth, the suckling pig, dashed up, hoping to find some bounty. Leah took a potato from a woven net hanging on the wall and tossed it to him. "There, you greedy thing," she said, then went back inside.

Her mother came in as Leah was mopping the spilled water. "If you'd empty that pan before it got full, you wouldn't have to mop it up, Leah." She began to pull the elements of breakfast together, asking, "Do you mind going to school in town so much, Leah?"

"Oh, no. It'll be all right, Mother."

Mabel Daniel cracked a number of eggs into an ancient white bowl. She was a small woman of forty, with brown hair and blue eyes. Traces of youthful beauty still remained, but years of hard work had drained her, and fatigue had drawn fine lines on her face. "I know you don't like it. Your father and Elder Sandifer did all they could to keep you from having to go." She stirred the eggs, then poured them into a skillet. "What's it like?" she asked as she turned the yellow eggs carefully with a wooden spoon.

Leah moved about the room, setting the table as she told her mother about her first day. She said nothing about Jack Clampett, for there was nothing her mother could do to help—or her father either, for that matter. She was an independent girl, having learned to handle her own problems. Typically, she spoke of the events of the day without giving her own emotional response. To have mentioned her fears would have been useless, so she kept a curtain over that part of her life. She knew that if tears had to be shed, the place for that was in her own bed in the darkness.

Albert Daniel came in and sat down as she was finishing. He was a tall, raw-boned man of forty-two, strong and slow moving, with light blue eyes and a scant crop of receding sandy hair. He wore dark blue pants and a chambray shirt, both faded by countless washings, and his eyes followed Leah as she moved around the kitchen. He worried about his children, wishing that he could live in a place where they could be kept away from the impurities of the world. He was not educated, but he was what southerners call "country smart," meaning that he had more than the usual supply of common sense.

A clatter on the steps leading up to the sleeping loft issued from the living area, and Leah's brother and sister came tumbling in—Bobby, age ten, and Esther, eight. They plopped down at the table, Bobby jabbering constantly, his red hair and freckles almost startling in color. He was a dreamer and in trouble most of the time for neglecting his chores. Esther's hair was a faded, sandy color that she hated. She was thin and often sickly, but she never complained.

When the food was cooked and on the table, Leah and her mother sat down. Albert bowed his head, glimpsing to be certain that the younger children did the same, then said, "Lord, we thank Thee for this food. Every good gift comes from Thee, and we are only servants." He hesitated, then added, "Be with Leah and keep her pure in mind and body. Shield her from the devices of Satan that would destroy her purity. In Jesus' name we pray—amen."

"What's 'devices of Satan,' Father?" Bobby asked, popping his mouth full of eggs after shooting the question at his father.

Accustomed to such queries from his inquisitive son, Albert said slowly, "Satan is in the world, son. He hates God and he hates the people of God. And he's smart. You know how we set traps, how we hide them? Well, Satan has his traps, and we have to be careful that we don't step into them."

Bobby swallowed a huge mouthful of eggs, biscuit, and bacon, then demanded, "What do they look like?"

"Sometimes they're right pretty," Albert said. He was a slow-thinking man, speaking with such hesitation that people often thought he was not very bright. This was not so, for he was simply careful—especially when something concerned his religion. He glanced toward Leah, then said, "The Book says that women are to have the ornament of a quiet spirit, but young women—and some who are old enough to know better—fall into the Devil's trap of fancy clothes and jewelry."

Bobby considered that, then asked, "Is that why Mother and Leah don't wear ear screws like the women in town?"

"Yes, that's right, son." Albert Daniel nodded with approval at the boy. "God hates pride, and when a woman gets to thinking of her looks and starts primping and wearing revealing clothes, the Devil has her."

"What happens to her?"

"Why, she goes to hell!"

Esther had been nibbling at her food, paying only slight attention to the conversation. Now, however, she looked at her father and nodded. "I'm never going to wear jewelry, Father. Hell is where people burn forever. That would hurt, so I'm not going there."

Albert Daniel had a soft spot for this child. He gave her a rare smile, reached across, and patted her hand. "Good for you, Esther," he nodded approval. He had a sudden thought and glanced at Leah. "I heard they had something called Physical Education at that school. What's it like, Daughter?"

Leah shrugged. "I think we play games. Yesterday we just went to the gym and the teacher said we'd be on teams—basketball and some other things—and do exercise."

Daniel moved his shoulders restlessly. "Don't see why they have to have that. You get enough exercise doing your chores."

"I guess those city children don't have to work so hard, Albert," Mabel Daniel said defensively.

"Another reason for not living in town. Those young people have too much spare time. And I don't hold with too many games. School ought to be for learning, not playing games."

They finished the meal, and after her father left to work in the fields, Leah gathered her books, put on her coat, and said, "I'd better go, Mother. It takes half an hour to walk to the main road."

"I fixed you a good lunch, Leah," Mabel said. She handed the paper sack to the girl, then hesitated. She was by nature a woman of warm feeling, but Albert Daniel was not, and over the years she had repressed most of her emotions. Now she suddenly put her arms around Leah, hugged her hard, then said as she stepped back, "You have a good time, you hear?"

Leah was so surprised by the unexpected gesture, she blinked and could only say, "Why—all right, Mother." She left the house, and when Mr. Chips started to accompany her, she had to speak to him several times in a harsh warning. "No! Go back, Mr. Chips! No dogs at school!" The small dog persisted until she slapped his nose and said, "Bad dog! Go back!" He gave her a mournful look, then turned slowly and plodded back to the house, his feelings injured. Leah ran to him, picked him up, and hugged him. "Don't be hurt, Mr. Chips," she pleaded. "I love you—but you can't go to school." She put the dog down, opened her lunch sack, and brought out a potted-meat sandwich. "There, go on home now," she said as he gulped it down. "After school I'll take you for a walk."

The sun peeped over the trees that crowned the low hills rising in the east, but the wind was sharp and Leah shivered as she walked along the road. The weather had been dry, but the deep ruts made by the wagons used on the Farm back during the wet springs were now hardened by summer's heat. Leah ambled along the road, her eyes moving constantly. She was aware of her world far more than most people and didn't miss the flight of honkers that made a ragged V high up in the sky, nor the scurrying white-footed mouse that nosed out of a patch of wild onions, his eyes beaded like black pearls.

When she reached the main road, she put her books and lunch down, and walked along the edge of the gravel road as she waited, then came back and sat down beneath a huge sweet gum tree that overshadowed the road. She picked up one of the balls that had fallen, studied the prickly arc of its circle, then tossed it toward the tiny creek that ran parallel to the road. It hit the water, and she saw a school of minnows come to investigate, their bodies silvery in the morning light.

A noise came to her, and she rose quickly, picking up her books and lunch. The yellow bus lumbered around a curve to her left. When it stopped and the door opened, she got on.

"Hi, there," the driver nodded with a smile. He was a fat man of thirty, with a moon face and prominent teeth. "Forgot your name—?" When Leah gave it, he spoke it aloud. "Leah—Leah. I gotcha. Take a seat and make yourself comfortable. My name's Mr. Small."

Leah moved down the aisle toward the back, but the bus started with a lurch and struck a pothole at the same time, so she fell awkwardly against one of the students—a short, black-haired boy who grinned at her. "Better sit down, Leah. Ol' man Small will probably hit a telephone pole or two before we get to school. My name's Lennie Leslie. I'm in your English class. I'm a junior, but I flunked English last year."

"Oh—I remember," Leah said. She would have moved on, but Lennie moved his legs aside, saying, "Hey, have a seat by the window." She sat down awkwardly and looked out to avoid his eyes.

"You get that dumb paragraph written ol' man Gifford assigned?"

"Why, yes, I did."

Lennie shook his head gloomily. "What a dumb subject! A duck for cryin' out loud! Why couldn't he let us write about something *important*—like Superman?"

Curiosity caused Leah to turn and look at the boy. "Superman? Who's he?"

Lennie's jaw dropped. "Are you kidding me?" he demanded. When she shook her head, he whistled. "Boy, you really *are* out of touch! Don't they let you read comic books out where you live?"

"No, they don't. I've never seen one."

Lennie grinned broadly, "Well, you're about to see one now!" He reached into his book satchel, pulled out a comic book with a lurid cover, and shoved it into Leah's hands. "There you go! It's a good one, too! Not Superman, but it's almost as good. *Amazing Comics* is its name. Go on—look it over."

A guilty feeling came over Leah as she opened the garish cover that showed some sort of a strange monster with many arms holding a scantily dressed woman. The monster had large white teeth and red eyes and was about to bite the woman in two, or so it seemed. But coming out of a grove of trees was a heavily muscled man with blond hair, charging toward the monster with a gleaming sword in his hand. Leah began to read and was so engrossed in the story that she started when Lennie dug his elbow into her side. "How about it? Pretty nifty, ain't it?"

Leah hardly knew how to answer. She knew that her father would have a fit if he ever saw such a thing in their home—but it was *interesting!*

"It's—very nice," she said haltingly. She handed it back, but when he offered to let her keep it, she said quickly, "No, I won't have time."

Lennie shrugged. "I've got about ten million of these things. You ever want any, just let me know." He opened his satchel, paused, then looked at her. "Hey, I bet you're good at spelling and stuff, ain't you, Leah? Yeah, sure you are." He nodded without waiting for her to answer. "Look, I got my theme all wrote, but my spelling ain't so good. How about you look it over and give me a few hints about fixing it up?"

"Is that against the rules?" Leah asked.

"Naw, we can get all the help we want with that kind of stuff.

Ol' man Gifford always says good writing is more than spelling. Here, take a look."

Leah took the rather grubby paper Lennie shoved at her and examined it. His handwriting was terrible—but his spelling was worse! She began to point out the misspellings, and Lennie waved his hand in the air. "Aw, just write 'em in over mine. I'll copy it over during history."

"Won't you miss what the teacher says?"

He stared at her with surprise. "Ol' lady Peabody? She ain't *never* said nothin' that anybody'd want to remember! Anyway, I can study my history in algebra."

"And study algebra in civics class?" Leah was amused at the boy, but he seemed nice. "Wouldn't it be easier to study the subjects as they come?"

"Oh, I don't give a dead rat about none of it, Leah!" Lennie protested. "I'm gonna be rich when I grow up—and rich men don't hafta spell good. They got secretaries for that, ain't they?"

"I suppose so." There were several flaws in Lennie's thinking, but Leah didn't want to argue the point. She circled all the misspelled words on the paper, put in some punctuation, and handed it back.

"Hey, thanks!" Lennie exclaimed. "You ever want somebody to push you in the creek, just give me a call!" He saw her eyes widen in alarm and laughed. "Just a joke, kid! Just a joke!" He turned to look out the window and nodded at some small signs. "Look, some new Burma Shave signs." He read the series of signs slowly and laughed: "LET'S MAKE HITLER . . . AND HIROHITO . . . LOOK AS SICK AS . . . OLD BENITO . . . BUY DEFENSE BONDS . . . BURMA SHAVE! Some guy probably got a thousand bucks for writing that! Now *that's* the kind of poetry I could go for. Give me a hundred bucks a word and I could be a poet myself!"

Lennie rattled on as the bus made its way over the gravel road. When they pulled into the school parking lot, he suddenly said with a trace of embarrassment, "Hey, Leah—I seen that creep Jack Clampett givin' you a bad time yesterday. I'd have stood up for you, but—" He shook his head and rubbed one scruffy shoe against the other, and finally he blurted out, "Well, I could probably stomp Jack—but Keith Demerie . . . he's pretty tough."

Leah was touched by his words. "Don't worry about it, Lennie." She got up and the pair filed off along with the other students. Leah was watching for Clampett and was relieved when she didn't see him.

"Hey, Leah," Lennie said, nudging her with his elbow. "See that big guy over there—the one with the football jacket on? Well, that's Mike Hardin. He's the toughest guy in school, I guess. Why don't you ooze over and play up to him? You know, just do like girls do when they want guys to do something."

"I—haven't learned how to do that, Lennie."

"No?" He appeared surprised, but after looking closely at her, he nodded. "I guess not. Some girls are *born* knowing how to do it—like Debbie Lambert. I could ask him for you."

"Ask him *what*, Lennie?"

"Why, ask him to stomp them creeps if they bother you again!"

"Oh, no, don't do that!" Leah spoke quickly and shook her head. "I'll be all right. Just don't worry about me."

"Well, okay, if you say so. Hey, thanks again for fixin' up my paper! There's the dumb bell—!"

The morning went by quickly for Leah. She moved through her classes, taking a seat as far back as possible and not speaking at all. She listened carefully to the teachers and took notes. The work seemed so easy that she feared she was not getting it right. *Mother and Mr. Dale make me do things harder than this!* she thought. Mr. Dale had covered all the arithmetic in the text two years earlier, and Leah was both pleased and worried. *I can't be this far ahead!* she thought. Several students were sent to the board to work some algebra problems, and she was amazed to see how poorly they did. When her name was called, she worked the problem given her very slowly, and pretended to have problems with it. Mrs. Simpson, a tall skinny woman of about fifty, offered her some help and seemed pleased with her.

The other classes were about the same, and by the time Leah went to gym class with all her classes except English behind her, she knew she'd have no trouble keeping up. She was a girl with a quick manner of observation and had seen in just one day of classes that the students who did *very* well were not admired by the other students. *I'll not do as well as I can*, she thought suddenly. *That way nobody will pay any attention to me.* It seemed dishonest, but she was determined not to draw attention to herself.

In gym class, she was met by an abrupt problem. Miss Janet Tennerman was the teacher, and after getting the girls together, she said, "Tomorrow you'll need to bring your gym clothes: tennis shoes and socks, a white T-shirt, and a pair of shorts. Better bring two of everything except the shoes. Now, let's play some volley-ball—"

Leah couldn't keep her mind on the game. *Shorts! My father would die before he'd let me wear shorts!* She went through the hour mechanically and made her way to Mr. Gifford's English class with a sickness in her stomach.

She took her seat, not even noticing Jack Clampett, who leaned over and whispered something to her as he went to his seat. All she could think of was shorts! *He'll never let me come back to this place!* It never occurred to her that this was exactly what she wanted—to stay on the Farm. At some point she had decided that Liberty High School was somehow—*necessary* for her.

Her thoughts kept her so occupied that she barely listened as Mr. Gifford lectured for twenty minutes. He was only talking about punctuation, and she was an expert in that. Finally, she heard him say, "Well, let's have some papers on ducks. Keith, I believe you mentioned that it'd be easy to write on that subject, so let's have your *magnum opus.*"

"My *what?*"

"Your masterpiece. Come on, let's hear it."

Leah watched as the class snickered. Keith read his paper quickly. "Ducks are dumb. They are good only to eat. My favorite ducks are Donald and Daffy. They're pretty funny. And that's all I've got to say about ducks." He looked up defiantly at Mr. Gifford. When the teacher said, "A fine paper . . . ," he grinned, but then Gifford concluded, "for a fifth grader! You can do better than this, Keith. Melvin, let's hear your paper."

Leah prayed that the bell would ring before he got to her! She scrunched down in her desk, trying to hide behind Judy Carouthers. Despite her efforts, she finally heard the dreaded words, "All right, Leah, let's hear what you've come up with."

Her hands trembled so violently she could barely read the words she'd written the previous evening. Lennie Leslie, sitting

next to her, whispered, "Go on, Leah! You can do it!" His encour-
agement spurred her on, and she began to read in a tight voice.

When the ducks come to me from the pond to get fed,
some of them are so far away, they fly over the water. Others
come sailing in, their white feathers like sails on old galleons.
They leave V's on the smooth water, ripples that keep going all
the way to the sides of the pond. They begin to answer me as
soon as I call, and they sound like toy buzzers with their high
nasal honking sounds. When they get close to the bank, I throw
the grain out, and they stand on their heads to dive for it. I
thought of a short poem once—"Whenever they sup—it's
bottom's up!" Not a good poem, but it's what they do!

All of them are so white! Whiter than a bride's dress or the
clouds in an April sky! They dot the dark water like white,
fluffy periods. When they have little ones, the ducklings are
yellow and follow their mother in single file as they come
through the water to be fed.

One is not white. He is so ugly that I feel sorry for him!
My father says that he is a Muscovy duck. He is very heavy and
much larger than the white ducks, and he has black-and-white
feathers. When he walks, he waddles from side to side like a fat
woman, and the other ducks all run past him to get the food.
He has tremendous red wattles around his beak and what
seem to be large red warts on his face.

He is all alone. None of the other ducks will have anything to do with him. I guess I felt sorry for him, because he
was so alone and so different. Now I save food for him and
feed him after I shoo the other ducks away. He's very nice, and
I call him Magwich because he reminds me of the poor criminal
who died in *David Copperfield*. Sometimes I sit down and he
comes and nestles next to me. He's wet and muddy, but I don't
mind. For some reason, though all the other ducks are white
and beautiful, I like Magwich best.

Leah put her paper down flat and stared at it, her heart beating
hard. Her lips were dry, and she knew by the silence that they were
all staring at her.

Leslie Gifford said quietly, "A fine paper, Leah. I never heard
of that kind of a duck. I always like to be surprised when I read a
paper, to learn something." He hesitated, then said abruptly, "All

right, hand your papers in." He seemed to be a little ashamed of showing gentleness and added caustically, "I've laid in a gallon of red ink for this year. I'll start slopping it on your papers tonight. Now, the assignment—"

When the bell rang, Lennie said, "Hey, that was a nice paper about the duck. I'd like to see Magwich. Can I come over sometime?"

"Of course—"

"Leah—" Mr. Gifford said, coming up to stand by her. He waited until all the students were gone, then fixed his eyes on her. "I really liked your paper. Have you written much?"

She hesitated. Her writing was a secret she had never shared with anyone, but somehow she found herself saying, "Y-yes, sir. I write all the time—but nobody else has read it."

"I see." Gifford paused, then smiled. "Sometime—after we get better acquainted, maybe you'll let me see some of your writing. Not now. Writing is very personal. I don't share mine with many people. It's something private, isn't it?"

Leah stared at him. "I didn't know anybody else felt like that!"

"Some very fine writers have felt that way," he nodded. "I hope we get to be good enough friends to read each other's writing. But in the meanwhile, I have a book or two you might like to read. I'll bring a couple tomorrow."

By the time Leah got on the bus, she was not over her surprise about how easily she'd told Mr. Gifford about her writing. But by the time she got off the bus, the thought of writing was far behind her.

Shorts! I've got to tell Father about the shorts!

A shiver ran though her, and she began to pray that God would do something. "You'll have to, God," she said aloud, her lips drawn tightly. "You know my father—and You know how I want to stay in high school. Somehow, You have to work a miracle!"

3

"LOOK OUT FOR NUMBER ONE, KID!"

*S*mall southern towns are microcosms of the entire United States—or perhaps the planet. In the large world, a single shot can upset the balance of civilization. One bullet in the breast of Archduke Francis Ferdinand in a village called Sarajevo may have been only a slight popping sound—but before 1914 had passed, Europe was deafened by monstrous cannons, and nations were bled white by the slaughter.

The question of Leah Daniel's wearing shorts did not come to shedding blood in Liberty, Georgia, in the fall of 1938—but it was close. If there were no corpses in the physical sense, several reputations were slain and lay cold and dead. The principal, the superintendent, the chairman of the school board, and several of the more liberal members of that august board set their teeth, *vowing* that the blasted girl would wear what the other girls wore or else!

Usually these dignitaries got their own way, for the Middle Ages knew no stronger hierarchy than Liberty. At the top of the pyramid were two or three wealthy families who pretty much owned the town—namely the cotton gin, the hardware store, ad infinitum. Below this nobility were the professionals riding the shoulders of the middle-class small businesses. As the pyramid grew larger, there were the blue-collar workers, those who did the actual *work* necessary to keep the ship afloat. Then the poor whites, whose only pride had to come from the knowledge that there was *one* class below them, the Negroes.

The wave that rocked the town began when Leah Daniel went to the office of Alvin Ditweiler with a note. She was admitted to the inner sanctum, and Ditweiler grunted as he took the note she silently handed him. His mind was on the meeting of the Liberty Rebels with the Conway Tigers on the following Friday night. He loved his farm, the Rebels, his church, and his family—though not necessarily in that order. Taking the note, he pulled his mind away from the upcoming contest, scanned it, then frowned. "What's this, girl?"

Leah's face flushed pink. "My father says I can't wear shorts, Mr. Ditweiler."

"Nonsense! You can't wear overalls, can you?" He grinned at his little joke, adding, "Just run along now and do as Miss Tennerman tells you." He tossed the note into his wastebasket, then turned his mind to what sort of play he might suggest to Coach Bonner Ridgeway. *Stop throwing the ball!* he'd probably say. *When a quarterback throws a pass, three things can happen—and two of 'em are bad!* His lips moved as he rehearsed the speech, and he felt, unless Ridgeway were a total fool, he would take good advice.

"Sir—?"

"What? Oh, are you still here?"

Leah saw the irritation on his face and swallowed hard. Desperately she said, "I can't do it, Mr. Ditweiler—wear shorts. None of the girls or women at the Farm are allowed to wear anything but dresses."

"That's foolishness! We're not living in the Dark Ages!"

Leah shook her head. "My father says if you don't change the rule, he'll keep me at home."

"He can't do that! The law says you have to go to school." The heavy-bodied principal shot his lower lip out in a gesture of anger. "He'll go to jail if he breaks the law!"

"He'll go before he lets me wear shorts!"

Ditweiler huffed and puffed and set out to blow someone's house down. He fired off a note for Leah to take home to her father, then later in the faculty lounge boasted of how he'd "put a stop to the nonsense of those fanatics!"

Most of the faculty agreed with Ditweiler's handling of the problem, but Leslie Gifford remarked, "I'd be careful about getting that bunch riled up. In some ways they're more rigid than the Amish they broke away from years ago."

Ditweiler slapped his meaty thigh, snorting, "They'll soon learn they can't dictate the policies of Liberty High School. This is a democracy, and these kids are going to do what I say or take the consequences!"

Gifford smiled at the wrenched logic, saying only, "It's people like these who allow themselves to be burned at the stake, Alvin."

The wave gained considerably throughout the day, for if Liberty lacked many modern conveniences possessed by New York and Chicago, it did command an effective system of gossip. Everyone in the school knew of the thing by noon, and Leah was tormented by crude remarks from callow youth all day. Jack Clampett's loud comment heard by half the school was typical: "Hey, Leah, you must have a gorgeous set of pins if your old man's so careful to keep them under wraps! Let's have a preview!"

Leah endured the day and carried Principal Ditweiler's message home that afternoon. That night the ruling body of elders of the Farm met for three hours.

She went to her room and was as tense as a watch spring. Leah turned her lamp down and approached the heavy box in which she kept her work. It was a masterpiece made by Caleb Dale, the carpenter. He was a widower who had lost his wife and three children in a house fire. He spent his life building and teaching the children of the Farm. Though he'd never admitted it, Leah had been special to him. When he discovered that she needed a place to keep her notebooks, he'd made her a special "table." It looked like a heavy box and seemed to be built of solid oak. Leah kept her lamp on it, and no one ever knew that the back dropped down when pressure was applied to a certain point.

Holding her breath, Leah opened the back of the box. Inside were dozens of notebooks. The early ones were Red Horse notebooks, with a picture of a thoroughbred's fine head on the cover. The paper was so coarse one could almost see chips of wood, and Leah often smiled at the primitive pictures and stories inside, all in a childish hand. She glanced at the stacks of notebooks, all colors and sizes, thinking of how many hours she'd put in on them. Taking a blue spiral notebook from the top, she went to her small desk and began writing at once.

> *What a terrible day! And tomorrow will be worse, I know. If I could run away, I'd do it in a second. But where would I go? What would I do? No, I'll go to school, and father will go with me, and I'd guess the entire board of elders from the Farm. They'll have faces like death, and Mr. Ditweiler won't scare them as he does the kids who go to his office to get a thrashing!*

What must it be like to be a girl like Debbie Lambert? So pretty! Such nice clothes! And all the boys are in love with her. She's laughing about me tonight. The whole town is laughing. That crazy girl from that crazy place run by crazy people—that's what they'll say!

She paused and rested her chin on her cupped palm. For a long time she sat there, then her eyes narrowed and she got up and crossed the room and opened the closet door. An ancient mirror was affixed inside. Her father didn't know it was there or he'd have taken it down. She'd found it long ago and managed to smuggle it into the house. She kept her coats hanging over it so that even her mother didn't know it was there.

Silently she stood there, staring at herself. She wore a thin flannel gown and turned around slowly, studying her face and her figure. Finally she picked up a coat, covered the mirror, then shut the door and went back to sit at the desk.

I'm not pretty. I've got no more curves than a rake handle! When does that happen to a girl? I thought I'd fill out by the time I got to be fifteen. My face is as skinny as the rest of me. I'm not a woman. No man will ever want me.

Leah stopped writing and stared down at the words. For a long time she sat there, the amber light of the flickering flame in the lamp casting shadows over her. Slowly she closed the notebook, rose and replaced it in the box, then carefully closed the secret door. She blew out the lamp, crawled beneath the covers, then settled into the featherbed.

She listened as the tree outside scratched at her window with skeletal fingers. When she closed her eyes and tried to pray, all she could think of was, *God, I don't think even You can handle this!* Her doubt shocked her, and she shook her head fiercely, thrusting the blasphemy from her mind.

* * *

When the ruling body of elders from the Farm drove into the school parking lot in a wagon pulled by a magnificent team of draft horses, conversation among the students fell off abruptly. The six big men who climbed down from the wagon and trooped into the front door looked as much like a posse out to hang a rustler as they did anything else. All wore black suits and wide-brimmed black hats, and there was a fire in every man's eyes.

"Good night!" Taylor Spain whispered as the men disappeared into the depths of the school. "Who *are* those guys?"

"I dunno," Larry Parsons responded. "But I'm glad they're after somebody besides me!"

Miss Agnes Quince, a maiden of advanced years, looked up from her desk at the six men, and her hands flew to her scrawny bosom in an involuntary gesture of fright. For years she had had nightmares about big men dressed in black—and now they were here!

"We want to see Superintendent Sloan," the leader said in a rumbling voice that seemed to make the lamp on Miss Quince's desk tremble.

Miss Quince asked in a quavering tone, "Who shall I say is calling?" It was her first grammatical error in forty years, and the fact that she didn't even recognize it was evidence of the palpitation of her heart.

"I'm Elder Cletus Sandifer," the leader announced, and it was almost as if he'd said, *I'm the commanding general!* so firm was his tone.

Miss Quince scurried into the office and was back shortly to say, "You may come in."

The posse marched inside, and the smile on the face of T. P. Sloan faded at once. He was, as all high school superintendents must be, a skilled politician. This meant he knew how to read men—and these men, he recognized instantly, were not the usual group of Rotary Club boosters.

"Ah—won't you gentlemen have a chair?"

"We'll stand." The leader announced his name and grouped the others together as simply, "The Ruling Elders of the Farm." Then he fixed his close-set brown eyes on Sloan and said, "We've taken time from our work to come here, and we won't tarry long."

"What seems to be the problem, Elder Sandifer?"

"One of our young ladies is enrolled in your school. She's been told she will have to wear shorts. She will not wear shorts."

Sandifer was six feet tall and bull-strong. His will was as strong as his neck, and the words he dropped seemed to be set in

concrete. There was no room for discussion or debate in his manner—none whatsoever.

"Gentlemen, we're always glad to discuss any problem with
parents—"

"There'll be no discussion," Elder Sandifer stated flatly. "You
may choose to let your young women parade around half-dressed.
You must answer to God for such things. But we will obey God,
and that is final!"

Outside Sloan's office, the faculty drifted by, all of them aware
of what was happening. Ora Peabody said caustically, "If Mr. Sloan
lets those—those *fanatics* have their way, what would come next?"

Leslie Gifford said, "I absolutely agree with you, Ora. Why,
the next thing they'd refuse to let you wear a revealing dress!"

Ora Peabody was plump as a partridge and was always
baffled by Gifford's remarks. She could never tell if the English
teacher was making fun of her or not. "Why, I never would do such
a thing!" she snapped angrily.

"Sorry to hear that," Gifford remarked. "It might put a little
life in this dull place."

The faculty watched until the first bell rang and were treated
to the spectacle of their principal, Alvin Ditweiler, and their athletic
director, Bonner Ridgeway, as they were summoned into Sloan's
office. Gifford and Ridgeway were sworn enemies, and the English
teacher said acidly, "If they argue with you, Bonner, penalize them
for delay of the game."

Ridgeway, a gravel-voiced, bulky man, cast a vitriolic look on
Gifford. "I may do worse than that," he snapped, then disappeared
into the office.

For over an hour the meeting went on, and various members
of the community were summoned, including the chief of police
and the judge. Rumors flew around the school. Peggy Jackson said
boldly, "I'd play volleyball stark naked before I'd make a fuss like
this!" She cut her eyes around toward Mike Hardin who was leaning against his locker talking to Debbie Lambert. He looked at her,
grinned, and said, "We'll talk about that privately, Peg."

By noon the wave was so large it threatened to swamp the entire school system, if not the entire town. Gifford was eating lunch
with Janet Tennerman, teasing her about creating such a problem.
Janet was an attractive young woman of twenty-five. Some said

that she was too pretty to be a teacher, and it was rumored that she would not say no to a drink—under the right conditions. She liked men, and she liked Gifford. Smiling, she said, "What will come of all this, Les? The whole school board can't cave in, can it?"

"Ever hear of a *tsunami*, Janet?" he asked lazily.

"A what-ami?"

"Means a giant wave."

"Like those on the West Coast?"

"No, not like that," Gifford corrected her. He sipped his milk slowly, then said, "A giant wave, sometimes over a hundred feet high. They're made by an underwater volcanic eruption. They pick up speed until they're moving faster than you can think. And when they hit the mainland, nothing stands before them. Trees, houses, office buildings, people—they all disappear."

The pretty blonde girl shuddered. "Sounds awful!" She looked in the direction of the offices, then asked, "You think those hicks from the Farm are going to wipe out Liberty?"

"I think so."

"But—how? Les, there's only a few of them out there. And only one girl in school."

"There was only one Martin Luther, but he turned the world upside down," Gifford said. His thin face grew angry, and he said, "I wouldn't care if those birds sunk this whole system!"

"You don't like Liberty?"

"The idea I like—but not the town."

"Why not, Les?"

"Because a bunch of pompous people think they can make the rules for everybody to live by."

Janet stared at him. "Do you mean the school board—or those preachers?"

Gifford ducked his head. "You've got me there, Janet. Wherever you get a structure—a club or a nation or a church—you get people who want to run the other people."

"Don't see why they're making such a big fuss about a pair of shorts," Janet shrugged. "Poor kid's going to get hurt by all this. The other kids are making fun of her as it is. This will finish her off—no matter how it comes out."

Gifford stared at her. "We all draw different lines, Janet. What would you die for?" When she stared at him blankly, he asked,

"There must be *something* you absolutely wouldn't do. What is it?"

Janet gave him a sudden wicked smile. "I guess I'm just a coward, Les. I can't think of much I wouldn't do—if the circumstances were right. Why don't you ever try to find out?" She looked at his arm, then said, "Is it because of that? Is that why you never ask me out?"

Gifford's face grew pale. He rose suddenly and limped away without a word. Janet watched him go, thinking, *Poor guy! He's really hurting. Too bad. I could go for him, even crippled.*

At ten minutes until noon, the door of Superintendent Sloan's office opened, and the black-clad elders marched out. They said nothing to anyone but climbed into their wagon and drove stolidly away.

"Well, what's it going to be, Mr. Sloan?"

T. P. Sloan sat in his chair, wilted and exhausted. He stared at Alvin Ditweiler, who asked the question. The two of them were alone, and Sloan said wearily, "We're going to compromise, Alvin."

"Compromise? How can we do that?"

"Let the girl wear slacks."

Ditweiler's face grew angry. "I say we throw her out!"

"You tired of your job, Alvin?" Sloan asked idly. He was staring out his window at a gray squirrel making one of his periodic forays across the power line that led to the top of the school. He was fascinated by the jaunty assurance of the animal. Once he'd seen one fall off the wire, and it hadn't harmed the furry acrobat in the least.

"Why—no, I like my job," Ditweiler said in surprise.

"I like mine, too—and I'm going to keep it." He glared at the other man, saying, "It's one of the reasons why I'm superintendent and you'll never be, Alvin. I know when to hunt for cover—when to fold 'em. Those fellows are death. They'd get their way one way or another, and we'd be the villains. But you go on, Alvin. You fight the battle. I'll just watch, and when I get a new man to fill your shoes, I'll be sure I get one who's smart enough to know when the woods are on fire!"

The students never heard that a decision had been made—but when Leah wore a pair of white cotton slacks to play volleyball the next day—they knew!

"Hey, for once the good guys won!" Lennie Leslie said. He was standing with a group of older students who'd come to watch the girls play.

Mike Hardin cocked his eyebrow, asking, "What's that mean, Lennie? Those guys didn't look too good to me."

Lennie shrugged his thin shoulders. "Hey, they're pretty grim, but they got a right to have their kids wear what they want. Besides, some of the guys been giving Leah a bad time."

Hardin looked over to the slender girl in the white slacks. "What kind of a bad time?"

"Hey, you know, Mike," Lennie answered. "Because she has to wear those ugly clothes and no makeup and stuff like that. Poor kid needs a break, Mike. I'd take care of it, but Keith Demerie's too tough for me to handle."

"Demerie?"

"Yeah, and Clampett. You know what a creep he is!"

"None of my business."

Lennie was the youngest of the boys in the group—and the smallest. But he faced Hardin squarely, saying, "If I were your size, Mike, I'd take care of it."

"Take care of number one," Hardin smiled easily. "That's my motto."

Lennie admired Hardin—or had. But now he said bitterly. "I guess that's okay if you feel that way. But I thought there was more to you than that, Mike."

The small boy turned and walked away. One of the other boys said angrily, "You gonna take that, Mike?"

"What am I gonna do, Mick? Fight him?"

"Well—you ought to do something!"

Hardin cared little, as a rule, what people said. Mostly they said good things; he was easily the most admired student at Liberty. But something about the way Lennie had looked at him was troublesome. He said, "See you guys later," and left them there.

That afternoon Leah was walking toward the bus with Lennie, and, as usual, Clampett and Demerie showed up. Both were grinning, and they began ragging her about her legs. "Hey, let's just see a little of those famous legs, Sweetie!" Clampett said. He planted himself in the middle of the walk and turned to leer at Demerie. "Like to have a glance, Keith?"

"Sure," Demerie grinned. "They must be something!"

Clampett grabbed Leah suddenly, pulling her ankle up so that her long skirt began to slide up. She cried out, and Lennie suddenly lashed out, catching Clampett on the nose with a hard fist.

Jack yelled and threw himself at Lennie. The two went at it, and when Lennie began to get the best of Clampett, Demerie reached out and struck the smaller boy on the cheek. "You're not big enough to save the damsel from a fate worse than death," he grinned. "You've been seeing too many movies. In real life, the good guy gets stomped most of the time." He turned to Leah, caught her skirt, saying, "Now, let's see those—"

He never finished the sentence. A hard hand closed on his neck, and he gasped and tried to turn. The hand was like a vise, and he suddenly found himself lifted high in the air—and then the earth seemed to reel as he flipped in a complete somersault. He struck the ground on his back, the air rushing from his lungs with a whooshing sound. The back of his head hit the hard-packed ground, and bright lights seemed to explode in his head. He crawled around blindly, trying to get his breath, then looked up to see who had manhandled him.

"Come on, Keith, get up." Demerie climbed to his feet and glared at Mike Hardin. "I intend to save this maiden in distress— just like Errol Flynn! Unless you stop me, that is."

As always when a fight breaks out on the schoolyard, a crowd collects as if by magic. Demerie, his head aching from the blow on the ground, looked around to see a ring of students. He was a rough fellow and had lost few fights in his life. But one look at the powerful shoulders and knotty fists of Mike Hardin, and he knew he was beaten.

"What's wrong with you, Hardin?" he asked. "What'd you jump me for?"

"Just wanted to make a point," Hardin said. He had been certain that Demerie would back down and he dropped his fists. "You've been having too much to say about this little girl. I think you've had enough fun. Don't you agree?"

"Why, sure, Mike," Demerie said quickly. He was no fool, and could be a smooth talker. "I didn't mean any harm. Guess I did go too far." He turned and said, "Sorry, Leah. Didn't mean to make a pest of myself. Okay?"

Leah, her face as pale as it had ever been, nodded. "It's all right," she whispered.

Hardin looked around the crowd, then remarked, "I hope this is the end of this thing. Hate to have to deal with it again." He looked straight at Jack Clampett, who dropped his eyes at once, then smiled at Leah. "Glad the shorts thing came out all right for you," he remarked. "Glad to have you at Liberty." He walked away but hadn't gone far before he heard footsteps and turned to face Lennie.

"Hey, Mike, that was great!" he said.

Hardin grinned. "I'm your hero again?"

"Aw, come on, Mike!" Lennie protested. But he put his small hand out. "Might not have been much to you—but it was a great thing for Leah."

Mike took the small hand in his big one and smiled. "You did pretty good back there yourself, Lennie. You and me, we make a pretty good team."

A flush of pleasure illuminated Lennie's face, and when he went back to get on the bus, he found the kids all staring at him as if he were ten feet tall.

He sat down beside Leah, saying nothing. But as the bus rolled along, he felt her hand fall on his. He looked up quickly and saw tears in Leah's beautiful eyes.

"Hey, don't turn on the waterworks!" he protested. "It wasn't nothin'."

"Yes, Lennie," she whispered, and her hand tightened on his fiercely. "It *was* something!"

"Mike, he did it."

"No, he's so big he knew he'd win. But you didn't! I'll never forget it, Lennie!"

The bus hit the gravel road, dropping into the potholes with enough violence to snap someone's neck.

But Lennie didn't care!

4

ALL OR NOTHING!

*T*he three dominant religions of Liberty, Georgia, were Catholic, Protestant, and Football. When the leaves turned to shades of rust and red and flaming gold and the air from the Canadian wilderness rushed down upon the little town, bringing the first sharp chill of autumn, Catholic and Protestant took seats on the back pews for the duration of the football season. They were pretty much relegated to the status of second-class citizens except for an occasional funeral or wedding, when the townsfolk had little choice but to tolerate them.

The coffee shop of the Liberty Hotel and the counter, booths, and tables of Ollie's Drugstore filled to capacity each morning with throngs of the faithful. The air rang with somewhat less than fabled accounts of aging athletes recounting their past exploits on the gridiron and of the havoc their sons would wreak on their Friday night foes. Some of them unabashedly wore their blue-and-gray letter jackets, tattered and faded through the years, with sleeves riding up above their wrists and the fronts splayed open over middle-age paunches.

After working hours in the autumn afternoons, those too old or as yet too young to play on the hallowed varsity would gather on the bleachers and watch the practice sessions. With the band thundering on a distant practice field, they talked of off-tackle plunges and end runs, discussing the weaknesses of the opposition and the unflagging strengths of the Rebels.

Leather popped loudly in the crisp air as the offensive and defensive lines snapped together, and the ball, on its way to a receiver's outstretched hands, spiraled high against the hard blue sky. The young boys saw their futures, bright with the promise of girls and glory. The men looked back through the drab clutter of their years, laying the awful burden of their dreams on the backs of their sons.

Liberty had an 8–2 record that season and was tied for first place with the Centreville Bobcats. Tonight's game would decide the district championship.

All year long it had been rough going for the Rebels. Their line averaged 155 pounds, small even for a school the size of Liberty, but what they lacked in size they more than made up for in slowness. Their quarterback was slower than most of the linemen, and with a strong wind at his back he could throw a pass maybe thirty-five yards. Of the three backs, one weighed 140 pounds and had some speed, while the fullback was twenty-five pounds heavier with more guts than ability.

Mike Hardin played left halfback, and the fate of the Rebel football team rested in him. At six feet even and 185 pounds he was the fastest man on the team, although his speed was no more than slightly above average for a high school back. His strength and balance made it difficult for even the strongest defenders to knock him off his feet, and his iron will made them less than eager to attempt it.

What made Hardin an exceptional athlete, however, were his peripheral vision and uncanny reflexes. He appeared to have a sixth sense for finding holes in the defensive line and for avoiding tacklers on downfield runs. He loved the game that had brought him the adulation of the crowd and his classmates, but he abhorred the self-discipline that football required of him.

* * *

"We're gonna send them Bobcats home with their teeny little tails tucked between their legs tonight!" Kyle Hardin sat at the kitchen table, the *Liberty Herald* scattered in front of him. Thick black hair hung down over his brown eyes, slightly glazed from three shots of bourbon he had knocked back since coming home from work. The fourth sat in front of him. At 220 pounds, he weighed thirty pounds more than when he had played halfback for a year at Georgia Tech. "Yes sir, this district championship is in the bag."

"Anything can happen in football, Kyle." Darla Hardin stood at the stove frying hamburger steaks, but her red satin dress, heavy makeup, and high heels spoke of a night on the town. Since the years when her father had lost all his money in the Depression, she had taken refuge in the dubious art of overdressing.

"Not tonight," Hardin smirked. "Tonight's a sure thing."

Darla glanced over her shoulder at her husband. "Nothing's a sure thing in football! If you didn't learn that at Georgia Tech, you never will."

Oh, no! Here it comes again. Same ol' thing week after week. Mike sat with his chair pulled back from the table, slipping into his brown-and-white saddle oxfords. Jeans and a white T-shirt completed his outfit. The Rebel letter jacket hung over the back of his chair. His black hair, still wet from the shower, was combed straight back. "Mama, let's don't start that again."

Darla turned and stared at her son as if she had no idea what he was talking about. "I just think you might do better to put in a little more time on your studies, that's all. Football can't teach you to be an executive."

"You mean like your daddy, don't you, Darla?" Kyle Hardin turned to his son. "She's right, Mike. You study real hard in school and you can learn to jump off the roof of a bank building just like your granddaddy did."

Darla spun around toward her husband, the spatula in her hand flinging grease across the table. "You're a cruel man, Kyle. And you can't blame that on losing your business."

Hardin looked up sheepishly at his wife. "I'm sorry. I shouldn't have said that."

She opened her mouth to speak, then dropped the spatula back in the skillet and whirled out of the kitchen.

Mike got up and stepped over to the stove, listening to his mother's high heels clicking down the hall on the hardwood floor. He flinched involuntarily as her bedroom door slammed shut. Turning the steaks over, he mumbled, "You gonna eat, Daddy?"

Hardin gulped the whiskey. "Naw. I ain't too hungry."

Mike turned the burner off on the stove, grabbed his jacket from the chair, and headed for the kitchen door.

"Wait a minute, Son. I'll drive you."

"I'd rather walk, Daddy," Mike called back over his shoulder as he left. "See you at the game."

Hardin rubbed his eyes with both hands. Getting up wearily, he walked over to the cabinet. He flicked the knob on the cathedral-shaped radio on the counter next to the breadbox. As it glowed, the vacuum tubes warming up, he took a bottle of bourbon down from the cabinet and poured a water glass half-full. As he sipped it, he listened to the Glenn Miller band play its lively version of "In the Mood."

Hardin pulled back the red-and-white-checkered curtains over the sink and stared out at the streetlight near his front walk. *I can't remember the last time Darla was "In the Mood."*

As he was about to close the curtain, Hardin saw a slim man shambling down the street. He was dressed in a worn sport coat with the collar turned up. *Well, there's one man who drinks more'n I do. Here's to you, J.T.,* he thought as he drained his glass.

* * *

Sweat poured down Mike Hardin's face. His breath was raspy and labored as he grabbed a towel from the team manager, wiping his face, neck, and arms. "Let me take the punt, Coach."

Bonner Ridgeway knelt on the grass next to the bench. A bear of a man with close-cropped, thinning blond hair, his voice was gravelly from years of yelling at hard-headed jocks. "You shut up and take a breather, Hardin. I'll tell you when to go back in."

The Liberty fans rose to their feet as the ball wobbled off the foot of the punter, bouncing out of bounds on the Bobcat thirty-two yard line. A collective groan rose up from the crowd on the opposite side of the field. Men slammed their hats down on the hard bleachers and women clasped their hands to their throats.

Mike glanced at the scoreboard. *Rebels-14. Visitors-21.* "Coach, you got to let me in now!"

Ridgeway glared at Mike as he sent a play in by his right guard. "When you're rested. You played every play and made both touchdowns. Ain't that enough?"

Mike watched their fullback drive straight up the middle for a two-yard gain. Both sides cheered for their teams. He shook his head slowly, glancing to his left. The cheerleaders were doing cartwheels along the sidelines, their legs flashing against the blue-and-white pleated skirts. They stood in a line in front of the stands and led the crowd in the Liberty fight song as the team left the huddle.

Go, Rebels, go.
Your power shows.
Fight on
A little bit, more a bit, lots a bit
Rebels go!

What a stupid song, Mike thought. *I hope they do a little better than this when I get to college.*

The quarterback approached the line, glanced to the right and left, barking signals. Dropping back for a pass to his right halfback out in the flat, he saw his line collapse. A huge red-helmeted tackle drove him to the ground before he could get the ball off. Third and fifteen. A loud groan went up from the Liberty stands.

Mike jumped off the bench, pacing up and down the sidelines, his tanned face dark against the white towel draped across his neck. "Coach! You gotta put me in!"

Ridgeway opened his mouth to reply but was cut off by the resounding chant that rose from the Liberty stands. "We want Mike! We want Mike! We want Mike!"

Glancing back over his shoulder, Ridgeway saw that T. P. Sloan and Alvin Ditweiler were among the more enthusiastic chanters. He considered the consequences of keeping Mike on the sidelines and having Centreville score again, putting the game out of reach. Ridgeway loved the power and respect of his job as head football coach. "Hardin! Get in there!"

Mike grabbed his helmet off the bench and sprinted out onto the field. The crowd behind him roared with approval. Cowbells clanged loudly. Horns blew. Fans stomped the bleachers, the noise rumbling out across the field.

"Off tackle," Mike mumbled as he bent into the huddle next to the quarterback, carrying the play in from Ridgeway.

"Everybody in the stadium knows what the play's gonna be! That's what he always calls!"

"He's the coach," Mike complained along with them, as though he had no desire to run with the ball.

The Rebels peeled out of the huddle. A silence had descended over the stadium. The only sound was the flapping of the Stars and Stripes high on its pole, popping loudly in the night wind. The quarterback bent behind his center, studied the defense, and barked his signals.

Mike dropped into a three-point stance. As always, when the pressure was on, time seemed to slow to a crawl. He stared at the left tackle for the Bobcats. He weighed two hundred pounds and had a face that was far too big for his helmet. Digging his cleats into the scarred surface of the field, the big lineman waited for the inevitable off-tackle play to begin. Glaring at Mike out of his tiny helmet, he bared his teeth and spat on the ground.

The quarterback took the snap from center, took two steps backward, and spun with the ball held outward in both hands. Mike hesitated one count, then exploded from his stance, felt the ball snap into his midsection, and cradled it tightly with both hands clasped over its ends. His fullback threw a body block on the defensive end, swinging around to turn the play inward so his interior linemen could all have a shot at Mike.

Mike's line had failed to open a hole for him. He expected that, but he still had a matter of honor to settle. The big tackle roared in ahead of the other linemen. Mike feinted to the outside, throwing him off balance slightly, then lowered his head and rammed his helmet directly into the solar plexus of the charging lineman. The boy's face went white as the air in his lungs left him with a whoosh. He doubled over, wheezing and gasping for breath.

Bouncing off the tackle, Mike sprinted for the sidelines. In his left periphery, he saw that two defensive backs had the angle on him, and would hit him before he could turn the corner. Instinctively, he stopped almost in his tracks as the first back sped past him, clutching onto his jersey. Ripping loose, he felt the second back slam his shoulder pads into him at thigh level. His balance was such that Mike had seldom been knocked off his feet by anyone hitting him above the knees. This time proved no exception. Churning his powerful legs, he broke free into the open field.

A lone defensive back stood between Mike and the end zone. With a grimace on his freckled face, he put his head down and came on with a full head of steam. *The boy's got guts. Got to give him that much.* Mike summoned his reserves, lowered his right shoulder, and charged at full speed. He caught the back on his numbers with a loud slap of leather, sending him flying through the air. The boy landed on his back with a grunt and lay there motionless, his arms and legs splayed outward.

Mike trotted the last ten yards into the end zone. He turned and stood there like a gladiator, victorious and shining in the bright glare of the arc lights. Tossing the ball proudly over to the referee, as though it were the head of a slain enemy, he trotted toward the sidelines.

The Liberty fans went wild. Pennants waved brightly, cowbells clanged, and the bleachers thundered as they stomped their feet. Mike's teammates rushed off the bench to greet him. Debbie Lambert, bouncing away from the other cheerleaders, took his sweaty face in her hands and kissed him soundly on the cheek.

High in the stands, Ollie Caston slapped Leslie Gifford on the shoulder. "You ever see anything like that? We got 'em now for sure!"

"A fine run," Gifford replied, flinching under the hearty blow to his crippled shoulder. "The boy's got real talent." He glanced at the clock. "It's not over yet though."

"Aw, Leslie, don't be such a spoilsport," Caston complained. "With Mike out there, they ain't got a chance."

Liberty kicked the extra point, tying the game at 21–21. After the kickoff, the Bobcats managed to move the ball down to the Rebels' own twenty yard line, but they were stopped cold on an incomplete fourth-down pass attempt. After two plays up the middle and an end sweep, it was fourth and three for Liberty.

"All right, get back in there and punt that thing clear back to their end zone, Mike." Calling for a time-out, Ridgeway stood on the sidelines with his beefy arm around Mike.

Mike was furious. "But, Coach, we won't have time to get the ball back again."

"Do as you're told, Hardin!" Ridgeway pushed him roughly back onto the field.

Mike stood twelve yards behind the center, shaking his arms loosely to relax them. Holding his arms out in front of him, he called the signals, a slight smile on his lips. He watched the defense loosen up, preparing to block for their back who would return the punt. The ball spiraled through the air from the center's hands. Mike took it easily, stepping forward in a kicking motion as the ends swept in to block the kick. He let them leap into the air after a ball that wasn't there.

Tucking the ball under his right arm, Mike sprinted up the middle of the field where only a few scattered defenders stood in amazement, unable to respond in time as he flashed past them. In his element now, broken field running, Mike stiff-armed a would-be tackler and saw only the same skinny freckled-faced defender between him and the winning touchdown.

Sensing the easy victory, Mike relaxed. But the last tackler had managed to hold onto his arm. With a terrible sinking in his chest, Mike felt the ball pull free, saw it bouncing crazily in front of him and reached desperately out for it. It brushed past the tips of his fingers teasingly and landed squarely in the arms of the freckled-faced back. Running against the flow of the play, he cut toward the sidelines and sped past the shocked Liberty players.

Mike saw the slim boy sprinting toward the end zone, victory cradled in his arms. *No! You can't do this to me!* He charged with all his remaining strength after the boy, his legs churning, heart pounding, the chill air burning deep within his chest. Closing the gap between them, he made a desperate leap on the five yard line, his fingers clawing at the boy's legs. Mike hit the ground with a groan, not of physical pain, but of the sharp stab of defeat in his chest as he watched the clock run out.

The Centreville crowd rushed onto the field, banners waving as the band played their fight song. They carried their hero off shoulder-high as his teammates jumped wildly about, clapping him on the back.

On the opposite side of the field, the Liberty fans were stunned into silence. The pompoms of the cheerleaders hung down like the wilted hopes of their owners. Mike lay on his face, tasting the dirt in his mouth. Victory's wings brushed softly against him as it flew high above the glare of the arc lights, disappearing into the autumn darkness.

* * *

"C'mon, Mike," Keith Demerie called out from the locker room door. "We're all going over to Ollie's and drown our troubles in root beer and Coke floats."

I must really look down if Demerie's tryin' to cheer me up. "No thanks. Y'all go ahead."

The last of Mike's teammates banged their lockers shut and shuffled out of the room, grumbling under their breaths about rotten luck and how they would rip the heads off the Centreville players next year. He sat on the hard bench with his head down, water dripping from his hair onto his muscular thighs and puddling on the bare concrete floor. The smells of sweat and liniment and dirty socks filled his nostrils.

In his mind, he kept diving flat out for the elusive back from Centreville, feeling his hands brush against the heels of the player's flying shoes. He looked at the tip of his index finger where a cleat had ripped the skin off.

After another hour, Mike walked home by himself. He went straight to bed with the sound of his parents' argument drifting down the hall as he fell into a restless sleep.

Mike decided to forego his usual Saturday night date, claiming an unspecified injury. He moped around the house all day, reading magazines and listening to "The Green Hornet" and "Gangbusters" on the radio. Several friends came by. He shut himself in his room while his mother told them he wasn't feeling well.

"Your friends said to tell you that you shouldn't feel bad about the game, Mike," his mother called through his door.

Sunday morning dawned gray and wet. Mike lay in bed feeling as sad and cloudy as the November weather. His chest still ached where he had slammed into the ground in that last desperate attempt to tackle the freckle-faced back from Centreville.

Later in the morning, Darla knocked on his door. "I'm going to church, Baby. You want to go with me?"

"No ma'am," Mike mumbled into his pillow.

"You sure? We haven't been in three or four weeks."

"Yes ma'am."

"Well, okay. I'll leave the eggs and sausage in the oven to keep them warm. Your daddy's still sleeping. See that he eats something, will you? If his hang—if he's not too sick."

"Yes ma'am."

Mike dreaded the next day at school. *Why do they have to be so nice to me? That only makes things worse. I hope they just leave me alone.*

He reached over and turned the knob on his radio. As he watched the raindrops tracing their silver patterns on his window, Mike listened to the voice of Deanna Durbin, full of sweetness and light, as she sang "Someone to Care for Me." He flicked the knob abruptly, rolled over, and buried his head in the pillow.

* * *

"Hey, Mike. Too bad about the game." Jack Clampett sauntered by on his way to join Keith Demerie, who was talking to a group of girls over by the front steps of Liberty High. "Don't worry though. You'll get 'em next year."

I won't be here next year, you idiot! "Yeah," Mike mumbled, unable to tell whether Clampett was rubbing his nose in the defeat or trying to encourage him.

"Good game, Mike."

Feeling the friendly pat on his shoulder, Mike turned and saw Ben Logan walk by. He had no doubt about Ben's sincerity. "Thanks, Ben." He watched the easy grace and controlled power of Ben's movement as he walked toward the school building. *If I had you at the other halfback position, we'd never lose a game. Too bad you have to work all the time.*

Mike's first class was geometry, and his teacher was Bonner Ridgeway. Ridgeway glared at him as he took his seat. No one else knew that Mike had disobeyed his orders to punt. He couldn't tell them for fear of losing discipline among the team members, so he was saddled with the blame for their loss to Centreville.

Seeing the rage that burned in Ridgeway's slate gray eyes, Mike knew it was not finished between them. Football was over, but he knew the coach would make him pay dearly during the coming basketball season and might carry it over for track.

After the class had settled down, Ridgeway tapped his yardstick on the blackboard. "Mr. Hardin, would you come to the board and work any three problems on page 123 of the text? I'm sure it'll be a big help to your classmates."

Preparing for the big game with Centreville, Mike hadn't opened his geometry book in two weeks and Ridgeway knew it.

By the time the morning had ended, Mike had heard more "Sorry, Mike's" than he had scored points in three seasons of football.

One more and I might just bust somebody in the mouth. He lingered in the hall as the throng of students pushed and laughed their way downstairs for the lunch hour. Standing at a tall window, he watched the thin November light cast shadows straight down around the base of the live oaks.

"Hi, Mike."

Mike thought he was alone in the third-floor hallway. Turning around, he faced a tall, slim girl wearing a plain dress with a high neck and long sleeves. At first he couldn't remember who she was.

"I never did get to thank you for—for what you did when Keith Demerie and Jack Clampett were teasing me." Leah felt awkward in the presence of the school hero. Mike's deep-set hazel eyes were startling in his dark face. His nose had a slight crook to it where the elbow of a beefy lineman had broken it in the first game of the season. She thought it gave him character.

Mike remembered her first name. "Thanks, Leah." He looked at her bright blue-gray eyes, the clear skin with its apricot glow. *You might be a real looker if you didn't try so hard to hide it.*

"I—I heard what happened in the game," Leah stammered. "I know it wasn't your fault."

Feeling a burning in his chest, Mike merely grunted in reply.

"I know it's hard, but sometimes God lets us go through hard times so we can be strengthened by them." Leah began to feel more at ease. "My daddy says they either make you better or bitter and . . ."

Something suddenly snapped in Mike's mind like a shutter banging loudly in a strong wind. "I've heard enough of this! Get away from me you ugly ol' hag!"

Leah felt like someone had punched her. She stepped back, her hand against her throat. Tears welled brightly in her round eyes.

"Go on! Get out of here!" Mike no longer tried to control the fury that had been building up in him the last three days. "You look like a scarecrow!"

Leah turned and fled down the hall, the sound of her shoes on the pine floors echoing loudly off the high ceilings. Blinded by tears, she tripped on the first stair, clutched the banister for balance, and disappeared down the stairwell.

Mike stood looking back out the window, breathing heavily.

"You may be a big man in this school, Mike Hardin, but you're just a dwarf in my book!"

Mike whirled, seeing Lennie Leslie standing in front of him, his fists clenched at his sides. The frustrated halfback pushed him aside with an oath and stalked off down the hall.

5

HANDLE IT LIKE LOU

*H*ey, Mike, don't take it so hard!"

Nolan Delcamp stood beside Mike Hardin, ignoring the crowd that milled around the Greyhound Bus depot. Delcamp wasn't as big as a mule, but then he wasn't a great deal smaller. He weighed fifty pounds more than when he'd been a pulling guard for the Packers, and his face was scarred and dented by a thousand abrupt collisions with behemoths on many fields. He was happy in his job, which was to make all-American running backs out of the young men that came to Georgia Tech.

I missed out on this one, Delcamp thought sadly. *He's got all the tools—size, strength, speed, and lots of quick.* He glanced at the sullen look on Hardin's face and wondered if the young man could take the jolt. *I should have kept up with his studies more. But his high school grades fooled me. Now he's out for a year—but that ain't got to be bad. He'll come back bigger and stronger.*

Slapping his meaty hand on Hardin's shoulder, he grinned. "Not the end of the world, Mike," he shrugged. "I flunked out my freshman year. Had to catch up on basics."

Mike stared at Delcamp, a smoky anger in his hazel eyes. "If I'm too dumb to pass classes in summer school, what chance would I have in regular classes?"

"You're not dumb," Delcamp shot back. "You just got blind-sided. All your life you been handed grades 'cause you can play ball. I told you when you enrolled you'd have to work at the books —but you spent all your time at parties and goofin' off." The bulky coach saw the resentment in Hardin's set lips and shook his head. "It's up to you, kid. Go find a junior college and make good grades.

Work out regular. Come back next fall, and I think you can be the best running back Tech's had in a long time." A hard light came to Delcamp's light blue eyes. "But it's up to you. You want to hang it up, you can be one of them fat-bellied guys in the pool room bragging about how they *could* have been a pro—but they got rooked out of it."

Angry words rose to Hardin's lips—but when he looked at the battered face of his coach, he knew nothing he could say would change what had happened. The diesel fumes of the bus bit at his nostrils, and he let his anger pass before he answered.

"I'll be back, Coach," he said quietly. "You save me a place."

Delcamp laughed aloud and slapped Mike on the rump. "Now you're talking, kid! You're gonna be a great one, I'm telling you."

Mike noted the driver was waiting impatiently and said, "I'll send you a copy of my grades, Coach. And I'll be in shape next fall." He turned, got on the bus, and from his seat by the window felt a great loss as Delcamp waved, then turned and left the station.

The diesel revved up and the driver spun the massive wheel, easing the Greyhound out of the station. Thirty minutes later Atlanta gave way to the open country, open fields, and pine. Mike slumped down in his seat, his lips drawn together in a hard line. As the trees shot by, he looked out at the fields, the August heat baking the red clay of the plowed fields.

He put his head back, closed his eyes, and thought of how different his trip away from Tech was. He'd come with an eagerness from Liberty, no doubt at all in his mind that he'd be the hottest prospect that had come to Tech in a long time. He'd been met by coaches and some of the players, and he had thrown himself into the life of the school. The classes he'd treated with contempt. Boots Otterman, his roommate, had said airily, "Aw, nobody works in summer school. The profs just teach to make extra jack. They don't care what the students do! We're gonna have a good time, 'cause when the fall semester starts, they get *serious!*"

Mike thought bitterly, *I picked a great guy to listen to! Why didn't I have sense enough to know that Otterman didn't know beans about college?* He let his head rest on the window, the vibration of the road running though him. *Now I go back home and everybody in town will say I'm a stupid jock who can't read or write!*

The bus droned on and Hardin sat there, eyes closed, trying to doze off. When the dean had called him in and told him he couldn't play football because of his grades, the world had seemed to drop out from under him. He'd argued and lost his temper, but the dean had only stared at him, stating flatly, "Go get a year's work at a small school. Take English and basic math over. Then if you want to come back, I'll be glad to work with you."

Mike stirred restlessly at the memory, opened his eyes, and stared out the window, not really seeing the landscape as it flowed by. He discovered suddenly that his legs ached and found that he had been pressing them against the floor—looking down he saw that his brawny fists were clenched so tightly that the veins stood out on his wrists.

Taking a deep breath, he forced himself to relax. *Can't go around wound up like a spring for a whole year,* he thought. *It won't be so bad.* But he knew deep down it *would* be bad. He thought of some of those in Liberty who'd be glad he'd failed. There were always that kind, smiling and slapping a fellow on the back when he was winning, but secretly hoping to see the big man take a fall. Why were they like that? Did it make them feel better?

Restlessly he plucked the *Saturday Evening Post* from his bag and studied the cover. It was by Rockwell, who did most of their covers. This one made him smile; it depicted a young couple, no more than sixteen, all dressed up for their first date. They were sitting at the counter of a small drugstore, and the soda jerk was leaning over and smelling with a rapturous expression the flower pinned on the girl's dress. Mike shook his head. "That guy sure knows drugstores and kids. This might be June Haltom and me on my first date—and this is more like Ollie Caston's Drugstore than the real thing!"

As he flipped through the magazine, reading the cartoons, he thought of how simple life had been for him at the time of that first date. "Guess life gets more complicated as you get older," he muttered. And the thought made him wonder what lay ahead. He was not a young man to worry much, so he began to read the story about Kate Smith, which explained very carefully that her success proved that fat girls could be stars. Mike grinned, sang the first line of "When the Moon Comes over the Mountain," and then thought, *Kate can sing—but she'd look pretty out of place in a skimpy bathing suit!*

She'll never star with Randolph Scott either—they'd never get her on a horse!"

He read the magazine, tossed it on the seat, and took out the Atlanta newspaper the coach had stuck in his bag. The headline read, NEW WAR THREATENED BY CRISIS OVER DANZIG. It was another story about that funny-looking German, Hitler, but what was happening wasn't so funny. Mike was not much interested in politics, but he read the story.

> The newest flash point of tensions in Europe is the hotly disputed and strategic free city of Danzig. Adolf Hitler is making it quite clear he wants to absorb Danzig into the Reich. But France and Britain have both warned him that the action could precipitate another war.
> The warnings were the strongest yet to the Führer, but he shows no sign of heeding them. His military commanders have already assembled a strike force of tanks and cavalry that could easily be used in an invasion of Danzig and the arm of Poland known as "the corridor," which stretches into the Baltic . . .

Mike thought about that part of the world—and it seemed to be as alien as if it were on Mars. The Pathé News at the theater had shown the German troops "goose-stepping" down the main street of Berlin, and it had seemed comic to most of the high school kids. "They'll be so busy learning how to do that nutty goose-step, they won't have time to learn how to fight!" Mike had scoffed. But now Hitler and his Brownshirts were no longer funny. If a war came, that would be the end of his hopes of fame on the gridiron! Nothing much could be worse than being in the army for a few bucks a month!

He turned the paper back, scanned the comics, laughing at "The Katzenjammer Kids," then found the sports page. He scanned it, slowing down to read a story on Lou Gehrig. He'd seen the film in July of Gehrig's tribute in Yankee Stadium. Mike was not a crying man, but the sight of the dying man standing before sixty-one thousand people and saying with tears in his eyes, "I consider myself the luckiest man on the face of the earth!" had moved him. He'd sat in the darkened theater, the screen suddenly blurred, and had to pretend to sneeze to cover up. The story went over Gehrig's life, which included a string of 2,130 consecutive games, and stressed how the great home-run hitter was handling his fatal illness with courage and dignity.

Boy, there's a real man! Mike thought. *Going down for the count without a whimper—just like he lived! I hope I can handle it like Lou when it comes to me.*

The bus pulled into the Greyhound station at Liberty at 4:15. Mike disembarked and considered taking a taxi. The walk to his house wasn't that far, and he wasn't in the mood for talking. But it would cost a buck and a half, and he was almost broke. He left the station and walked down Main Street, wondering how his parents were going to take the news that he'd flunked out of summer school.

As he passed the Liberty Theater, he glanced at the posters. James Cagney and Humphrey Bogart were squared off in *Angels with Dirty Faces*. The lineup for the next few weeks included Errol Flynn in *The Adventures of Robin Hood* and John Wayne in *Stagecoach*. *Turn those guys loose on the Nazis and they'd have 'em whipped!* Mike grinned sourly, wondering just how tough the movie stars actually were. On the screen they could whip any five guys at the same time, but he'd read a story that had told of the stunt men who did all the really dangerous tricks.

"Hey, Mike . . ." Hardin turned to see Ollie Caston standing in the door of his drugstore. "Come on in and have one on the house!"

Hardin hesitated, then nodded. "Sure, Ollie." He shook the proprietor's hand. Caston was in his mid-thirties, a pale man with clear brown eyes and a round face that usually glowed with humor. He wore his uniform—dark pants, a white shirt with sleeves rolled to the elbows, and a white apron that reached to his knees. He dashed behind the counter and grinned broadly as he said, "The usual, Mike?"

"Sure, Ollie."

Mike sat down at the soda fountain and watched as Ollie yanked a stainless steel container from the shelf and began filling it with ice cream, milk, and chocolate. As he put it on the green mixer and hit the switch, he said, "Missed you, Mike. Things go all right at Tech?"

Mike blinked and for a moment was tempted to lie. His mind raced, but he knew that once he started down that road there was no end to it. He waited until Ollie yanked the frosty container from the mixer and poured a small Niagara into the tall glass, then said, "No, Ollie. I wiped out."

Ollie blinked and he stared at the young man in disbelief. "Why—what happened?"

"I goofed off." Mike pulled two straws out of the container, stuck them in the rich mixture and pulled at them. "This is too thick to drink," he said. "You always did make the best malts in the world, Ollie."

Ollie nodded, but he was stunned by what he had heard. He had followed Mike's career for years and taken pride that one of Liberty's own had gone to Tech. But he was a keen student of human nature, and as he stood there, he thought hard, then asked quietly, "You failed?"

"Flat as a flounder!"

"Can't understand that, Mike!"

"Sure you can, Ollie," Mike took the spoon the small man handed him, dipped out a frosty mound, and put it in his mouth. "You know, I remember when I was about eight and used to come here. It took me about a week of yard work to save up for a malt, and I'd squeeze the straw to make it last longer." He took another bite of the malt, let it run down his throat, then looked at Ollie. "Wonder what makes a fellow remember stuff like that?"

Ollie saw the pain in Mike's eyes and said, "Well, you're handling it right. I've seen you take some rough licks on the field, but you always got up. You can do this one." He hesitated, then added, "It might be the best thing that ever happened to you."

Mike frowned. "I don't buy that. The best thing would have been for me to have passed, to make first string, then all-American, then gone to the pros."

"Maybe not. Sooner or later you're going to get a bad lick. We all do. You've had it pretty good," Ollie remarked. "Maybe too good. If you handle this right, it'll teach you something."

"Well, Ollie," Mike shrugged, "I learned that if I'm going to play football, I've got to learn to write a theme and do some math. Those were the two that wiped me out."

"What's the master plan? You going back to Tech in the fall?"

"Nope. Going to go to Liberty Junior."

Ollie stared at Mike, shock in his eyes. Then he grinned. "Quite a comedown—from Georgia Tech to Liberty Junior College."

"Tell me about it!" Mike picked up the stainless steel container, filled his glass, then tilted it. "This always gives me a headache—but I can't help it," he said. He drank long and then put the glass down, closing one eye. "Boy—does that hurt!"

"Why Liberty?"

"Good question. For one thing, I can live at home and save money. I can get a pretty good job and buy me some wheels—use the high school athletic equipment and get in the best shape of my life." He picked up the glass, drained it, then put it down. "Ollie, you're a good man. Not everybody in this burg is going to be as nice about the mess I've made." He got up, put his hand out, and squeezed Caston's hand warmly. "I thought I'd go by and tell old lady Simms about flunking out." A humorous light came into his eyes. "She can get the news out quicker than the *Herald*."

Ollie nodded, a smile on his lips. "Hang in there, Mike. You'll make it."

Mike left the drugstore and walked home. His father's Dodge was not in the driveway, so he knew that he wasn't home from the office. *He's going to blow his stack,* Mike thought, and his jaw hardened. He loved his father, but this was the first time that he'd let him down. Kyle Hardin had never missed one of his games, and Mike knew that his father's life was tied up in his future as an athlete. Other fathers could go to the games, enjoy them, then go home. But as Mike entered the house and went to his room, he thought of the altercations—and on two occasions, actual fights—his father had engaged in at his games.

He entered his room, put his suitcase on the bed, then looked at it. "Might not have to bother unpacking," he said aloud. "Dad might show me the door." He shrugged, unpacked the suitcase, then turned on the small radio and lay down on the bed.

"And now, let's see what's going on down in Pine Ridge," the mellow voice of the announcer said. Mike half-listened to the problems of Lum and Abner at the Jot-Em-Down Store while thinking about the scene he knew would take place when he broke the bad news. He'd gone over it more than once and knew it was going to be unpleasant. Closing his eyes, he lay still, thinking, *Well, it's a year—but there's guys who do that much time in prison for drunk driving. This won't be that bad.*

But he was wrong—it was *worse!*

That evening when his father came home and Mike told him he'd failed, he knew just how bad it was going to be.

"You've had a chance every young man in America would give his eye teeth for!" Kyle Hardin had raged. His face was red with anger, the veins standing out as he stood shaking his finger in Mike's face. "And you blew it! You threw it down the drain—and for what?"

"Aw, Daddy, I can go back—"

"And you'll miss your freshman year!" the older man shouted. "You think you're the only good back who wants to play for Tech? Not by a long shot! You've fallen flat on your rear, and now you come crawling back—"

"Kyle, don't shout at him!" Darla Hardin hated it when her husband went into one of his rages. She put her hand on his arm, saying, "It's not the end of the world. Mike can study hard and go back next year."

But Kyle Hardin was not blessed with the gift of reason. He'd been robbed of his big chance. He'd boasted for years of how his boy would make football history at Tech—and now it was gone, the big chance! For two hours he raged, and finally glared at Mike, saying, "All right, you say you can go back. But let me tell you something, young man, you're not getting a free ride from me. You'll work and if you go to school, you'll pay the tuition. And you'll pay room and board if you stay in this house!"

Mike left the house after the scene, trembling and biting his lip. It had been on the tip of his tongue to tell his dad to shove it— but he knew he could count on some help after the first rage was over. He walked along the tree-lined street, letting his nerves settle down, and then for an hour out into the country. He got to the swimming hole where he'd learned to swim, where he'd kissed his first girl, and where he'd had a fight with Thad Mahew when he was fifteen.

Sometimes lovers came there to park, but no cars were parked on the bank, and he walked over and took the rope swing in his hand. He thought about the times he'd swung out over the still green water, let the rope go, and tumbled joyously into the cold pond. A few stars glinted in the sky, and he finally sat down on the bank.

Going to be tougher than I thought, he mused. *Dad will help, but he's strapped. I've got to stay in shape, make some dough, and get some good grades.*

He tried many plans as he sat there, discarding them one after another. The mutter of the stream was calming, and the skies overhead were silent as the burning stars came out to spangle the darkness. Hardin was bright—when he had to be. Most of the time he'd powered his way through trouble by brute force, and on the field he'd have been a better runner if he'd learned to avoid tacklers. But he loved contact and welcomed smashing into his opponents.

Now the opponent wasn't a big tackle, but a more elusive foe. He thought of many things as he lay on the bank, staring across the water, but to combine all three needs for the next year was difficult. Finally a thought came to him, and he let it run through his mind. He stood up and tossed a stone into the river, speaking aloud.

"I can get a job loading boxcars or laying track," he mused. "Either one would keep me in shape and pay my expenses and tuition—maybe even buy some kind of car. That takes care of money and keeping in shape. But I hear Liberty's trying to become a four-year college and they've got a hot-shot, eager-beaver of a president who's hot for students making good grades." He frowned, shook his head. "That could be a problem. Got to be sure I make good grades. Might be tough working at a hard job." He walked down the bank slowly, trying to find an answer. A frog croaked hoarsely and plunged into the water making a miniature geyser.

Suddenly he halted, exclaimed, "A good tutor! But—they cost money." He thought hard, then smiled, "Hey, lots of girls are good at English and math. I'll find one and let her get me through. Hey—that's it!"

He laughed aloud, then turned and walked back along the bank, a spring in his step. The air seemed fresher and somehow more invigorating.

"Sure, it'll work," he said and smiled broadly. "All I need is a girl who's good with books—and wants to help ol' Mike make it through his freshman year!"

He broke into a run, a feeling of relief sweeping through him. When he got home, he showered, then went to bed, still excited and making plans. He thought of different girls who might do and rejected them one by one. *Can't have one of them getting serious,* he thought suddenly. *I don't need romance; I need to pass English!*

Finally he had a thought—which he rejected at first. But as he lay there, it came back to him, stronger than before. Finally he nodded. "Sure. She'd do it. And she won't be expecting me to marry her like some of the girls around here!"

He smiled and drifted off to sleep, thinking of what kind of car he'd be able to manage. Maybe that 1936 Ford V-eight coupe he'd been looking at for months at Appleton's? White sidewalls and plenty of chrome on the grill? And enough power to pass most anything on the road!

6

FORGIVENESS

A breeze freshened from the northwest as Leah walked across the sparse dry grass of the backyard toward the henhouse. As usual, Mr. Chips followed her, leaping up at her skirt, begging to be petted.

She knelt down and rubbed him behind the ears. "Might as well get this over with. You won't give me any peace until I do."

The little dog's dark eyes peered at her through the black and gray hair hanging over his face. He moaned with pleasure, then snuffed and shook himself when she had finished.

"There," Leah announced, "that ought to hold you for a while."

Mr. Chips stood on his hind legs, pawing the air and yapping excitedly.

"I thought you'd agree," she remarked, stepping into the darkness of the henhouse. The hens were clucking in undertones like gossips at a beauty salon. Leah had taken an interest in the chickens' noisy social structure and had even come to take a certain pleasure in observing their fractious ways. As she gathered the eggs, to the disdain of some of the more intolerant residents, she thought of the story she had begun only last night.

Leah had come to feel that somehow a birth process, every bit as mysterious as that taking place inside the eggs of the setting hens, was at work in her intellect and her emotions. *Maybe that's what writing is all about, giving birth to something new, something this old world's never seen before.*

Lifting the warm, smooth eggs from the nests as she moved down the line of wooden boxes, Leah placed them side by side in

her white oak basket. She had finished, bade the grumbling, feath-
ered ladies good evening and stepped outside when Bobby, her
younger brother, came bounding like an antelope across the yard
toward her, his red hair blowing back from his freckled face.

"Sis! Oh, Sis! Somebody's here to see you!"

"Gracious sakes, Bobby! You act like you've never seen anyone visit the Farm before."

"Ain't seen many," Bobby responded excitedly.

Leah started briskly back toward the house. "Well, who in the
world is it?"

"Never seen him before," Bobby chirped, bouncing along beside his older sister. "But he's a grown man and he's—crippled. Got
a bad leg and one arm hangs down kinda funny."

Mr. Gifford! Leah smoothed her hair back, glancing down at her
high-topped work shoes. *He would catch me looking like a field hand.*

When she came to the front porch, Gifford greeted her
warmly. "Hello, Leah. Thought I'd take you up on your invitation.
You promised to show me around the Farm. Remember?"

Leah looked shyly at her mother and father who were standing with Gifford next to the front porch. "Would I have time, Father?"

Albert Daniel smiled at his daughter. "A promise is a promise,
child. Mr. Gifford here's been telling us you're a real fine student."

"Mind you don't show up late for supper, young lady," Mabel
Daniel warned. "Nice meetin' you, Mr. Gifford." She turned and
walked back toward the house.

"Well, go on, child," her father admonished mildly. "I expect
Mr. Gifford would like to get back home before midnight."

Leah escorted Gifford down the rutted wagon trail toward the
fields. As they passed the barn, they could see the land rolling gently downward toward a dark line of trees where the river ran. Two
men in gray shirts, black trousers, and suspenders plowed the rich
dark soil. Plodding steadily along behind their braces of oxen, they
appeared to have stepped out of a painting from the last century.

They passed other homes, all sturdily constructed with hand
tools wielded by expert craftsmen. Leah showed Gifford their
church, the small one-room schoolhouse, and the barns and out
buildings. They walked through the peach orchard, the trees already
dropping their thin leaves with the first touch of the cool nights.

Standing next to a split-rail fence, they gazed out at a huge field of cotton, white and almost ready for the harvest.

"This is all very lovely, Leah," Gifford remarked, wiping the sweat from his brow with a frosty white handkerchief, "but what I really came for was to see some of your work."

Leah noticed that he kept his gray tweed jacket on in spite of the warmth. *To hide his bad arm. He's such a handsome man, too.* "Well, I'll have to go back to the house and bring it out here."

"Couldn't we just sit on the front porch?"

"Well, I—uh," Leah stammered, unwilling to explain that she had kept her writing secret. "I know, let's go down by the pond!"

"Fine with me," he agreed.

"See you in ten minutes," she assured him, pointing toward the pond that gleamed darkly through the willows that lined its banks.

As Leah ran lightly back down the wagon trail toward the house, Gifford shambled across a field of high grass toward the pond. True to her word, she ran across the levee ten minutes later, sitting down next to him under the graceful sweep of the willow branches.

"I assume that's Magwich," Gifford remarked, pointing to a black-and-white duck plying the still waters of the pond. "Apparently he swims better than he walks."

"Oh, yes sir!" she agreed readily. "He's a real good swimmer."

Gifford watched the big Muscovy glide by, easily and with no apparent effort. He wished there were an element for him, somewhere on this earth, where he could move so easily and effortlessly. *You have that advantage over me don't you, Magwich? But we're both loners,* he thought, glancing at the other ducks waddling about on the far shore.

"Are you OK, Mr. Gifford?"

"What? Oh, sure I'm fine," he replied, coming back from his reverie. "I was just admiring your handsome beau."

"I'm afraid he's much too independent for me," Leah smiled. "Besides, we have religious differences."

Gifford laughed easily. "Well, are you ready to read another of your literary jewels for me?"

"All I brought was this one little story." She opened her blue spiral notebook to the last pages.

Gifford lay on his side on the long grass of the levee as Leah read in her soft, musical voice. The story told of a couple who lived on the Farm. They had a child, a girl, who grew to be a dreamer—not the daughter the mother wanted to help with the chores or the son the father needed to work in the fields, but a girl who saw beauty everywhere, even in the tiny everyday things that went unnoticed by everyone else.

Her parents thought her vain and tried to force upon her the somber and difficult nature of the life they lived. But the girl saw the Farm as a Garden of Eden and told fantastic stories to anyone who would listen. The younger children followed her wherever she went, and their laughter and cries of delight rang down the lanes and hidden paths of the Farm.

Before she reached the age of twelve, the girl died of a fever one raw January day just after twilight. Her parents felt the brightness fade from their lives as the drab world closed in about them—leaving them with no dreams at all.

When Leah had finished reading, she closed her notebook, glancing expectantly at Gifford, then staring down at the still, dark water of the pond. She heard nothing but the persistent drone of the cicadas from the woods. *He hates it.*

"It's a moving story, Leah." Gifford glanced at her, then watched Magwich making his evening rounds of the pond. "I can help you improve some of the mechanics, but the way you handle the language—no one can teach a person to do that."

"Thank you," Leah mumbled, trying to control her elation.

"I'd like to see more of your stories."

Her mind worked feverishly. "I know, I can bring some to school for you."

Gifford stood up, pulling on the base of a willow limb with his good arm. "I almost forgot. A former student of mine came by the other day looking for someone to tutor him in English. He just enrolled in Liberty Junior College. I told him you'd be perfect for the job, but he'd have to make his own arrangements."

Leah remained silent.

"You might remember him. Mike Hardin. He played football."

Leah trembled inwardly, remembering their encounter in the hallway.

"He's laying track for the Missouri Pacific, so he can pay you for your time."

"It's not the money," she said softly.

"Well, I'll just leave it at that."

Walking together back across the rolling fields toward the house, they heard the frogs behind them tuning up for their nocturnal symphony. A line of wispy clouds along the horizon collected the last of the sunlight and colored it in shades of violet and rose.

* * *

Leah walked down the front steps of Liberty High School in the three o'clock bedlam. The wide concrete walk between the line of cedar trees, spider-webbed with cracks from blistering summers and infrequent freezes, led directly to the street where the school buses waited patiently for their noisy riders. A dark-haired young man with a tanned, smiling face sprawled casually on a concrete bench. He wore jeans and a white T-shirt and he kept his eyes fixed on Leah.

Oh, no! Not him. Leah cut across the school ground toward her bus, parked at the last of the line.

Seeing her veer away from him, Mike Hardin walked directly down the sidewalk along the line of buses, their exhaust pipes fouling the clear September air. *I've got the angle on her. No way she can beat me,* Mike thought, like a defensive back cutting off an end run.

Leah glanced at Mike out of the corner of her eye. *Oh, Lord! Why doesn't he leave me alone!*

Mike hopped jauntily up on the front fender of the bus, arms resting loosely on his knees, a big grin on his face. "Hi, Leah. You're lookin' mighty pretty today."

Leah kept her head down and got behind the four or five children waiting to get on the bus.

Sliding off the fender, Mike stepped next to her. "I just wanted to talk to you a minute or two."

Glancing up at him, Leah found herself drawn involuntarily to his deep-set hazel eyes and dark good looks. "I think you said it all the last time we spoke."

Mike tried very hard to look humble and repentant, but then he had very little practice with those expressions. "I'm real sorry about that, Leah."

"I accept your apology," Leah mumbled, her foot on the first step of the bus.

Mike persisted. "It's no excuse, I know, but that was about the worst day of my life." He remembered the day Coach Delcamp told him he had flunked out of college—no more football! "Well, almost the worst day," he corrected himself.

Leah took the next step onto the bus.

"Wait!" Mike realized with alarm that she was actually turning him down. "I'm in the college here now. Mr. Gifford said you might help me with my English."

"I'm not responsible for what Mr. Gifford tells you," Leah muttered, disappearing in front of a tall, gangly boy in brand-new overalls.

Mike stood transfixed on the sidewalk, staring at Leah through the reflections and bursts of sunlight in the windows of the bus as it started to pull away. He turned and walked away slowly. *I must be losing my touch. Looks like when football goes—everything goes!*

The bus rumbled along the shady streets of Liberty, sunlight and shadow flickering through the windows. Turning left toward the highway, it passed the Negro quarters next to the railroad tracks. Children played noisily in the hard-packed dirt yards among the dog houses, rusted hulks of ancient automobiles, and the clean wash hanging on drooping clotheslines.

Ahead of her, Leah saw Jordan Simms turn into the overgrown driveway leading up to the big house where she lived with her aunt, Butcher Knife Annie. *That might be a good house to put in a story*, she thought, gazing at the rambling old mansion with its turret rising in front as though it had aspired once to become a castle, then abandoned its dream as the owners abandoned theirs.

Poor Jordan. She has it rough with no mama or daddy and old Annie drinking all the time.

"That wasn't very nice of you."

Leah, startled out of her thoughts, turned to face Lennie Leslie, who had sat down next to her. "What do you mean?"

"I mean the way you treated Mike Hardin." Lennie's usually cheerful face had clouded over.

"You—you don't know what he did to me." Leah stared back out the window. They were passing the cemetery with its gray-bearded oaks and piked iron fence. The slanting afternoon light cast long shadows from the tall, tilting old tombstones.

"Yes I do."

Leah turned around abruptly.

"I was there in the hallway that day," Leslie explained.

"Then you heard those names . . ."

"Yeah. I also saw how you treated Mike today." Lennie stared directly into her eyes. "Did it make you feel better?"

"No—no, it didn't. I feel even worse now." Leah looked back out the windows. Beyond the barbed-wire fences, Jerseys grazed contentedly in the rolling pastures.

"Christians are supposed to forgive their enemies, ain't they?" Lennie asked bluntly.

"Yes."

"Mike was having a real rough time that day, Leah. I never saw him act that way toward anyone before. It wasn't anything personal. You just happened to be there when he reached his limit." He watched Leah struggle within herself.

"What do *you* think I should do?" Leah realized how little experience she had dealing with a situation like this. She had always kept her distance from boys, except for a few friends like Lennie, and the way she felt around Mike Hardin was nothing at all like the way she felt around Lennie.

"Well, I heard Mike say he was sorry." Lennie got up and moved to another seat, leaving her to figure it out for herself.

That night after Leah had prepared for bed, she pressed the small knothole on the side of the oak table next to her bed. When the back panel dropped down, she removed her newest notebook and lay across the fluffy feather mattress. The light from the coal oil lamp cast a warm amber glow across the brightly patterned quilt her mother had made. After bumping her tablet with her eraser a few times, she began to write.

I found out a frightening thing about myself today. I've hated Mike Hardin since that day at school when he called me all those terrible names. Lennie Leslie made me realize it on the way home from school today. Mike seemed so violent that day, I guess I've been afraid of him, too, and fear can make people do things they wouldn't do otherwise.

I have to forgive him. There's no other choice. And I have to apologize for the way I treated him today. Tomorrow on the bus to school, I'll tell Lennie to call him for me since we don't have a telephone out here at the Farm. He can tell Mike that I'll talk to him—that is, if he still wants me to.

I'm not afraid of him anymore—not the way I was that day in the hallway when he was so mad, but I'm afraid in another way that I don't know how to explain. I believe he *will* get in touch with me.

Leah chewed on her pencil for a few seconds, listening to the bugs thumping against the screen. Then she sighed and carefully wrote a few more words.

I hope things go well between us.

Returning her notebook to the compartment behind the table, Leah turned down the lamp and slid between the cool sheets, still carrying the smell of the sun.

* * *

Leah's classes were interminable that next day. She stared so much at the big schoolhouse clocks in her rooms that two of her teachers remarked on her lack of attention—something that had never happened before.

At the end of the day, as soon as Leah walked through the heavy oak doors of the main entrance, she saw him sitting on the same bench. Even from that distance, she could see his bright smile. All the way down the long front walk, she tried to think of something to say. A dozen things came to mind, but she discarded them.

"Hi, Leah," Mike said easily while she was still ten yards from him. "You think maybe we could be friends again?"

Leah gazed at his smile and thought of a toothpaste ad she had seen in a *Life* magazine one of her classmates had brought to school. "Hello, Mike."

"I'm real sorry about what happened that day." Mike stood up in one quick motion. "It was a terrible day."

Leah was fascinated by the way Mike moved. *I wish I could*

_____

have seen him in a football game. "I'm sorry I treated you the way I did. I'm not usually like that."

"Well, I guess we're just a couple of sorry people then," Mike laughed.

Leah looked puzzled at first, then smiled when she understood what he meant. "I guess we are."

"Is your bus leavin' now?"

"I've got a few minutes," she replied, glancing down the line of buses.

Mike motioned at the bench and they sat down together. Most of the students at Liberty remembered Mike from his football days and a lot of them greeted him as they walked past. Most wondered why the former resident Romeo was spending time with a girl who acted and dressed like Little Orphan Annie.

"I've got a little problem that Mr. Gifford said you might could help me with," he began.

"What is it?" Leah asked innocently.

"I'm stupid."

She looked puzzled, then smiled again.

Mike grinned back at her. "Actually, I have two problems," he continued. "English and math. Not too much with math, but English drives me crazy. You think you could help a bonehead like me?"

"Sure I could," she replied quickly. "No—I don't mean to say you're a bonehead, I just . . ."

"I know what you mean," Mike laughed.

Leah found the conversation confusing. Mike handled the spoken word in his own way better than she did. "I'll be glad to do what I can, but you'll have to come out to the Farm."

"Fine with me. How about tomorrow?"

Again he caught Leah off guard. "Well, I guess it would be all right. My parents have to approve of it though."

"They'll love me," Mike said confidently.

*   *   *

"Mama, Daddy, this is Mike Hardin." Leah stood in the front parlor of her home. Her mother, coming from the kitchen, was drying her hands on her apron and her father was in his stocking feet, having left his plowing shoes on the back porch.

"How do you do," Mike said formally, shaking hands. He wore a tan sport coat and dark brown slacks. His shave was so fresh his face still shined.

After the introductions Mike sat in a wing-backed chair while Leah and her parents took the sofa.

"Leah tells us you're enrolled in Liberty College," Mabel Daniel said. "Yes ma'am." Mike shifted uncomfortably in the chair.

Albert Daniel stared at Mike's strong arms and chest. *What work he could do on this farm with strength like that! A shame to waste it on football.* "You think our Leah could help you with your studies at college, young man? She's only in high school."

"Oh, yes sir!" Mike answered quickly. "Mr. Gifford says she's one of the smartest students he's ever had." Shaking his head slowly, he added, "And I'm a real dummy."

"That's a shame, son," Albert spoke solemnly. "But we all have our shortcomings. God will help you."

Mike glanced at Leah. She rolled her eyes back in her head, making sure her parents didn't see her.

"Well, I've got stock to feed," Albert announced, standing up and heading toward the hall.

"But, Daddy." Leah was on her feet. "What about my helping Mike with his studies?"

"Certainly, child," he replied soberly. "God expects us to help the less fortunate among us." He walked off down the hallway.

"Would you like some lemonade, Mike?" Mabel Daniel asked, rising from the sofa.

Mike was still trying to figure out how things got so off track with Albert Daniel. He usually had the fathers of his girlfriends charmed within the first ten minutes. But then they were all football fans who lived conventional lives, not at all like the imposing and deliberate Albert Daniel. "Uh, yes ma'am, I sure would," he mumbled.

After Mabel Daniel had served them, Leah and Mike sat on the sofa with texts and notebooks scattered on the coffee table in front of them. The light was fading outside, going from pale yellow to a thin misty gray behind the lace curtains. Leah lit the two lamps on the tables next to the sofa.

"I've already been assigned a theme for next Monday," Mike remarked mournfully—as if he were announcing the date of his execution. "We're supposed to describe the shape of an egg in five hundred words. Nobody can write that much about the shape of an egg."

Leah's eyes narrowed in thought. "I think the teacher doesn't really want to know the shape of an egg. I think he wants to dig into your imagination."

"Well, he'd hit rock bottom with the first shovelful in my imagination," Mike shrugged.

Leah smiled. She was beginning to like the way Mike never seemed to take himself too seriously. It was very different from the way most people on the Farm viewed themselves. "I have an idea."

"Anything at all! I don't even know where to start."

"First, we'll describe a few things that are nothing at all like an egg: a porcupine, a river maybe—tell the readers it's so they won't get them mixed up with an egg. Then we'll describe a walnut and tell them the similarities it has to an egg—maybe something else that has a similar quality. Before you know it, we've got an egg." Leah glanced over at Mike, hoping he approved.

"That's amazing!" Mike was truly impressed by Leah's idea, although he had no idea at all if it was what his teacher wanted. "Let's get started on it." He eagerly took up his notebook and pencil, sitting poised and waiting further instructions.

When they had finished, Leah began organizing her study materials neatly. Mike stared at her auburn hair shining in the gleam of the lamps as it fell softly about her shoulders.

Leah finished and turned toward Mike. "Well, I think we got a lot done for the first meeting."

"More than I could have done in a month," Mike nodded. "Now, I want to give you something for your help."

"No," Leah said softly. "I'm happy to do it."

"You sure? I've got a pretty good job with the railroad."

"I'm sure."

"Well, if that's the way you feel about it," Mike shrugged, returning his wallet to his back pocket. He reached over and took Leah's hand in his. "I really appreciate this." *She's really nice. Not man-crazy like most girls. I'll get her something real nice when I bring my first grades—to show her how much she helped me.*

Leah gazed into Mike's deep-set eyes, mysterious looking in the lamplight. *I wonder what it would feel like to run my fingers through his hair?*

7

A NEW ACQUAINTANCE

*L*eah—Mike's here!"

"I'll be right there, Mother!" Leah stood before the mirror, turned and tried to see what her new dress looked like from the back. She'd gotten it through the mail from Sears and Roebuck, the result of a plan she'd devised weeks earlier. Mike had come to the house at least twice a week all the first semester to study with her, and as the new semester began, Leah had determined to get something to wear—anything but that ugly gray dress!

She'd known that going shopping in Liberty for an attractive dress was out of the question—but it came to her that no one actually *knew* what the clothing from Sears would look like until it arrived. She'd studied the thick catalog for hours, finally discovering a dress that had a chance of getting by her parents' inspection and yet was pretty. She'd caught her mother alone, talked her into ordering it *after* her parents had made out the order. She'd waited until her father was gone, then had taken the catalog into her mother, saying, "Mother, can't I have this dress? I've outgrown my only go-to-meeting one."

As her mother had studied the dress, Leah had held her breath, actually praying. "Why, this is too ornate for you, Leah!" her mother had said. Whereupon Leah had launched her carefully planned campaign. The dress wasn't a bright color, no, it was a simple blue-gray, and no, it wasn't too short—just a little shorter than her old ones, and didn't you realize that I've got to go to some things at school that call for a new dress?

Leah had carried the day, and when the dress had come and she'd tried it on for her parents, she'd been terrified that her father would declare it to be too fancy and worldly. But all he'd said was, "Little short, but not too bad. Maybe your mother can let it out."

But there had been no letting out, and now Leah was pleased with what she saw. The past few months had brought changes to her figure, a promise of future ripeness. She leaned forward, peered at her face in the dim light, and then glanced at the door nervously. She hesitated, then nodded as if she'd made up her mind. Quickly, she moved across the room, took a small box from her desk drawer, opened it, and took out a small vial marked "Evening in Paris." Quickly she unstopped it, applied some of the perfume to the tip of her finger, then touched her neck and her ears. It gave her a sinful feeling, but at the same time was rather delicious. Capping the bottle —which had been given to her by a classmate for her birthday—she concealed it in the box, then turned and left the room.

Mike was talking to her father, the two of them looking at some pictures through the stereopticon. Mike was wearing a pair of Levi's, a white shirt, and a charcoal pullover sweater. He grinned at her as she entered, saying, "Be more fun to look at these than to do math, Leah."

She smiled at him, hoping he would say something about how nice she looked. On the other hand, that wouldn't be so good. Her father had been very suspicious of Mike at first. He'd had a long talk with her about how young men can be dangerous and had managed to stay close at hand as the two of them studied. But as the weeks rolled by and he never heard anything more daring than, "A linking verb always takes the nominative case," he relaxed. Usually he went to bed by eight and Mike usually stayed until ten. Leah's mother and the children kept out of the way, and on the whole the tutoring had worked out wonderfully well.

Mike handed her the instrument, saying, "Look at that picture of the Eiffel Tower, Leah—it's just like being there!"

She had seen the picture at least a thousand times, but she obediently looked into the viewer, stared, then remarked, "It is good, isn't it? I'd like to see the real thing some day." She handed the viewer back, then said sternly, "We can look at pictures after you've shown me you can handle your algebra problems."

Mike groaned and turned to her father. "You're raising a hard woman here, Mr. Daniel! Can't you get her to give me a break?"

Albert Daniel had grown very fond of the young man. After his initial suspicions were overcome, he'd spent some time talking with him and found Mike to be very interesting. Now he smiled slowly, saying, "She was always a hard worker, Mike. You'd better mind her." He got up from his rocker, asking, "The studies at school, they go all right?"

"Better than I'd hoped. But Leah here gets all the credit," he added quickly. "Got all A's and B's the first semester, and if she keeps my nose to the grindstone, I'll do it again this time."

"That's good," Albert nodded. "Well, I'll let you get to your work."

When he was gone, Mike grinned at Leah, "He thought I was going to steal you when I first came here," he remarked. "It was pretty scary working with his eyes fixed on me."

"He likes you," she smiled.

Mike grew thoughtful. "You've got a fine family, Leah. I always get a sense of peace when I come here."

Leah wasn't surprised; she'd learned that Mike's home life was not a happy one. He said little directly to criticize his family, but a few remarks had revealed that his parents were not suited to each other. Leah nodded slowly, "Yes, it's peaceful enough. Boring, I guess a lot of people think. No radio, no going to the movies— every evening at home."

Mike was silent for a moment, then said, "There are worse things than being bored." He blinked with surprise at his own statement, then laughed shortly, "Well, guess you better start trying to get this stuff through my thick head."

They sat down at the big tiger-oak library table, pulled their chairs close together, and opened his book. Leah began looking over the work he'd done and said in surprise, "Why, you've gotten every one of these right!"

Mike grinned. "Proud of your star pupil?"

"I really am!" She looked up at him, her eyes bright. "You won't need me much longer!"

He hesitated, then shook his head. "Maybe not for the problems. But I'd miss our evenings together."

"Really? I'd think you'd be glad to escape your schoolmarm. I've done everything but take a switch to you!"

Her eyes were filled with humor, and Mike admired the silken sheen of her fine complexion. "Yeah, well—I needed it." He thought back over the past months, then said slowly, "I wanted to quit lots of times. Oh, making the grades wasn't the problem. But it was tough living with the fact that I flunked out. Lots of folks let me know they thought I was a dummy." He leaned back, the yellow lamplight casting its glow on his strong features. There was a repose in him that didn't come often and he commented on it. "I guess you'll never know how many times I wanted to punch some guys out and hang it up. Hasn't been too good at home either."

"I knew you were unhappy."

"You did?" Mike gave her a surprised look. "I thought I covered up pretty well. But what pulled me through was these nights at your house. I'd work like a mule all day laying track, then rush to classes, then run for five miles to keep in shape. I'd want to just lie in my room—either that or go out and get drunk! But I'd drag myself out here."

"I—I'm glad you did," Leah said softly.

"Don't know why," he shook his head slightly. "I was pretty grumpy lots of times. But those evenings sort of—well, they seeped into me, I guess. This place is so quiet; there's no pressure." Suddenly he realized that he was telling Leah more about himself than he'd planned and said hastily, "Well, let's get at this theme. That new professor, he wants something written by a genius. Says he wants us to put down our thoughts as honestly as we can. Not me! I don't want him reading what's going on inside me!"

Leah said thoughtfully, "I guess most of us feel like that. But let's see what you've written . . ."

Two hours later they were leaving the house. Leah walked with him to his car, saying, "I think your teacher will like your paper." She led him to write about one of his experiences on the football field. He'd been astonished that she'd chosen that, but he'd thrown himself into it. It had been *fun*, he'd discovered to his astonishment. He'd written about an incident from his junior year, telling about a player he'd hit after the whistle blew—and how bad he felt about it.

They paused beside the Ford, and he turned to her. "Well, I wish you'd take money for helping me, Leah. But you won't do that, I know."

"Oh, no, I couldn't do that!"

Mike stretched his arms over his head, looked up, and said, "Pretty sky tonight. Look at those stars."

"They're doing their great dance," Leah remarked, looking up.

He stared at her, then said abruptly, "I like your new dress."

She flushed with pleasure and was glad that the darkness covered it. She was not accustomed to handling compliments from young men and stammered, "Oh—thank you, Mike."

The moonlight threw pale silver over her cheeks, and Mike noticed how the planes of her face were very strong. She was not pretty in the way of Debbie Lambert and other glamour girls, but he found the symmetry of her features pleasing. "You're growing up, Leah," he remarked, noting the lines of her figure. "I expect the young guys will be lining up here to court you."

"My father would furnish the reception," she answered.

"Well—you won't take money for helping me," Mike said, "so you'll have to take this—"

Leah was caught completely off guard when Mike stooped down and kissed her on the lips. He did it easily; he had kissed many girls. The pressure of his lips and arms around her sent powerful sensations through the young woman. She had never been kissed on the lips; her family was not the kissing kind. The strength of his powerful body and the touch of his hands aroused something in her that she had not known was there.

Mike held her a moment, shocked at her fragility, and yet there was a promise of womanhood in her slender form. He released her at once because she stirred him unexpectedly.

"Can't say I'm sorry for that, Leah," he whispered. "You can blame it on your new perfume."

Her heart was beating rapidly, and her throat seemed to be closed. But she managed to say, "I—I've never kissed anyone."

Mike, accustomed to girls who'd had a bit too much experience, was touched by her straightforward honesty. "No other girl in the world would say that," he said, and looking down he saw tears glittering in her eyes. "Oh, Leah, don't cry!" he said quickly. "You haven't done anything. I just feel—that is—I wanted to—" he broke off his stammering speech, then said huskily, "You're growing up to be a woman, Leah. I never noticed it before."

He stepped back, nodded, and asked, "Are you mad at me? Want me to stay away?"

Leah shook her head. "No, Mike."

He smiled and said, "Good night, Leah. I'll see you Wednesday."

She watched as the Ford pulled away, watched as it disappeared into the darkness. She stood there listening until the throbbing of the engine faded and she could hear only the sound of the crickets' thin voices. Then she turned and walked slowly back into the house, knowing that if she lived to be an old woman, she'd never forget these few moments.

*   *   *

"Leah?"

"Yes, Mr. Gifford?" She was on her way out of English class and turned to face the teacher. He had a slight smile on his lips and seemed amused. "What is it?" she asked curiously.

Gifford waited until the last student left the room, then leaned back in his chair, saying, "I'm fishing for an invitation to dinner."

"Why, that would be nice," Leah said at once. "We all enjoyed your last visit."

He shrugged his slight shoulders. "An old bachelor like me has to get all the home cooking he can. Your mother's a fine cook. But this time I'd like to bring a friend of mine."

"I'll ask my parents, but I'm sure Saturday will be fine."

The next day when Leah came into the classroom, she smiled, saying, "You're supposed to be at our house for supper tomorrow night. Who will you be bringing with you?"

"An old friend named Dave Stone. You'll like him, I think. And he'll enjoy some good southern home cooking." Lennie came in just then, and Gifford said quickly, "We'll be there about five o'clock."

On Saturday Leah helped her mother cook supper. "Who is this man Mr. Gifford's bringing with him?" her mother asked. "Is he a teacher?"

"I don't know," Leah answered. "Mr. Gifford didn't say. Can we use the good dishes—and the linens?"

"Why, I suppose so. But you'll have to wash the linens."

At 5:30 Leah looked out the front window and saw a car coming. "There they come," she called out. Her parents were both in the kitchen, but they came to the front porch to greet the visitors.

Leah stepped to the ground and spoke to Mr. Gifford, then looked at the man with him as Gifford said, "Leah, this is Lieutenant Dave Stone of the U.S. Navy. Dave, this is Leah Daniel."

Stone wore a light khaki uniform with some odd looking boards on the shoulders and a cap with a polished bill which he took off as he greeted her. "I'm happy to meet you, Miss Daniel. Les has told me all about you."

Leah had never been called "Miss Daniel" by an adult and for a moment couldn't answer. Then she smiled, saying, "It's good to have you, Lieutenant." She turned and said, "I'd like you to meet my parents and my brother and sister . . ."

While the officer was greeting her family, Leah was able to study him more carefully. He was of no more than average height but seemed taller because of his erect posture. He had crisp chestnut hair with a red glint, fair skin, and sharp brown eyes. Though he didn't have Mike Hardin's heavy muscular build, he was trim and looked very fit. Leah guessed that he was about twenty-five years old.

"Come into the house, sir," Albert Daniel said. "I hope you like plain food, because that's what we have."

Stone smiled, his teeth white in his tanned face. "After eating mess hall food for the past six months, I'm ready for some home cooking."

Bobby Daniel was staring at Stone with awe. "Are you a soldier?" he demanded.

"No, young fellow," he answered promptly. "I'm a sailor."

Bobby looked at his uniform, then shook his head. "That don't look like a sailor suit to me."

Stone grinned at the boy. "Well, I'm in that part of the navy that flies airplanes instead of sailing ships." Bobby looked dubious, and as they followed Leah's parents into the house, Stone walked beside the boy explaining the naval air force.

The table was set, the plates all turned upside down, and Albert Daniel took his place at the head of the table, then indicated the two places on his left. "You two gentlemen can sit there," he nodded, then sat down. When the others were seated, he bowed his head and prayed a brief prayer of thanksgiving. As soon as he was finished, Leah's mother said, "I didn't cook much of a meal, but Leah and I did the best we could. "

The two visitors started in on Mrs. Daniel's idea of "not much of a meal": steaks pounded and floured and fried and drenched in gravy, an enormous bowl of red beans laced with onions, green peppers, and tomatoes seasoned hot enough to scald one's throat, potatoes boiled until their fluffy interiors burst out of their jackets, hot blackberry pie gently steaming through its open-work crust, sliced cucumbers soaked in vinegar and cream, spongy-fresh bread with a thick golden crust, a chunk of butter out of an oak-leaf mold, and all the accessories of corn relish, pickled beets, huckleberry jam, and a jug of milk on which the yellow cream lay an inch thick.

Finally Lieutenant Stone dropped his white napkin on the table, shoved his chair back and groaned. "If I eat another bite, I'll die!" he announced. "Mr. Daniel, I don't see for the life of me why you don't weigh three hundred pounds!"

"Mabel's a fine cook, just like her mother was," Albert nodded. He had said little during the meal, but now began to question the young officer. "How long have you been in the navy?" he asked, and soon the family learned that the young man had been working in an office in New York up until a year ago, when he'd quit his job and joined the navy.

"Wasn't it a good job?" Leah asked timidly.

"Oh, it was fine," Stone shrugged, "but I'd spent my whole life in classrooms and offices. I wanted a little adventure, besides—" he hesitated, then added, "the country's going to need men when the war comes."

"Maybe it won't come," Mr. Daniel said. "I pray it won't."

"So do I, but it looks inevitable. Hitler won't stop. He's said so himself. The only way to stop him is with an army and a navy. Force is the only thing he understands."

For some time the talk was of the rising winds of war in Europe, and then Mr. Gifford said, "I'd like to see some of those old family pictures, Mr. Daniel. We'd just started looking at them last time I was here. Could you show me some more?"

"Why, sure!" Albert Daniel possessed many fine old prints of his family in the old country and loved to show them to visitors. He led Gifford off to the parlor, and Leah said, "Mother, I'll do the dishes."

"And I'll help," Stone spoke up. "I want to do something to pay for that fine meal." Mrs. Daniel protested but finally agreed.

"You two come along with me and do your work," she said firmly.

"Aw, Mother—!" Bobby protested, but was hauled firmly off, along with Esther.

Leah looked at Stone with some embarrassment. "You should go look at Father's pictures, Lieutenant," she protested.

"Nope, I'm the hired help," Stone announced cheerfully. "You wash and I'll dry, okay?"

Leah agreed, and soon they were washing the huge pile of dishes together. As he stood beside her at the sink, he spoke of some of his experiences, mostly making light of his ability. Leah listened, smiling at him from time to time, and when the last dish was washed and put away, she said, "I've got to go to the barn and see to the new calf. Would you like to wait here?"

"No! I've never seen a new calf."

"Well, barns are pretty messy—" she said, eying his spotless uniform.

"Lead on, McDuff!" he said.

Leah said at once, "And damned be him that first cries, 'Hold, enough!'"

Stone stared at her, astonishment in his face. "You know your Shakespeare," he said. "Les said you were a great reader."

"Oh, not really," Leah protested. "I haven't had a chance to read much. Our people don't hold with such things as fiction and poetry." She was embarrassed and said, "Well, let's go see the calf."

They left the house, visited the calf, and Stone was astonished at the velvet softness of its nose. After they left the barn, Leah said, "Mr. Gifford's been so good to me. I don't know what I would have done without him."

"Fine fellow," Stone nodded. He stopped beside a fence to look out at the rolling pasture, and Leah stopped with him. He turned and said, "I believe confession is good for the soul, don't you, Leah?"

"Why—yes, of course."

"Well, let me confess," Stone said. The moonlight was very bright, and Leah could see that he was very serious. "Did Les ever tell you what my job was in New York?"

"No, he didn't."

"I worked for a publisher—a big one. I was an acquisitions editor. That's someone who finds writers and gets them published."

Stone hesitated, then said, "Now for the confession. I hope you won't get mad and kick me off the place!"

Leah smiled, saying, "I don't think there's much chance of that."

"No, you're much too gentle. Well, here it is, then. Les sent me one of your stories. I liked it, so he sent me another, and it was even better."

He paused, and Leah looked at him with a puzzled expression. "But—what's your confession?"

Stone laughed, "We were both worried that you might be upset that a stranger read your work. I'm glad you're not."

She shook her head, her eyes lustrous in the moonlight. "Mr. Gifford would never do anything to embarrass me."

"You're right. He's very proud of you." Stone stood there for a moment, then asked, "Could I see some more of your stories?"

Leah blinked in surprise. She said cautiously, "I—I guess so, Lieutenant."

"And one more favor?"

"Yes?"

"Could you call me 'Dave'?"

"Well—I guess so—Dave."

"See? It was easy. Now, tell me how you got started writing."

Later, when the two men were on their way back to town, Gifford asked, "What did you think, Dave?"

"Fine girl! The real thing—like you don't see much anymore."

"Yes. What about her writing? Think there's a chance you could get it published?"

Stone thought about the question, then nodded, "It's better by far than lots of fiction being printed. Needs some work, but not much. I'll let you know, Les. She's sending me half a dozen stories."

"I appreciate it," Gifford murmured. "Like to see her make the grade."

Stone looked curiously at his friend, then nodded. "Me, too, Les. Me, too."

*   *   *

Gifford's old Ford bounced over the rutted road that led to the small airport two miles north of town. As they drew near to the field, he said, "Look, there's Mike Hardin—the fellow I was telling you about."

Stone glanced up at the runner, then said, "I'd like to meet him, Les." Gifford had given him the history of Hardin's exploits and had ended by saying, "He's just using Leah, but you'd never convince her of that."

Gifford shrugged and pulled to the side of the road. Both men got out, and when Mike looked up and saw them, Gifford said, "Mike—somebody I'd like you to meet."

Stone took in the strong figure, and when he was introduced, put out his hand. He thought Hardin would try to crush his hand, but received only a firm handshake. "Glad to meet you," Mike said. He was breathing deeply, and asked, "Is that your plane at the field?"

"Not exactly. It belongs to the U.S. Navy. I get to fly it sometimes." He saw the interest in Hardin's eyes and said impulsively, "Come along and you can look it over if you like."

"No kidding? Hey, I'd love to!"

The three men got into the car, and a few minutes later they were all standing beside the large yellow biplane parked at the end of the airstrip. "This is a Stearman N2S," Dave said. He patted the side of the plane affectionately, adding, "We call it 'The Yellow Peril.'" He pointed out the various details of the plane, then asked, "Ever been up, Mike?"

"No—but I've always wanted to!"

Stone cocked his head to one side, considered the broad-shouldered young man, then shrugged. "It's against regulations—but climb in."

Hardin stared at the young officer, his eyes wide open. "Do you mean it, Lieutenant?"

"Sure—but if you get killed, don't complain to me!"

Ten minutes later the yellow biplane took off and for the next thirty minutes Mike Hardin enjoyed life as he never had. When Stone yelled, "Want to do some acrobatics?" Mike had responded, "Sure!" and Stone did loops, rolls, dives, and even a stall.

When Stone put the plane down and the two men stood on the ground, Mike's face was beaming. "If I ever *do* go into the service," he said, "this is what I want to do!"

"Not all peaches and ice cream and acrobatics," Stone said quickly. "When a dive bomber makes his run on a ship, every gun will be aimed at him. And the deck of a carrier looks about as big as a postage stamp from up there."

Mike listened, but shook his head. "I know it's tough, but, boy! What it must be like to have all that power under your hands!"

"Get your college finished, Mike," Stone said warmly, "and then you can apply for naval aviation. Let me know if I can help."

Gifford gave Mike a slight smile. "The navy doesn't pay as well as the Packers, Mike. What about your dream to be the greatest running back since Jim Thorpe?"

Hardin blinked, then grinned with embarrassment. "Guess you meet lots of guys who'd like to fly fighters, don't you, Lieutenant?"

"Sure—but some of them stick with it. Maybe you'll be one of them. Good to meet you." He turned and shook hands with Gifford, saying, "Hey, let's get together. Come on down to Pensacola first chance, okay?"

Gifford and Hardin watched as Dave took off, and as the Stearman rose over the clouds, Mike said with admiration, "He's some fellow, isn't he, Mr. Gifford?"

"Yes, he is."

Mike asked wistfully, "Do you think I might be good enough to fly for the navy?"

Gifford gave Mike a considered stare, then said, "You've got the eyesight and the reflexes. But I guess being a pilot calls for a special kind of courage. And you'll never know if you've got it, I'd guess, until you try."

Mike Hardin watched the small yellow dot as it faded from sight. "Yeah," he whispered, "it'd take a real man to fly one of those babies!"

8

FIRST DATE

*T*hanksgiving really began for Leah with a letter in the mailbox from Dave Stone. She got off the bus, walked down the road that led to the Farm, stopping to open the mailbox. Eagerly she shuffled through the advertisements and letters with windows, and when she saw her name on the large white envelope postmarked from Pensacola, Florida, she went at once to sit beneath the big hickory tree. Tossing her books and the rest of the mail on the ground, she sat down and for a time simply held the letter without opening it.

In the bottom of her lower dresser drawer lay a small bundle of letters tied with a blue ribbon—all but three from Lieutenant David Stone. Ever since his first visit, he'd written at least twice a month. His letters were long and filled with witty descriptions of what he was doing—and long critical paragraphs on the stories Leah sent him. He had provided, Leah realized, a fine course on the art of writing fiction, and she marveled at how much better her writing had become since he'd begun pointing out ways for her to improve.

She hated to open the letter, for the first reading was always such a pleasure to her. It was, she thought with a slight smile, like having a Hershey bar, so good that you hated to eat it, because it would soon be gone. *No, that's not right,* she thought at once. *I can always go back and read Dave's letters—and lots of times I get things out of them that I missed the first time.*

Still, she sat there holding the letter for a time, thinking about the past months. The fall semester of her senior year was almost over. She'd finally heeded Leslie Gifford's advice about her work.

You don't have to play dumb, Leah. If others don't like it because you get good grades, that's their problem. But if you want to go to college, you'll need a good record. She'd made straight A's during the spring semester and had found with pleasure that most of the students were happy for her. Lennie Leslie had been as proud as if he had made the grades himself! And her parents, though they had warned her to beware of pride, had offhandedly let it be known throughout the fellowship at the Farm.

A flight of crows flew over, filling the air with their raucous cries, and Leah traced them until they lit in the top of a tall fir. As if their caws had been a signal, Mr. Chips came flying down the road to throw himself at Leah, striving to lick her face and barking ecstatically.

"Oh, Chips!" Leah laughed, hugging him and trying to avoid his rough tongue. "Every day you greet me as if I'd been gone a year! Get down now; you're going to mess up my letter—get down, now—!"

Mr. Chips ducked his head, lay down as close to her as he could get, and Leah remembered how much Dave liked the small dog. On both his visits to the Farm since his first, he'd made much of Chips, bringing him a can of Vienna sausage each time. She had gone over those visits often in her mind, for they'd been times better than any others. She and Dave had spent hours talking, sometimes sitting in the swing on her front porch, sometimes walking along the roads around the farm, or through the fields. Her parents had been baffled by the smartly uniformed officer coming to see a sixteen-year-old girl, and Elder Cletus Sandifer had gone so far as to order Leah's father to forbid the visits.

Leah smiled as she thought of how her father had, for once in his life, flatly refused to obey the bulky preacher. "He's a fine young man, and Mr. Gifford says he's helping Leah with her work," Albert had said firmly. "He's a Christian and there's nothing wrong with his coming to visit our family."

Leah carefully opened the envelope and removed the bulky sheaf of pages, greedily happy over the length. *I'll read half of it now—and the other half tonight after I go to bed.* She began to read, and for the next few minutes was totally oblivious to the beauty of the Georgia landscape. She read slowly, lingering over each word, frequently going back to read passages again. Finally she forced herself to stop, to save half the letter for later, got to her feet, and picked up her books and the mail.

"Come on, Chips," she said absently, her mind still on the letter. As she walked slowly through the dried leaves that crunched beneath her feet, she suddenly wondered, *He never mentions any girls. A good-looking young man like that in a beautiful uniform must have lots of them.* The thought disturbed her, and she felt a sudden stab of emotion that she could not identify. Looking down at the small dog, she asked, "What's the matter with me, Chips? Am I like all those silly girls at school—like Debbie Lambert, always trying to make every boy she meets fall in love with her?" Chips followed her lips with his eyes and then began to run around her, trying to entice her into a game, but she shook her head firmly. "No, I won't play with you."

She walked more briskly, greeted Bobby and Esther, then said, "Mother, I'll change and help you with the canning." When she got to her room, she tossed her books on her desk, opened the bottom drawer and took out the small sheaf of letters. As she slipped the new one under the ribbon, she noted the three letters not from Dave. Hesitating, she pulled them free, opened one and read it again. It was the first letter she'd received from Mike after he'd gone back to Tech and was only a few lines. She knew them by heart, but let her eyes go over the brief sentences; then in a sudden flash of anger, replaced the letter in the envelope, then put it back with the others.

Three letters in one year! she thought bitterly. *I was just a tutor to him, that's all. Mr. Gifford tried to tell me that, but I wouldn't listen.* The letters had all been brief, telling mostly of his success on the football team and promises to write more and to come and see her when he came home for a visit. But she knew that he *had* been home, twice at least, but he had never come to the Farm.

She put Mike out of her mind, replaced the letters, then went downstairs and began working with her mother. She helped with the evening meal, spent some time afterward helping Bobby with his arithmetic, then went to bed early. Deliberately she ignored the letter from Dave, reading *David Copperfield* until after ten. Finally she closed the book, put it on her table, and got the letter. She read slowly, savoring his comments on her story, laughing at a funny story he told about a young recruit who'd made a mess of his first landing.

When she got to the last paragraph, she blinked with surprise.

Leah, I'll be coming to visit you for Thanksgiving. I hope you can wrangle an invitation for me! I've got big news for you! Hey, I've always *hated* people who say things like, *I know something—but I'm not going to tell you,* don't you? But in this case, I want to tell you this news in person! I've got a two-day leave and will be at your door at noon on Thanksgiving Day! Save a turkey leg for me!

Leah stared at the envelope, delighted and mystified. "What in the world can it be?" she whispered. A present? It didn't sound like it. She put the letter away, but was so excited she couldn't go to sleep for a long time. *He'll be here in two days,* she thought, and a smile was on her lips as she finally drifted off to sleep.

* * *

He came exactly at noon on Thanksgiving Day, getting out of Leslie Gifford's old Ford with a wide smile on his face. Leah had gone at once to meet him, and he'd greeted her with a question, "Well, do I eat here—or go back to Liberty and get the blue plate special at Joe's Diner?"

"Oh, Dave, don't be silly!" Leah was aware that her parents were watching, but when he put his hands out, she grasped them, saying, "I'm so glad to see you, Dave!" His hands were hard and warm, and when he squeezed her own, she flushed, pulling them back self-consciously. "Come on in—dinner's almost ready."

It was a fine meal with turkey, corn-bread dressing, cranberry sauce, pimento-cheese-stuffed celery, olives, green beans, hot rolls—and the choice between pecan pie or pumpkin pie. Dave chose a piece of each and finally put his fork down. "Albert," he said with a gleam in his eye, "I've got a problem—a biblical problem you're going to have to help me with."

"Why, what is it, Dave?"

"Is gluttony a worse sin than drinking a beer?"

Albert grinned unexpectedly. Despite his slow mannerisms, he had a sly sense of humor that surfaced from time to time. "Well, I'll have to take that up with the board of elders, I reckon—but my guess is they'll ignore gluttony. That's one of those failings we don't like to talk about too much."

"I'm a backslider for sure, and it's all your fault, Mabel!"

Mabel sniffed. "There's not an ounce of fat on you, David Stone! They don't feed you right at that place. I'd like to have you for about a month—I'd put some meat on your bones!"

Dave laughed, then said, "Soon as I let this dinner settle, I intend to whip the daylights out of you at horseshoes, Albert."

"Think so?"

"I've been practicing. Sure wish you were a betting man. I need a little extra cash."

Leah's father was the best horseshoe pitcher in the county. He secretly took great pride in his prowess and winked at Leah. "Tell you what, sailor boy, let's just make a little—oh, call it an *arrangement*. If I beat you, you can take us all into Liberty and buy us one of them things I been hearin' about—what is it, Mabel?"

"A banana split, Albert."

"'That's it," Albert nodded. "One of the hands got one and said it was the best thing he'd ever eaten. How about that, Dave—not a bet, you understand!"

Dave grinned with delight. "You're on!"

Leah and her mother washed the dishes while Dave and Albert walked out to inspect the farm. Dave had never been on a farm in his life before visiting here and was highly interested in every aspect of the operation. He questioned Albert about the use of horses and mules and oxen instead of tractors and listened as his host explained how, cost-wise, tractors were not the best way for small farmers.

By the time they got back, Leah and her mother were sitting in the porch swing. "Now, let's see you beat Father," Leah challenged, coming to where the two steel stobs were driven into the ground. "I think you've bitten off more than you can chew, Lieutenant David Stone!"

And so it proved, for though Stone *had* practiced, he was no match for the champion. After losing three straight games, he stared ruefully at the older man and shook his head. "Looks like I didn't practice *enough*," he said. "Let's go get those banana splits."

"Won't the stores all be closed?" Leah asked.

"A new ice cream parlor's just gone in. He's offering specials today," Dave said. He put Bobby in the front seat between himself and Leah, which provoked a howl from Esther at once. "You can ride in front on the way back," he said hastily.

The trip to town was delightful—for Leah's parents as well as for the children. Albert looked uneasy as he sat at the table inside the ice cream shop. He stared down at the banana split with three flavors of ice cream covered with various syrups and whipped cream dotted with pecans. "Sure is something," he murmured. "How do you get at this thing?" he asked Dave, probing at it with his long-handled spoon.

"Any way you can, Albert!" Dave grinned. "Use your hands if you want to." Looking toward Bobby and Esther, who were staring at the concoctions in front of them almost fearfully, he said, "Do it like this, kids—" and shoved a big spoonful into his mouth. "Let's see if you can eat the whole thing!"

They sat there, Leah and the children giggling at the mess they made trying to eat, the older couple blinking in surprise as they struck new flavors. Finally they finished, and when Dave paid the bill and they were back in the car, Albert muttered gloomily. "That thing has *got* to be sinful! Anything that good just can't be good for a feller!"

They drove around the town for a time, then back to the Farm. "Guess you and Leah want to talk about books," Albert said. "You sure do read a lot of stuff that ain't so."

Dave knew that was Albert's standard definition for poetry and fiction—anything, pretty much, that wasn't in the *Farmer's Almanac* or the Bible. He was, however, aware that Leah's father talked like that out of habit—and knew that Albert took a real pride in his daughter's literary bent. "I brought you a few new books," he said. "Left them in the trunk."

The two of them went out to the car, and when Dave gave Leah three paperback books, she smiled shyly. "Thank you," she said quietly. "You always give me presents—and I never have anything to give you."

Dave Stone looked at the happy expression on Leah's face, noting the long eyelashes that any girl he knew would die to have, and answered, "Oh, I don't know about that." He wanted to say that she'd given him more than she knew—but instead said, "Let's walk down to the pond. Maybe we'll see a deer."

"All right, Dave."

They ambled along, savoring the sharp, crisp air, and when they got to the pond, they sat down on a large tree that had fallen next to the bank. The water was still, reflecting the open sky, and there was a smell of burning leaves. They sat there talking idly, and finally Dave said, "You're not a little girl anymore, Leah."

"Why—what makes you say that?" Leah asked in surprise.

"Because little girls always want to know about their presents the first thing." He looked very handsome, she thought, his face tanned and his eyes clear. "I thought you'd come running out to the car demanding to know what I talked about in the letter."

"Well—" Leah grinned impishly, her gray-blue eyes narrowing. "Where's my present?"

Dave laughed with delight. He took her hand suddenly, held it tightly. Leah didn't know what to do but sat there as he said, "The story you wrote about the little girl who died—it's going to be published in the *New Yorker*." Stone watched the shock come to her face and nodded, "That's the surprise—but it's not a present, Leah. You did the work."

Leah was very conscious of the warmth of his square, strong hand—and the news that she was going to have one of her stories in an important magazine was too much for her to take in. "I—I can't think, Dave," she whispered. She pulled free, stood up, and walked to stand on the brink of the pond. He came to stand beside her, saying nothing. The silence seemed to settle on them, and Leah felt a joy that was fresh and strong. Turning to face him, she looked into his eyes and said, "It's all your doing, Dave."

"No—!"

"Yes, it is," she insisted. "I'd never have sent anything in to be read by strangers." Her lips were soft and vulnerable, and Stone had never seen anything like the gentleness and trust in her fine eyes. She was, he realized, still a child in some ways—yet the subtle curves of her youthful figure and the beginnings of feminine maturity in her face were unmistakable.

"You're going to be a fine writer, Leah," Dave said quietly. "The world is pretty jaded with itself. It needs a fresh voice like yours. One of these days," he mused, "you're going to wake up and find yourself famous—just as Lord Byron did."

"Oh, Dave, not really!"

He took an envelope from the inner pocket of his coat and handed it to her. "Your first royalty check," he smiled. He watched as she took out the check and stared at it. "Not enough to retire on," he ventured, "but there'll be more."

Leah stared at the check—which had her name on it and was for $200. "I never had any money of my own. What will I do with it?"

"Save it for college," Dave said at once.

"I don't think my parents want me to go," Leah said.

"Well, wasn't it you who quoted the Bible last time I was here?" Dave asked. "What was it? 'Trust in the Lord with all thine heart; and lean not unto thine own understanding—'" he paused and frowned. "I forget the rest—"

"'In all thy ways acknowledge him, and he shall direct thy paths,'" Leah said quietly. She looked at him with a touch of wonder in her eyes. "I didn't think you'd remember that."

"I've thought about it a lot," Dave confessed. "With a shooting war coming along, I figure I might need it."

"We all need God," Leah answered.

"Well, if I can trust God to keep me alive, you can trust Him to get you to college, can't you?"

Leah nodded slowly. "You're right. I—I guess I'm not much of a Christian." She smiled and shook her head. "All right, let's both trust God, Dave."

"That's a bargain," he said quickly. "Now, I think you ought to tell your parents, and then we ought to celebrate by going out tomorrow night. A real date—without cows and chickens."

"Oh, Dave, I'm afraid to tell them—and Father would *never* let me go out with you!"

"Bet he will," Dave said cheerfully. "There's a tent revival in town, on a vacant lot near the water tower. Your dad will let you go there, I'll bet."

Leah was shocked when Dave proved to be right! When she walked out to the car with Dave after talking with them, she said, "I can't believe it! The girls here just don't date men from town— especially sailors!"

"It's my wholesome face and stainless character," Dave nodded confidentially. "Be ready at 5:30. We'll have dinner at the best restaurant in town, then take in the preaching."

The next day Leah went about singing at her work—until Elder Cletus Sandifer came to pay a call. Leah answered the door, and her heart sank as soon as she saw who it was.

"Good afternoon, Leah," Sandifer nodded. He was wearing his black suit and hat, and there was a grim look on his face. "I'd like to speak to your parents."

"Oh, come in, Elder," Leah said quickly. She led him to the parlor, then said, "If you'll have a seat, I'll get them." She ran to the backyard where both her parents were working, telling them, "Elder Sandifer is here to see you."

Albert looked surprised. "What can the Elder want this time of day? Must be something wrong. Come along, Mabel." The three of them went back, and Leah said, "I'll be with the children—"

Elder Sandifer shook his massive head. "I think you'd better stay, Leah. I've come on a matter that concerns you."

Suddenly Leah knew what it was—her date with Dave! There were no secrets at the Farm, and all it took was one word for a matter to go all over the community.

"What is it, Elder?" Albert said. "Sit down and we'll talk."

"I don't think it'll take long, Albert," the minister said. He made a bulky shape in the room, dominating it with his presence. He had a tremendous voice that could fill any room, and it did so now. "I understand that you've given Leah permission to go out with a man who's not of our faith, Albert."

"Why—"

"It must not be!" Sandifer interrupted. "You and I have talked many times about the dangers in the world for innocent young women, Albert. I'm surprised that you've compromised your faith. Surprised and disappointed. But I think there's still time to put this thing right—"

Putting the thing right, according to the Elder, was forbidding Leah to go out with Dave Stone—or any other man who was not a practicing member of the Farm. He spoke loudly and Leah's heart contracted. She knew that her father had all confidence in Elder Sandifer and would never go against his will. Duly she listened as Sandifer went on and on, and when he rose to go, she wanted only to go to her room and weep.

"Now, that's settled, Albert," Sandifer boomed, satisfaction on his broad face. "You and Mabel are too sensible and spiritual to let your daughter do this worldly thing. Now, I'll be going."

Sandifer rose and was at the door when Leah's father said, "I'm afraid we're not all that spiritual, Elder Sandifer."

Sandifer halted as if he'd run into a wall. He wheeled, his face beginning to turn bullish as it did when he was crossed. "What's that you say?"

Albert's face was pale, but he faced the big minister squarely. "I've known the young man in question for nearly a year. As far as I can tell, he's a Christian young man and has more honor than some I could name here on the Farm." He turned to say, "Mabel, will you trust the young man with Leah?"

Mabel Daniel nodded instantly. "Yes, Albert."

Albert turned back to face Sandifer. "Thank you for taking an interest in my family, Elder. But in this case, as head of my house, I'm afraid I'll have to do as I think best."

Sandifer's face flushed with anger. He was not accustomed to being set aside, and for one moment he seemed about to break into a rage. Then he took a deep breath and forced himself to speak calmly. "All right, Albert. I don't agree—but it's your family. I trust that this thing doesn't get out of hand. Good day to you."

When the door closed, Leah ran to her father and threw her arms around him. "Oh, Father!" she cried and kissed him on the cheek loudly. Her eyes were shining and she cried out, "I'm so *proud* of you!"

"So am I, proud of you," Mabel said firmly. "He's a good man, but since his wife died last year, he's gotten too—well, *bossy*, I guess."

Albert said, "He's a good man, but no man can raise four children." He lifted his shoulders in a gesture Leah could not identify, then said, "Leah, your mother and I are trusting you. It's not what we'd like, but we feel you've got good judgment. Elder Sandifer is right about the world—it's a dangerous place for a young woman. Be careful, Daughter."

"I will!" Leah nodded. "Dave isn't like—some of the boys at school."

"Well, you can't go wrong going to a revival meeting," Albert smiled briefly. "I want to hear about it. Maybe your mother and I will go if he's a good preacher."

Leah was ready when Dave came, and the two of them had a fine time at the restaurant. Afterward they walked the streets, talking about books until time for the service. The preacher *was* good, and Leah said on the way back to her house, "I'll tell Father it's safe to go hear the evangelist. I'd like to go again."

"Well, I've got to go back to Pensacola tonight or I'd go with you."

"Will you come back soon?"

"I don't think so, not for a while. I'm an instructor now, and we're training as many recruits as we can get."

When he walked her to the door, he took off his hat, saying, "I won't come in. But I've had a fine time. Tell your folks for me—though I'll write and tell them myself."

"I can never thank you enough," Leah said. She looked lovely in the moonlight, though she did not think of that. "I'll send you my new story next week." She put out her hand awkwardly, saying, "Thanks for taking me out."

Dave took Leah's hand, studied it, then lifted it and kissed it. Shock ran though Leah—she had never seen such a thing done! "You're a sweet young woman, Leah," Dave said quietly. "Always stay the same!"

And then he turned and Leah watched as he got into the car and drove away. Slowly she went into the house, but when she was upstairs in her room, she sat down at the window and stared out at the moonlight as it washed over the gently rolling hills. Her eyes grew gentle as she thought of the evening, and finally she touched the spot on her hand that Dave had kissed. Her cheeks grew warm, and she smiled as she went to bed.

9

ANOTHER KIND OF WAR

When Leah got on the school bus that Monday morning, she knew something extraordinary was in the wind. There was an almost tangible excitement running like a current through the voices and mannerisms of her classmates. As she walked along the aisle cluttered with scrap paper, pencils, and stepped-on crayons toward a rear seat, she listened to their comments.

"They got the *Arizona*. My cousin was on that ship and now it's on the bottom. We don't know if he made it or not."

"We're gonna sink every Jap ship in the Pacific Ocean!"

"Yeah! I wish I was old enough to join up."

"I heard the Japs come ashore over at Savannah. Captured the whole town."

"Boy, I'd like to see 'em try that here in Liberty! I'd get out my daddy's shotgun and . . ."

"You'd wet your britches and cry for your mama first time you seen one of them little yellow rascals. That's what *you'd* do."

"Oh, yeah! Well, . . ."

Leah sat down next to Lennie Leslie. She felt compelled to ask the question. "How did it start?"

Lennie was one of the few on the bus who seemed to understand something of what lay ahead for his country. "They bombed Pearl Harbor yesterday morning."

Leah remembered Jed Crandell from the Farm who had joined the army two years ago. She could see him, looking more like a twelve-year-old than eighteen, when he told her he was going to join the army. "I had all of this place I can take. I'm gettin' out of here and see the world." He was stationed at Wheeler Field in

Hawaii and had written her several times. Once he sent a postcard with hula dancers on it.

"Sounds like they just about wiped out our Pacific Fleet," Lennie continued. "That's what I heard on the radio anyway."

Leah tried not to think of what had happened at Pearl Harbor, but her imagination, which was such an asset in her writing, conjured up images of death and destruction she couldn't seem to control. She saw the huge warships in flames, smoke billowing upward in tall black columns against the mild blue Pacific sky. The screams and moans of dying men came to her from thousands of miles away.

"Leah, are you OK?" Lennie asked, staring at her pale face.

"No."

"Can I do anything for you?"

She tried to smile but wasn't quite able to pull it off. "No. Thanks anyway, Lennie." All the way to school, Leah prayed for her country and that God would protect the men and women who would be risking their lives in its defense.

That morning was unlike any other morning in the history of Liberty High. It began with all the noise and excitement of a Fourth of July celebration, but this seemed to fall of its own weight, replaced by an almost eerie silence. Small groups of students whispered among themselves as though Japanese spies were hiding behind every tree and bush on the school ground. The sterile December air produced a bumper crop of rumors: the Japanese had poisoned the water supply; a Japanese carrier was sighted in the Gulf of Mexico; enemy bombers were headed for the American heartland.

The teachers finally gave up trying to conduct normal classes and let the students air their fears. Alvin Ditweiler called an assembly in the auditorium to let everyone hear the message from President Roosevelt requesting a declaration of war on Japan. Tears streamed down the faces of several teachers, men as well as women. Most of the students appeared to be either in a mild state of shock or a frenzy of anger.

Leah heard the voice of the president as if echoing from a great distance, so lost was she in her thoughts of David Stone. She knew enough from what he had told her of the navy that it was just a matter of time before he would be shipped out to the Pacific where pilots would be needed the most.

When the assembly was over, several of the boys, caught up in the fever of war, rushed off to join one of the services. They were accompanied by rousing marches from the band as they stood, announcing their intentions, and marched proudly down the center aisle.

"That won't last long," Lennie scoffed, sitting next to Leah. "They'll come sneaking back here in a day or two when they realize what they've done."

"It's a patriotic thing to do, I guess," Leah observed, watching the last of the boys leave through the wide doors.

"I guess so," he agreed, "but it's gonna take a lot more than bluster to win this war.

For the remainder of the day, Leah went through the motions of going to class, opening books, taking tests, and speaking with her classmates. The tests seemed so insignificant now in light of this national catastrophe; the books had lost their meaning for her; the conversations of her classmates were nothing more than a bothersome drone.

Liberty, stunned for the first few days by the news of Pearl Harbor, soon broke into feverish activity along with the rest of the country. Men joined the armed forces in droves. Scrap drives were organized to collect old pots and pans, used tires, newspapers, and anything else that could be used in the war effort. Air-raid wardens prowled the darkened streets, wearing their official helmets proudly and looking for any violations of the blackout code.

On the Farm, little changed. Some of the young men went off to war as young men have done for thousands of years, leaving behind weeping mothers and proud fathers. January and February passed with the feeding of animals and preparing for the spring planting. Calves and colts came wide-eyed and spindly legged into the world.

Leah spent much of her time studying for school and even more on her writing. She avoided most of her classmates, finding them boring and childish, preferring rather to be with Lennie or Rachel Shaw. Most of all she enjoyed the lunch hours with Leslie Gifford, discussing literature in his classroom, when he could find the time. Nights in her room, as the cold rain swept across the desolate winter fields, she prayed for the safety of America's fighting men, especially David Stone.

* * *

The wind moaned in the eaves of the house as Leah lay across the colorful quilt on her bed, reading a volume of poems by William Butler Yeats. She had borrowed it from Gifford, who was helping her build a foundation for her own writing. One of the poems, in particular, attracted her because of its title, *On Being Asked for a War Poem.* But somehow the last lines had a troubling effect on her:

> . . . who can please
> A young girl in the indolence of her youth,
> Or an old man upon a winter's night.

Someone rapped lightly on the door. "Leah?"

"Yes, Mother?"

"We have company."

"Be right down." After brushing her hair and checking herself in the mirror, Leah went downstairs.

Seated in the parlor on the sofa, where Leah had spent such happy times with Mike Hardin, was Elder Cletus Sandifer. His black suit and tie were freshly cleaned and pressed and his big hat lay next to him where he had taken it off his big head. His muscadine eyes, fixed firmly on Leah, were so close to the bridge of his nose, she had always felt the urge to pry them out toward the tips of his hairy ears each time she saw him.

"Good evening, child." Sandifer rose, his dark bulk seeming to soak up the light in the room.

"Elder." Leah hurried over to take the chair next to her mother, who was twisting her hands together in her lap. She glanced at her father. He looked at the floor. Leah felt a slight chill working around the back of her neck. She felt as if a night crawler, the slick, slimy worms she had seen her father use for fish bait all her life, had been dropped beneath the collar of her dress and was sliding down her back.

The room lapsed into an uneasy silence. The ticking of the clock on the mantle reminded Leah of a death knell. A fly buzzed against the window.

"Well, I'm a straightforward man," Sandifer boomed, startling all three members of the Daniel family, including Albert, who was slightly hard of hearing.

Without being conscious of it, Leah leaned closer to her mother.

"Leah, child, it's time you were married. You're seventeen now and the state no longer has any hold over you. You don't have to go to their school anymore." Sandifer spoke as though he were an oracle direct from Olympus.

Leah was petrified. She felt her heart hammering wildly in her breast. *What is he talking about? This can't be happening to me.* She had heard of arranged marriages before, but not in a long while and certainly nothing as abrupt as this.

Albert Daniel glanced at his horrified daughter. "Elder, I think perhaps we need more time to discuss this with Leah—just her mother and me."

Sandifer turned his dark eyes on Daniel. They held the glazed unwavering look of a fanatic, a man so absolutely immersed in his own rightness that another's words had no meaning for him. "There's nothing to discuss, Albert. It will be as I have stated."

Leah sat transfixed, watching Sandifer. His wild gray beard was so stiff that it never moved as he turned his head from side to side. She would have been only mildly surprised if a young rabbit had bolted from it and scampered across the parlor floor. Suddenly the whole thing seemed ludicrous. That this man should come into her home, usurping her dreams. She felt herself bordering on hysteria and had to fight against it.

"There's always room for discussion, Elder." Albert Daniel tried to maintain his composure.

"Not when God has spoken!" Sandifer rose to his feet, pacing slowly back and forth in front of the sofa, hands clasped behind his back. "No room for discussion at all."

"What do you mean?"

Leah couldn't imagine what would come next. *What could be worse than this?*

Sandifer stopped in the middle of the floor. The gray light streaming in the window behind him cast his face in shadow and gave a mountainous appearance to his massive body. He glanced at Albert, then stared directly at Leah. "God told me that Leah is to be my wife!"

Mabel Daniel's hand flew to her mouth, suppressing a gasp.

Leah felt herself becoming numb. Her mind could no longer comprehend or tolerate the words it was being fed. She felt herself drifting somewhere in a gray fog. Through it she could see Sandifer resume his slow pacing. His mouth was moving in speech, but the words had a hollow, dead quality to them as though he were speaking with a barrel over his head.

Even Albert Daniel was shocked at the latest revelation. "God spoke to you?"

"In a dream," Sandifer replied. "My children need a mother," he hastened to add.

Albert's expression softened at the mention of Sandifer's children. He knew the man did the best he could for them, but they were often unkempt with dirty clothes and sad faces. They were also beginning to have a certain smell about them. This had never been the case when Sandifer's wife was alive. "You have no argument with me there, Elder. The children do need a mother."

"I thought you'd see things my way, Albert," he concluded as though the matter were settled. "Now I must be on my way. The two of us will speak further of this in private."

Albert merely nodded his head in reply.

The elder picked up his big black hat from the sofa and squeezed it onto his head. "Good day, Mabel—Leah."

Albert Daniel walked stiffly down the hall to the front door with him. Leah could hear them speaking in undertones but couldn't catch any of the words.

Mabel reached over and patted her daughter's shoulder. "Don't be upset, child. Things have a way of working themselves out. You'll see."

Leah felt wooden, as though she was no longer in control of her own body. She tried to speak. "Oh, Mother, I . . ." Great wracking sobs shook her body. She bent over, putting her face in her hands.

Mabel knelt beside her daughter, putting her arms around her, cooing to her gently. "There, there, Leah. It'll be all right. Things will work themselves out. You'll see."

Albert stood at the door to the parlor for a few seconds. His face pale and drawn, he walked softly down the hall toward the back of the house.

In a few minutes, Leah's sobs began to subside. She felt the awful hopelessness and pain being replaced by anger. "Mother, you can't let this happen! He must be a hundred years old!"

"Nonsense, child. He's not much older than your father." Mabel patted Leah on the shoulder as though by that simple gesture she could make the world bright again.

That night Leah lay in bed listening to the wind. She had tried to pray but felt that the windows of heaven were bolted shut against her supplications.

She turned from side to side, lying on her stomach with her pillow over her head to shut out the terrible thoughts that came to her. Finally she called out in desperation. *Oh, God, please don't let this happen! This can't be Your plan for me! Nothing that causes a person this much pain could be Your will! I don't know what to do! Give me peace so I can sleep. In Jesus' name!*

Leah lay on her back, staring at the high ceiling. At first she thought someone was in the room with her, but she could see by the pale moonlight streaming through the window there wasn't. A soothing warmth seemed to flow over her. Her mind slowed its turbulent journey and, succumbing to a drowsy, pleasant weariness, she drifted off into a restful sleep.

The next week seemed to last an eternity for Leah. She couldn't concentrate on her schoolwork and would sit for an hour at a time, tablet on her lap and pencil in hand, without writing a word. Her mother and father had interminable closed sessions in their bedroom, discussing their daughter's future. Albert made two visits to Sandifer's home, returning both times after Leah had gone to sleep.

Finally, just before bedtime one night Leah's mother called her into the parlor. "Your father has something to tell you," she murmured, then disappeared up the stairs.

Albert motioned for his daughter to join him on the sofa. Putting his arm around her shoulders, he spoke in a tone softer than Leah could ever remember his using before. "Leah, your mother and I have decided . . ."

Leah didn't listen to any more of her father's words. When he put his arm around her shoulder, she knew what the decision was, as he had never been an affectionate man. She sat stiffly while her sentence was pronounced.

". . . and Elder Sandifer has graciously agreed to allow you to finish high school. The wedding will be celebrated after your graduation ceremony."

10

"THE ONLY THING WE HAVE TO FEAR IS FEAR ITSELF!"

*A*merica was suddenly and deliberately attacked by naval and air forces of the Empire of Japan."

Mike Hardin leaned toward the massive floor model Philco radio that dominated one wall of the living room of his dorm. The room was packed with young athletes, all frozen into silence as they listened to the reassuring voice of President Franklin Delano Roosevelt. Jay Stockton, the bulky first-string center, cursed the Japanese, then grunted, "Why don't he declare war and get on with it?"

"Close your trap, Jay!" Mike snapped, leaning closer. The news of the Japanese attack had affected him in a strange manner. When the line coach had come crashing into the dorm the day before, yelling, "Hey, guys, the Japs are bombing Pearl Harbor! We're at war!" it had been as though he'd been felled by a hard blow. The other jocks had cursed and raved as they'd sat around the radio trying to get the details—but Mike hadn't said a word. Finally they had gone to bed, and his roommate, the second-string tight end, had asked curiously, "Mike, ain't you sore? You ain't said a word."

Mike had nodded slowly. "I'm sore all right, Dwight—but it's going to take more than cussing the Japs to satisfy me."

Now he listened silently to the president ask the Congress to declare war against Japan and end his speech by saying: "We will gain the inevitable triumph, so help us God!"

Instantly the room burst into applause and cheers. Jumbo Highlander, the left guard, had a booming voice to match his massive body. He declared, "I'm gonna join the army. Them Japs can't get away with this."

Others began boasting of how they'd join at once, and finally Jumbo eyed Mike, asking, "What about you, Mike? What branch you headed for?"

Hardin said instantly, "Naval air force."

"Hey, the thing will be over by the time they teach you how to fly!"

"I doubt it, Jumbo," he answered. He got up and left the room, walking aimlessly around the campus, his mind filled with the crisis. He sat down beside a large fountain, sharing a concrete bench with some dulcet-voiced pigeons. "No peanuts today," he said quietly. "Sorry about that."

For a long time he sat watching the pigeons and the water as it bubbled and fell to the fountain below. It had been a mild winter; whoever decided such things had opted to leave the fishpond undrained. Now the large goldfish moved their tattered fins languidly in the murky water, gaping with open mouths as they hung suspended.

Daddy will kill me if I join the navy—but if I don't enlist, sooner or later I'll have to go. And I'd hate to spend the war carrying a pack through the mud!

He glanced up at the slate-colored sky, wondering what it would be like to fly a powerful plane armed with deadly guns and bombs—and at that moment he made up his mind.

Dave Stone said he'd help me get into naval aviation—well, I'm going to give him a chance to fish or cut bait! The thought of quick action stimulated him as always, and he got up and walked quickly along the sidewalk. His mind ranged over what must be done, and by the time he'd walked around the campus twice, he knew what he had to do.

*   *   *

"Do you remember me, Lieutenant Stone?"

Dave Stone had just come close to death, but the only sign of strain on his face was a tight pressure of his lips. A green recruit had nearly flown a trainer into the ground, and only after a struggle had Stone regained control of the airplane. He'd sent the young pilot away, and now stared at the large young man who was waiting for him beside the hangar. Recognition came slowly.

"Sure—Bill Hardin, isn't it? From Liberty?"

"Mike," Hardin corrected. He'd bribed and bullied his way onto the airfield, and a corporal stood watchfully ten feet away to make sure he was not a spy. Hardin nodded toward the corporal, saying, "If you could tell him that you know me, Lieutenant, he might not be so suspicious."

"It's all right, Corporal," Stone said. "I'll be responsible." As the corporal turned and left, Stone said, "I'm surprised to see you, Hardin. How's Les Gifford?"

"Well, I haven't seen him in some time," Mike said. "I've been at Georgia Tech." He hesitated, then blurted out, "I guess you've forgotten what you said to me back at Liberty."

"No, I remember. Did you come to see about getting into the program?"

"I sure did!" Mike was relieved at the officer's words. He had feared that Stone had spoken carelessly, but now he plunged in, speaking earnestly. "I know it sounds crazy, Lieutenant Stone, but I want to get in *now!*"

Dave Stone said, "Let's go find a place to talk, Mike. I think I can get you into the Officers Club as a guest." He led the way to the one-story stucco building, and when the two had gone inside and were seated at a booth, Stone said, "Mike, every time a war begins, young fellows rush out to enlist. In some wars, there wasn't room for them all—like the Spanish-American War. And I think that's not bad." He took a long pull on his Coke, adding thoughtfully, "The best and the most courageous are the first to fill the ranks."

The jukebox suddenly blared out, Tex Beneke singing, "Pardon me, boys, is that the Chattanooga Choo-Choo?" and Stone had to lean forward and speak louder. "What do your parents say about your joining up?"

"I haven't told them," Mike confessed. He looked down at his big hand, his brow wrinkled. "They won't like it, though." Then he turned his eyes on Stone and his lips were firmly set. "My mind's made up, Lieutenant Stone. I'll be in this war anyway—and I want to pick my own brand of action!"

The two men sat at the table, Mike speaking earnestly, desperate to convince Stone of his sincerity. Finally Stone said, "Well, Mike, it's not going to be easy. First, you'll have to finish your two years in college. Then you'll have to do basic flight school."

Mike grinned at the smaller man. "I took a full load last summer, Lieutenant. I'll have my two years at the end of this semester—in about three weeks—with good grades, too!" Mike noted the
surprise on Stone's face and added proudly, "*And* I went through
the CPTP program this year!"

"The Civilian Pilot Training Program?" Stone leaned forward
with interest. "How'd you do?"

"Top of my class!" Mike nodded. "Look, Lieutenant, I'm serious about this. Somehow ever since you took me up, I've thought
of nothing but flying. I made the football team, but my heart wasn't
in it." He paused and there was a brooding look on his face. The
voice of Sinatra filled the room as he crooned, "I'll never smile
again—until I smile at you," but neither man really heard it. Mike
gave his shoulders a shake, then looked directly into Stone's eyes.
"Will you help me, Lieutenant?"

Stone stared across the table, thinking of all that Leslie Gifford
had told him about this young man. *He's totally selfish and has to have
the limelight,* Stone thought. *But he's done his homework—and I guess
lots of good pilots have a healthy ego.*

"All right, Mike, I'll do what I can," he nodded suddenly.
"There are a few shortcuts, and I'll see what I can do."

Mike felt relief wash over him, and he slumped against the
back of his seat. "Gosh! That's a relief! I wasn't even sure you'd remember me."

Stone said idly, "Why not? We've got a mutual friend, remember?"

"Oh, sure—Mr. Gifford."

"Yes, but he's not the only one. Leah Daniel is the one I
meant."

Surprise came to Mike's eyes, and he nodded. "Why, sure, I
forgot about Leah." He dropped his eyes, wondering if Leah had
mentioned to Stone how he'd gone away and failed to write. "I—
I've gotten behind on my letter writing. Is she doing okay?"

"That young woman will always do okay," Stone said. He
drank the last of his Coke, got to his feet, and said, "Well, I've got
another future ace to risk my life with. Give me your address and
phone number, and I'll start the ball rolling."

Mike returned to Tech and was shocked to receive a letter
from the navy two weeks later. He tore it open and read it quickly:

22 December 1941

Mr. Michael Hardin
Box 2231
Georgia Institute of Technology
Atlanta, Georgia

Dear Sir:

You are advised that if we receive your educational record by the third of January, your papers will be forwarded to the Navy Department for training in the class commencing 15 January 1942. The January group is now in the process of being selected and their papers will leave this office the latter part of this month.

We suggest you obtain the transcript as soon as the college will release it and forward same to us promptly. Your application will be given every consideration at such time as you can meet the educational requirements. We trust that you will be one of the successful candidates.

Yours truly,

R. G. Ratton
Lieutenant, USN
Commanding

Mike moved faster around the campus than he'd ever moved on a football field! The day after this letter arrived, he'd managed to get tentative grades from all his professors and, by a minor miracle, got his transcript while he waited. He posted the letter, and settled back for a long wait.

He received another surprise when a brief letter from the Navy came, directing him to appear for a physical in Atlanta, but it encouraged him that something was being done. "That Dave Stone is really getting things done!" he murmured as he came out, having passed the exam as expected. But he had barely finished his finals (doing so well that he lived up to the grades he'd been given!) and was packing to go home, when a third letter arrived.

Tearing it open, his knees were weak with a premonition that he'd failed to make the cut. The letter read:

You are directed to report to commanding officer, Jacksonville Naval Air Station on 3 January 1942 for enlistment into the United States Navy. Elimination flight training as a member of the January class will begin immediately upon completion of enlistment procedures. You will be reimbursed for expenses incurred in carrying out these orders.

> R. G. Ratton
> Lieutenant, USN
> Commanding

"That's it—I'm in the navy!" Mike shouted. His shout drew a crowd, and when he showed them the letter and said, "I'll soon be mowing the Japs down in my trusty fighter!" nothing would do but an all-night party to celebrate. He got home in time to pack and catch the morning bus to Liberty, escorted by those few of his friends who were still conscious. Jumbo said, "I'm too drunk to walk—but I'll drive you to the bus station, Mike."

"No, Jumbo, I think that'd be more dangerous than bombing a Jap carrier," Mike grinned. They all went in a taxi, and as the bus pulled out, Mike felt a moment's sadness, thinking, *No more football for me. Now I'll never know if I had the stuff to make it in the pros.*

He slumped in the seat, thinking of what lay ahead, but soon his eyes closed and he slept soundly all the way to Liberty. As the bus passed the water tank, he sat up and tried to think of a good way to break the news to his parents. But there was no way, so he squared his shoulders, got off the bus, and headed for his house.

He'd lived in Liberty all his life and knew every street. As he passed down Main, he wondered suddenly, *What if I get killed? I'd never see this again. Never have another malt at Ollie's Drugstore or see another movie at the Liberty Theater.*

Mortality suddenly came on him, like a heavy mantle, and as he passed along the sunny streets, he was acutely aware of shadows that he'd never known existed.

*   *   *

"I hear they're gonna have a big homecoming for Ben." Mike Hardin walked along the sidewalk next to Billy Christmas. "Are you gonna try to come in for it?"

"Yeah. They say he's been recommended for the Congressional. I don't want to miss that." Billy brushed his thick black hair back from his face. His dark blue eyes darted nervously about the street in a furtive manner.

"If I know Ben, he'd just as soon forget all this drum-and-bugle stuff and stay with his shipmates." Mike noticed Billy's nervousness. "What's the matter with you, Son? You act like you're on the lam from J. Edgar himself."

Billy laughed uneasily. "I've been spending too much time away from college. I should be there right now. The general doesn't suffer truants gladly. All that doesn't seem important anymore, though, with the war and all. I hope I can see Ben a few minutes during his homecoming. Find out what it's really like to be in battle. I'm thinking about joining up myself."

"The general would stand you before a firing squad if you tried that," Mike laughed. "You gonna get your degree, be an officer, son. A real chip off the ol' West Point block."

"I just might fool you, Mike," Billy grinned. "By the way, what's going on with you now? I don't see anybody much since I went off to college. I heard you went back to Tech."

"Yep. Playing football, making decent grades, the whole thing." Mike stared at Billy, nodding his head slowly. "You're right, though, it all seems like kid stuff next to joining up and whipping a few Japs. I been thinking about that ever since Pearl."

"What'd you have in mind?"

"I've already done it."

"Done what?"

"Joined the navy. I report to Jacksonville on the third."

Billy's blue eyes flashed with excitement. "You're gonna be a sailor like Ben?"

"Not exactly," Mike smiled proudly. "I finished the CPTP over at Tech."

"The what?"

"It's a flight-training program. With that and my two years of college I managed to get into the navy's pilot training program. A navy flyer—that's my idea of going first class." Mike grinned at Billy. "You serious about this joining-up business?"

"Getting more serious every day."

"What branch?"

"Marines."

Mike whistled loudly. "Marines! How long you had this death wish, Son?"

"I never knew you to play things safe, Hardin," Billy shot back. "What kinda flying are you gonna do?"

"Dive bombers."

"I rest my case." Billy pointed across the street to the drug-store. "How about a malt at Ollie's?"

"Nah. I gotta get home and check the mail," Mike explained. "Expecting a letter from a flight instructor down at Pensacola. Trying to pull some strings and get me into his section of the pilot program."

"Well, I hope you make it through, if that's what you want."

"You too, Billy. Take care."

Ten minutes later, Mike shuffled through the stack of mail his mother had laid on the kitchen table. Seeing a letter with Dave Stone's return address on it, he ripped it open. He scanned it briefly, then leaped high into the air. "Yeehaaah!"

Darla Hardin came rushing down the hall to the kitchen. "Mike, are you all right?"

"Better than all right, Mama," Mike grinned. "A whole lot better!"

11

INDEPENDENCE DAY

When I walk across that stage and take that diploma in my hand—my life ends! Jesus, if it weren't for Your strength, I'd just be done with this world—I think I'd kill myself! But I believe there's something better waiting for me. I have to believe that! Maybe this is just a test of my faith.

Leah sat in the auditorium watching the first of the few students to graduate at mid-year walk across the stage to receive their diplomas from Superintendent T. P. Sloan. The Liberty High band played "Pomp and Circumstance" with one trombone slightly off-key. Then her turn came. The second row stood and marched toward the stage and up the steps. Waiting in the wings, she glanced out at the bright faces of her classmates. They all look so excited, so happy. *Why can't this be a happy time for me? I've worked as hard as anybody else!*

Then Leah was walking toward the rostrum where Sloan waited. She imagined that she walked toward a scaffold where a black-hooded hangman waited with his noose.

"Miss Leah Daniel." Sloan's voice reverberated in the auditorium as he waited, a thin smile on his face.

Leah snapped back into reality. The scaffold became a simple rostrum—the noose, a diploma—and the hangman, merely a small-town schoolmaster named T. P. Sloan.

As Leah took the diploma in her hand, changing her tassel from the left to the right side of her mortar board, she could almost hear a coffin lid slamming shut on her liberty—on her career as a writer.

"God bless you, Leah." Sloan's voice was steady and pleasant.

At the sound of his voice, Leah felt instantly better. He was the last person in the world she would have expected to be a source of comfort for her. His words were like water in a parched land. "Thank you," she mumbled. *I guess God does work in mysterious ways.*

Returning to her seat, Leah watched her robed classmates marching toward an uncertain future in a world ablaze with the fury and power of war. The music the band played sounded like a dirge. Her thoughts returned to the all-too-certain future that she faced with Elder Cletus Sandifer. She saw his wild, dark eyes—felt his bushy beard rasp against her soft skin. *No!*

Suddenly, a passage from the fifth chapter of Romans seemed to impress itself on her mind. "But we glory in tribulations also: knowing that tribulation worketh patience; And patience, experience; and experience, hope."

Well, Daddy says there's always hope, even in the worst of times. And this is sure the worst time I've ever had! Maybe I can have courage like David did during his hard times. "Be of good courage, and he shall strengthen your heart, all ye that hope in the Lord."

Leah tried to hold on to the words of comfort, but still, at the edge of her courage where the light failed, she could feel despair lurking like a yellow-eyed beast.

*   *   *

Leah walked through the late-winter woods strewn with dry leaves. As she came to the meadow, she noticed a few wildflowers that the unusually warm weather had coaxed forth. Yellow and blue and white, they waved in the breeze, a dazzling dance of color in the pale sunlight. She thought of Wordsworth's poem about daffodils. *"I wandered lonely as a cloud." That's me all right. Can't remember how the rest of it goes. Something about the daffodils dancing in the breeze. Oh, I do remember the last two lines about how he feels when he remembers them!* "And then my heart with pleasure fills, And dances with the daffodils."

Coming to the pond, Leah sat down beneath the willow where she had spent such happy hours with Leslie Gifford discussing the great writers, dreaming that someday she would be among them. She smelled the damp, rich earth at the water's edge. The wind rippled across the pond, shattering its surface with light.

Mr. Gifford! Maybe he could tell me what to do! He's always been a good friend. I certainly can't talk to my family about this anymore. They can only see things one way—the way Elder Sandifer sees them. How could I get in touch with Mr. Gifford though? Lennie! Maybe he'd take a message to him for me. Father always liked Mr. Gifford. He'd give his permission for me to spend some time with him.

And he did. Three days later, Leah sat next to Leslie Gifford in his Ford coupe spinning along the dusty gravel road toward town.

"I received a letter from David Stone." Gifford leaned back against the seat, holding the steering wheel with his good hand. "He said you had another story published."

Leah stared out the window at the fence posts flashing by. A single blue jay screeched at her from his perch on the barbed wire. "Yes sir. They sent me another two hundred dollars."

"You'll be rich and famous by the time you're twenty-one, Miss Daniel," Gifford smiled. "I expect I'd better get your autograph now before it gets too expensive for a poor schoolteacher to afford."

Leah laughed softly. "I don't think there's any chance of that. Not anymore."

Gifford noticed her despondent look, but decided to let her broach whatever it was that was bothering her.

A few minutes later they pulled over to the curb near Ollie's Drugstore. Inside, the coffee and newspaper club had already gone to work and the lunch crowd hadn't yet arrived.

Ollie stood behind the counter at his sink, washing the last of the breakfast dishes. "Morning, Leslie. Haven't seen you since school let out, Leah."

After exchanging a few pleasantries, Gifford and Leah took their fountain Cokes over to the last booth next to the jukebox while Ollie disappeared into the back of the store.

"How about some music?" Gifford took two nickels from his jacket pocket, dropping them on the table.

Leah had listened to the jukebox a few times, but she had never actually played a song on one. "I—I don't know very much about music. We don't have radios at the Farm."

"I know. Just pick whatever strikes your fancy."

Leah picked up the two nickels from table and stood before the jukebox, leaning on it with both hands as she had seen some of her classmates do. Scanning the selections, she came to "Boogie Woogie," by Tommy Dorsey. *Elder Sandifer would just hate that!* she thought grimly, pushing the button much harder than she had intended. Then she played "Over the Rainbow," by Judy Garland. *Wish I could have seen that movie,* The Wizard of Oz.

When she sat back down, she was startled to see a gift on the table. It was badly wrapped with the gold foil crumpled on the ends where it had been folded. She knew Gifford had wrapped it himself. "What's this for?"

Gifford smiled. His strange, sad eyes held a tender light. "I didn't have a chance to give you a graduation present. Hope you like it. I had to order it out of New York."

Leah carefully unwrapped the gift, reading the book jacket. *The Heart Is a Lonely Hunter,* by Carson McCullers. Her blue-gray eyes grew bright with tears. A sharp pain stabbed at her chest as the thought came to her that some day there might have been a book published with her name on it.

"What's wrong, Leah? I didn't mean to upset you." He reached over and lay his hand on hers.

"Oh, Mr. Gifford! My life's such a mess!"

Gifford handed her his handkerchief. She wiped her face, regained her composure, and poured out her story.

Gifford sipped his Coke, his eyes fixed in thought.

Leah listened to the sweet, perfect voice of Judy Garland. "And the dreams that you dare to dream really do come true . . ."

"Leah, you don't have to marry that man."

"But my father and mother . . ."

"I believe in the family as strongly as anyone, Leah," he interrupted. "It's where we get strength and direction for our lives. It's also the bedrock of this country. That may sound strange coming from an old bachelor, but it's the truth."

Leah listened intently, suddenly feeling a ray of hope.

"But," Gifford continued, "there comes an independence day for all of us. The day we start living our own lives—laying the foundation for our own families."

"The Bible says we're supposed to honor our fathers and mothers," Leah observed.

Gifford smiled, the gentle light still flickering in his eyes. "I don't believe God intended for *honor* to mean that we have to be ruled by our parents all our lives. If that were the case, none of us would ever grow up—learn to make decisions for ourselves—make our own contribution to the world."

Leah considered Gifford's comments thoughtfully. "But what could I do? I don't have any place to live."

"What do you want to do?"

"I want to go to college and study writing," she responded immediately.

"Well, we'll just find a way for you to do that then." Gifford placed his right thumb under his chin, rubbing his lips with his forefinger. "I've got a place for us to start!"

"What is it?" Leah asked eagerly.

"Florence Myles, the librarian over at the college, is a friend of mine." Gifford grinned like a mischievous boy. "If I take her out for a good steak dinner, I just bet we can get you a job in the library. With that and the money you've got from selling your stories, you should be able to make it okay. Renting a room near the campus should be the easy part. You can probably sell some more stories, too."

Leah sipped her Coke, tasting how good it was for the first time since she sat down in the booth.

* * *

"Mother, I've told you I'll be just fine. I've got a nice room two blocks from the school. Two home-cooked meals a day. Miss Myles seems to like me already. I think we're going to get along just great." Leah knelt next to her mother's chair in the parlor. Her few belongings were packed in two cardboard boxes tied with string. They sat on the floor next to the front door.

"But you've never been away from home for even one night before!" Mabel Daniel wiped her eyes with a tiny white handkerchief. "You're still my little girl!"

"I'm eighteen now, Mother," Leah said gently, trying to put more conviction in her voice than she actually felt. "And everyone has to have a first night away from home."

Albert Daniel stood at the arched doorway that led from the parlor into the hall, thumbs hooked in his suspenders. He thought of Cletus Sandifer's tirade when he told him of Leah's decision to leave the Farm. The storm was calmed when Mabel told Sandifer she'd come over three times a week to help with the cooking and the cleaning.

"Leah, you don't know anything about the ways of the world. It's wicked. There are men who . . ." Mabel almost sobbed, unable to finish the sentence.

"Mother, you and Father raised me as a Christian," Leah encouraged. "I don't intend to live any other kind of life."

Albert's face brightened. He felt a bittersweet pang of joy as he gazed at his daughter.

Leah took her mother's face in her hands and kissed her on the cheek, wet still with her tears. "Mother, I'm going to make you and Father proud of me. And it's not like I'm going to the ends of the earth. I'll come out every weekend. Lennie's working in town now. He said I can catch a ride with him anytime."

"We have to let her go now." Albert glanced out the window to where the Ford coupe was idling next to his wagon. "Mr. Gifford's waiting on her."

"You're not mad at him are you, Father?" Leah glanced anxiously up at him.

"No, Child. He only wants what's best for you." Albert held his hand out to his wife. She took it and stood up next to him.

Leah embraced her mother, kissing her again on the cheek. She looked up at her tall father, seeing the trace of a smile at the corners of his mouth. Standing on tiptoe, she kissed him on the cheek.

Albert and Mabel Daniel laid their hands on their daughter and prayed for God's protection over her. Leah heard her father's voice as he spoke from his favorite psalm. "For he shall give his angels charge over thee, to keep thee in all thy ways."

Part 2

MIKE AND DAVE

12

LIBERTY

More than once as Mike Hardin went through flight training, he felt more like a piece of equipment than a living man. He learned that every recruit was observed carefully—as if under a microscope—to determine if he possessed the combination of aptitude and attitude required to warrant the expenditure of thousands of tax dollars to transform him into a first-class pilot.

All his fellows in the program had several traits in common: good health, unmarried, young, at least two years of college, and an intense desire to fly airplanes. Most of the fledgling pilots had blue eyes, so Mike's hazel eyes made him stand out.

But it was his aggressiveness, more than the color of his eyes, that drew the attention of everyone. He threw himself at the difficulties of flight school with the same reckless abandon he'd used on the football field.

"You're going to have to sit on this one, Dave," Captain Pete Lassiter grunted just two weeks into the training. "Hardin's a hot dog—the worst I've ever seen."

"Sure, he's that, Captain," Stone agreed. "But he's the best pilot in the group." He thought carefully, then added, "Maybe the best we've *ever* had."

"Yeah? Well, you watch him, Dave," Lassiter snapped. "I've seen these hot shots before. They're grandstanders, every one of 'em. Sure they outshine the rest of the men in drills and gunnery, but they're glory hunters. Can't be counted on for teamwork."

Secretly Dave Stone agreed with his commanding officer, but he refused to admit it. "He'll be okay, sir. I'll sit down hard on him if he gets out of line."

"See you do. He'll be on somebody's wing when we go into combat. He's just the kind who'd leave you and go off after another scalp for his belt!"

Later in the week, after Stone had given Mike a lesson in formation flying, the two of them were walking along toward the hangar, discussing the flight. "Mike, you're leading the group in most of the numbers," Stone said. "But formation flying is your weak spot."

Mike shrugged carelessly. "I'll work on it, Lieutenant—but according to all I've heard, once a group goes into action, it's every man for himself."

"Wrong!" Stone stopped abruptly and his expression was so stern that Mike blinked with astonishment. "Wrong! Wrong! Wrong!" Stone spat out, his eyes hard. "When you go into action—*if* you ever do!—you'll probably live or die because of the pilot who's guarding your wing. And the fellow on your left is counting on you to keep him alive! If you don't learn that, Hardin, I'll never sign that piece of paper saying you're qualified as a pilot in the Naval Air Service!"

Mike licked his lips nervously. He'd never seen Stone angry, not even when some of the less gifted recruits had done some pretty dumb things. A streak of resentment fell across his nerves, and he wanted to remind his instructor that he was leading every other man in the group in every aspect of training. However, he'd learned to handle coaches and made himself say humbly, "Sure, I see that, sir. I just get carried away; I forget sometimes." He saw Stone's face relax, and added, "I'll put my mind on it from now on, Lieutenant."

Stone nodded, pleased that Hardin had responded so well. "You're the best natural pilot in the group, Hardin. But we're headed for combat, and we've all got to learn group integrity."

Group integrity! It was a phrase that came to nauseate Mike in the weeks that followed. "Your group! Your group!" Stone and the others hammered at the recruits. "You're responsible to your group! Never forget that. Your flight is designed to get maximum effort out of a certain number of planes. When you leave your group, you've robbed your group of its integrity!"

Mike had heard this sort of thing before—from his coaches. They all talked about putting the good of the team first—but Mike had noticed than when he pulled away from his blocking and made a touchdown, none of them had ever gone into a rage. *All this team stuff is okay*, he finally decided, *but the name of the game is to finish off the enemy. If a guy has to leave his group to do that—why, no commander's going to mind!*

He worked on his formation flying as he'd promised, and with no trouble became an expert at it as well. As the days went by he perfected takeoffs, landings, aerobatics, spins, and stalls to recovery. He felt sorry for those who dropped out, but never once did it occur to him that he might fail.

The time flashed by, and when the orders came to move from Jacksonville to Pensacola Naval Air Station, it caught Mike off guard. His group joined others to become flight class 4B–42–PC (166–C).

Pensacola Naval Air Station possessed a charm and a dignity that came from age and permanence. From its imposing main gate entrance to the brick hangars along the bay front, the base exuded a pride peculiar to naval aviation. It was a complete base, with distinctive officer housing on the hill overlooking Chevalier Field, a large overhaul and repair facility, a beautiful beach and Officers Club (with tennis courts), and even a regulation eighteen-hole golf course. A new aeronautical ground school complex had just been completed with auditorium, movie house, armory, and classrooms equal to the finest college or university in the country.

The training began with Stearman N3N trainer biplanes with open fore and aft cockpits. After a twenty-hour check, the cadets were moved into acrobatics, learning how to do snap rolls, loops, wingovers, Immelmanns, split-S's, and falling leaves. Mike said good-bye to several pretty good pilots who couldn't achieve the perfection demanded by the instructors, but he himself had no problem. He was moved with a few other choice pilots into Squadron 2, where he learned to fly heavier aircraft.

All of the cadets in Squadron 2 understood that their fate in naval aviation would be settled to some degree by the assignment they received. The carrier-type (VC) was the most coveted, and when the assignments were posted after a few weeks, Cadet Michael Hardin was assigned to that most glamorous duty!

"Congratulations, Mr. Hardin!"

Mike turned to find David Stone smiling at him. "I made it, sir!" Mike exclaimed. "I made carrier duty!"

"Never had any doubts about it," Stone nodded. "And I don't know if it's good news for you or not—but I'll be going with you fellows. No more instruction duty!"

"Hey, that's *great*, Lieutenant!" Mike beamed. "Between the two of us, we can shoot down the entire Japanese air force!"

"You'll never win a humility award talking like that," Stone shook his head. But he added at once, "I'm going to your hometown next week. Think you could stand three days' liberty? I'd enjoy your company."

Mike stared at the officer, then nodded. "Yes, *sir!* Can you fix that?"

"I think your group will get a short liberty before moving into the final phase of your training." He turned, saying, "We'll do it then. Don't mess up!"

"Not me!" Mike exclaimed, shaking his head almost violently. He could see himself going home in his new uniform. *I'll have to fight the women off with a stick!* he thought exultantly.

*   *   *

The first two days of liberty were all Mike had hoped. He was greeted by everyone in town, it seemed, as a conquering hero. His father seemed to have forgotten his anger over Mike's refusal to stay in college and play ball, and proudly pointed out that his son was the hottest pilot ever to hit Pensacola!

As for finding a date, the only problem was to sift through the applicants. T. P. Sloan insisted that Mike address the students at the weekly assembly. Mike had halfheartedly argued against it, but he allowed himself to be persuaded. He'd been properly modest in his remarks, but afterward he'd been swamped by hoards of students, the young men filled with envy and the girls' eyes filled with something else.

But Mike had avoided the high-school girls as companions; even the seniors seemed to him like children. For the first two evenings he found companionship with two of the more mature young ladies of Liberty. He had discretely borrowed his father's car and gone to a neighboring town, knowing that whatever he did in Liberty would be public at once.

On Friday, the last day of his leave, he slept late, having gotten to bed at three in the morning, and found himself thinking of Leah

Daniel. As he ate the breakfast his mother put before him, she asked him what his plans were.

"Oh, I guess I'll go out and see Leah Daniel." He ate a bite of biscuit, adding, "If I could get her out of that jail she lives in, I'd take her out on a date."

His mother answered, "Why, she's not at the Farm, Mike. Didn't you know that?"

Mike was lifting a bite of scrambled eggs to his mouth, but paused and stared at her. "Not at the Farm? Where is she?"

"Oh, when she graduated from high school, she went to Liberty College."

Mike slowly put the eggs into his mouth and chewed them thoughtfully. "I'm surprised they let her do that." He finished his breakfast and spent the rest of the day visiting old friends. That afternoon, after several sets of tennis, he went home, showered and shaved, then put on his uniform. When his mother encountered him going out the front door, she asked, "Where are you going, Mike?"

"Oh, I'm going to the college, Mama." He shrugged his broad shoulders, adding, "I'm going to take Leah out. She helped me a lot you know, and I thought I'd pay her back." He kissed his mother briefly. "Poor kid," he observed wryly. "She's a pretty plain girl and not good with guys."

"Well, it's nice of you to spend your last night at home taking her out. I hope she appreciates it!"

"It'll be a treat for her, I guess," Mike agreed. "I'll be in early tonight." He grinned as a thought came to him. "One thing about dating these plain little Christian girls—you can get in bed early and in good shape!"

He left the house and walked to the college campus. It was cold, with a hint of snow in the air. He'd drunk too much the night before and the snap in the air seemed to clean him out. He wondered what Dave Stone had been doing, thinking, *Not much to do in a small town like this. I wonder if Dave gave up and went back to Pensacola.* He'd called Stone's motel room twice without getting an answer and was somewhat put out. *We could have some fun together—but maybe he doesn't want to be seen with a lowly cadet.*

He put thoughts of Stone from his mind as he arrived at the campus. He was pleased with the thought of spending the evening with Leah. It gave him the sense of sacrificing something, and he'd had enough partying the past two evenings. He went at once to the girls' dorm and asked one of the students at the desk, "Would you tell Leah Daniel she's got a visitor?" he asked.

He waited in the lobby of the dorm, staring at the pictures on the wall and thinking that they hadn't been changed since he'd waited here for girls two years earlier. He was standing at the window staring out at the sky, when a voice startled him.

"Hello, Mike."

He turned quickly, saying, "Why, hello, Leah—!" But as he spoke, he was strangely rattled. He took her hand but was amazed at the transformation that had taken place in her. He'd been expecting the thin young girl he'd last seen, but the young woman whose hand he held was nothing like her!

Leah was wearing a light blue wool dress that matched the color of her eyes. She was still slim, but the contours of her figure were those of a woman, not a half-grown girl such as he remembered. She was smiling at him, and he noted that the mystery of womanhood revealed itself in the curve of her lips and in the steadiness of her blue-gray eyes. Her complexion was flawless, and he noted that she wore a little makeup.

"Why—Leah—" he said awkwardly, "You grew up on ol' Mike!"

She laughed softly. "People do that, don't they?" She pulled her hand from his grip, saying, "You're looking fine, Mike."

"So are you," he said, and felt that it was an inane reply. His nimble brain seemed to be paralyzed, and the speech he'd made up to give her seemed to be senseless. He blurted out, "I didn't know you were in college until this morning."

"Oh, I thought Dave might have mentioned it."

"Dave?"

The edges of her lips curved upward slightly, amusement in her eyes. "Yes, Dave Stone, your flight instructor."

"Oh—sure!" Mike said hastily. "Well, he's so busy trying to keep me from killing myself I guess he didn't have time." He felt awkward under her steady gaze, and somehow her remark grated on him. "You two been writing?"

"Oh, yes," Leah nodded. She glanced at the overstuffed chairs, saying, "Shall we sit down?"

"Well, I thought we might go out, Leah," Mike said. "This is my last night of liberty, and I thought you might like to help me celebrate."

Her expression was smooth as she answered, "Why, Mike, that's so nice of you to think of that." She shook her head slightly, saying, "I'd like to—but Dave and I are going out."

"Oh—" Mike grunted, and his brow wrinkled. He asked, "I haven't been able to get him at his motel."

"Well, we've been pretty busy," Leah smiled. "Would you like to come along with us?"

Mike stiffened his back, his answer rather short. "No thanks, Leah." He was angry and knew he shouldn't be. Somehow he felt betrayed and said curtly, "I'll find another date."

"I'm sure you will," she answered blandly. "There are several attractive girls here. Would you like me to introduce you to one of them?"

Mike shook his head, his eyes hard. "No, thanks. I can find a date without any help."

"I'm sure you can."

Mike could make nothing of her. She was not the same backward young girl he'd said good-bye to, and something in her bearing troubled him. He felt that he'd been bested in some way, though he didn't know exactly how. He said, "Look, Leah, I'm sorry I didn't answer your letters. I was pretty busy." His own words ran hollowly, and he tried to smooth them over. "If I'd known you were in college, I'd have written you."

"Would you, Mike?"

"Sure I would!"

"Then I wish you'd known it," Leah said easily. "And I'll be hearing from you now that you know?"

Mike knew she was laughing at him, though her words were innocent enough. But he read the slight gleam of humor in her eyes, and his irritation grew. He didn't answer her question, but put his cap on. "Well, I'll be moving on. Tell Lieutenant Stone I won't be riding back to the station with him."

"You can tell him yourself," she said, noticing Stone's car pull up. "Here he comes."

For some reason, Mike felt out of place as Stone came in. He wished that he'd gotten away before the man had arrived, but there was no way out. Stone was surprised to see him, but was friendly enough. "Hello, Mike. I just called your house."

"Hello, Dave," Mike said. He wanted to get away and said, "I just came by to see Leah."

"We're going out to eat," Stone responded. "Come along with us."

"No, thanks. You two don't need me along." Mike turned to go but halted long enough to say, "Don't bother coming by for me tomorrow, Dave. I've got a friend who wants to take me back to the station."

"Okay," Stone grinned. "I'll bet whoever it is is prettier than I am."

"Yeah," Mike managed a smile. "Well, Leah, so long. Glad things are working out for you."

"Thank you, Mike." When the door closed, Dave cocked one eyebrow and grinned at Leah. "Is he trying to beat my time?"

Leah blushed and laughed shortly. "You know Mike."

"I do indeed!" Stone was staring at her, and the color in her cheeks grew brighter. "He was pretty shocked when he saw you, I'll bet."

"Why—"

"Well, I can't blame him, Leah. You've grown up since he last saw you."

Leah was embarrassed by his steady eyes. "I'm still a growing girl, so let's eat."

"All right. Better get a heavy coat, though. It's a little chilly."

She took her coat and the two of them left the dorm. Dave insisted on going out to the Farm, where they spent several hours with Leah's parents, then they went to George's Steak House, the most expensive restaurant to be found. It was outside the city limits and Leah was impressed. After they had ordered from the menu, she said, "Dave, that steak costs four dollars!"

"But it weighs ten ounces," he grinned.

Leah did a quick calculation and looked at him. "I just figured out that Lady is worth a fortune at that price."

Lady was the calf that Stone had met on his first visit to Leah's house. He'd watched the calf grow up to a fine yearling and had become very fond of her. On every visit, Leah had taken him to visit her, and he said now, "Hard to think of that, isn't it? Someone eating Lady!"

"Don't talk about it!"

Stone grew thoughtful, his lean face handsome in repose. "Someone gave me a rabbit for Easter when I was seven years old. I kept him in my room. He'd get into everything! Once he ate the insulation off the electric wires. Wonder he didn't get electrocuted." He picked up the glass of water, sipped it, and looked at her thoughtfully. "My father decided to have him for dinner. Made me watch while he killed him and dressed him. I—vomited when Mother brought him out all cooked."

"Oh, Dave—"

He shrugged. "Long time ago."

"It still bothers you, doesn't it?"

"Lots of things bother me."

"What sort of things?"

Stone suddenly laughed at her. "The way that dress fits you so nicely and how pretty you are tonight. That bothers me."

"Oh, don't be silly!"

Stone shook his head. "Friends of Jane Austin got burned. She'd put them in her books—all their foolishness. Now the whole world will be reading in the *New Yorker* how a pilot in the navy with the job of blowing up enemy battleships is really grieving over the death of his pet rabbit!"

"Dave!" Leah protested. "I'd never do that."

"Sure you would," he jibed. "You writers are all alike. You know what William Faulkner said about his writing? He said a good writer would sacrifice *anything* for his stories. His exact words were, 'Everything goes by the board: honor, pride, decency to get the book written. If a writer has to rob his mother, he will not hesitate. The "Ode on a Grecian Urn" is worth any number of old ladies.'"

The two of them talked about writing, then when the meal came, they enjoyed it thoroughly. Afterward Dave said, "Will you dance with me?"

"Oh, Dave, I can't."

He cocked one eyebrow quizzically. "Part of you is still locked up out at the Farm, Leah."

She shook her head. "I hope I'll always believe in some of the things they hold dear there, Dave. But I meant it *literally*. I don't know how to dance. When would I have learned?"

"You can learn right now. Come on—" he said, ignoring her protests and pulling her out on the dance floor. Leah protested at first, but she was graceful and soon was moving around the room with some degree of confidence.

"See?" Stone smiled at her. "Nothing to it!" He pulled her closer, adding, "You can put *this* in a story, Leah!"

Leah felt very strange on the dance floor, acutely conscious of being held by Stone, but she danced twice more with him, then the two sat at their table drinking coffee and talking about her writing.

Dave was speaking when he suddenly broke off, his eyes going across the room. "There's Mike," he said quietly.

Leah quickly followed his gaze and saw Mike Hardin entering with a woman. They had both been drinking, she saw at once and turned away. Her brief glance had taken in the tight dress, the heavy makeup, and the loose smile on the woman's face.

Stone saw that Leah was embarrassed and said, "I guess it's time to go. Maybe we can go down and see the river before I take you back. I might not get a chance to see it for a while."

Leah agreed, "Yes, I'd like that—"

She was about to rise but felt a hand on her shoulder and turned quickly to see Mike standing there, the woman slightly to one side. "Hey, Dave, Leah—" he said, forming his words carefully, "Glad to see ya." He grinned foolishly, waving his hand at the woman. "This is—Betty. Betty—best friend I got—Dave Stone. Taught me all 'bout airplanes!"

The band started up, and Mike blinked, then said, "Hey, Leah—c'mon. Gotta' dance with Leah—!"

Dave moved forward, putting himself between Mike and Leah. "Mike, you're drunk. Better let me take you home."

"Gonna' dance with Leah!" he said, and when he tried to push Dave aside, the smaller man countered. "Come along, Leah," he said quietly. "Time for us to go."

Hardin stood there watching them, and the heavily painted woman laughed. "Too good for us, ain't they?"

Dave and Leah left. Mike's loud cursing followed them as they left the steak house, passing one of the managers hurrying to speak to the obnoxious drunk.

When they were in the car, Dave said, "Hate to see that. Makes the navy look bad."

Leah said nothing. By the time they'd gotten to the river and Dave had shut the engine off, she was calmer. "Why does he have to be like that?" she whispered.

Dave tried to explain. "He's got to be number one at whatever he does, Leah . . ." He talked for some time, then gave her a strange look. "He wanted you, and when you turned him down, he blew up."

"He's never been interested in me!"

Stone studied her smooth profile, admired the classic lines of her face. "He's never seen you as a woman, Leah."

They sat there in the car, then when it grew cold, he took her back to the dorm. She turned at the door, and her face was troubled. "I'm worried about you, Dave," she said quietly. "When will you have to go on sea duty?"

"Pretty soon," he nodded. "I'll try to see you before we ship out."

"Yes, do!" she whispered. Fear came to her, fear for him, and she whispered, "Oh, Dave! Be careful!"

He leaned forward, kissed her, then said, "I'll try." Stepping back, he added, "It's been good, Leah. Thanks for everything."

He hated drawn-out farewells, so he turned and walked to the car. When he got back to the motel, he went to bed at once. Sleep came quickly, but the phone went off with a suddenness that brought him bolt upright.

"Yes?" he mumbled into the receiver.

"Lieutenant, this is Ring Clampett. I'm the night marshal. We got us a problem here."

"What's wrong, Marshal?"

"It's like this. I got Mike Hardin down here at the jail," Clampett said. "Had to pick him up for drunk and disorderly—and assault."

"He hurt somebody?" Stone asked quickly.

"Oh, jest a fist fight—and he got the worst of it. But the thing is, I don't wanna throw him in the slammer. Won't look good for his people. You wanna come and take him off my hands 'fore it goes to the judge?"

"Yes, I'll be right there—and thanks, Marshal!"

"Always wanna do my part for our boys in the service, Lieutenant."

Stone got dressed, packed his bag, and left the motel. He found Clampett waiting for him in his office with Mike slumped on a chair. He looked pale and his lips were swollen from a blow.

"Better git him out of here before I change my mind," Clampett snorted. "He's been sittin' there cussin' me out—and I've just 'bout had it."

"Come on, Mike—"

Hardin came upright and tried to strike out at Stone, cursing wildly. Stone twisted his arm and led him outside, saying, "I appreciate this, Marshal—"

He opened the back door and shoved Mike inside. Getting behind the wheel, he drove away. He left town angrily, and when Mike began to curse, he said, "If you say one more word, Hardin, I'll turn you over to the shore patrol! You'll never fly a plane for the navy!"

The threat sunk into Mike's befuddled brain, and he suddenly lay down on the seat and dropped off into a drunken sleep.

When Stone got him back to their quarters and stopped the car, Mike got out carefully. He stared at Stone, who stood there reading him off. When Stone turned to go, Mike snapped, "You're pretty hot stuff, Stone—but I'm gonna show you what a hot pilot is really like!"

Dave said, "You can't even control yourself, Hardin! What makes you think you can control a dive bomber?"

Mike watched his friend drive away, and there was one thought in his mind.

He's going to find out who's the best pilot—me or him! He was sick and the memory of the night shamed him—and the only way he could think to wipe it out was to become the hottest pilot in the United States Navy!

13

A SET OF WINGS

*F*or Mike Hardin and the other pilots in his group the world seemed to shrink to a fragmentary portion of Planet Earth known as Miami Naval Air Station. In the larger world outside, great events were transpiring. The German super battleship *Bismarck* demolished the pride of the British navy, the *Hood*—and was herself destroyed three days later, which proved to be the worst naval defeat for the Nazis in the entire war.

The Nazis won victories, however, smothering Greece and smashing Belgrade as they overran Yugoslavia. President Roosevelt moved rapidly to mobilize the nation for war, freezing prices and declaring a national emergency.

Mike and the other pilots were aware of these massive movements, but they had no time to meditate on them. Their lives were bound by Opa-Locka Field northwest of Miami, an area of sand, scrub brush, and rattlesnakes under a blazing tropical sun. It consisted of two beautiful new fields, one for takeoffs and the other for landings.

But the fledgling pilots had no time to enjoy the rattlesnakes or the beach. They were shoved headlong into the final stage of naval flight training: advanced training in gunnery, dive bombing, fighter tactics, aerial navigation, and fleet-type formation flying. They flew the newer naval aircraft instead of the old trainers, and this last stage of their training was ruthless!

"You'll leave Opa-Locka," one of their instructors warned them, "either in a coffin, washed out and disgraced, or commissioned with wings and operational orders. It'll be up to you."

None of Mike's friends were killed, but several couldn't take the intense training. There were no good-byes as a rule. Their bunks would be empty and their gear gone—and the survivors would close ranks.

As for Mike, he was an instructor's dream. Top of the chart in every category! His instructors were fascinated by his flying skills and made a game out of trying to give him a problem he couldn't handle—but this rarely happened. Dave Stone grinned at his fellow instructors, "He's had a great teacher, that's all!"

Dave was satisfied with Mike's prowess as a pilot, but he was worried about their friendship. Ever since the steak house incident in Liberty, Mike had been cool, showing nothing but a civil respect for Dave. Stone tried to break the wall down and spoke of it in a letter to Leah:

> I've tried to let Mike know that I hold no resentment—but he's touchy and won't respond. I don't mind so much for myself, but I know we'll have to fly together when we get on a carrier. Leah, there's something about flying into combat that's different from most other activities. Men who are tense with each other are likely to make mistakes—and a mistake may mean death in an attack on an enemy. I tried to stress this today in a talk I had with the new pilots. I told them that we ought to be as close as circus fliers—the trapeze artists. Got a little poetic, I'm afraid! I said, "Think what that flyer is doing, men. He lets go of his bar and launches himself out into space—and his only hope is the hands of his catcher! Think what it would be like if those two had personal problems on the ground. The flier would be wondering if his catcher would fail him in the traps as he had down on the ground. Those two have to be *one*—and that's the way *we've* got to be when we're launched at a Japanese carrier!"
>
> Pretty corny, eh? And it didn't seem to mean much to Mike. He has a way of staring at me that's pretty disconcerting when I'm giving him some instruction. A cool look in those hazel eyes of his that tells me he's listening because he has to.
>
> The problem is that if he has trouble with me, he's likely to have trouble with his fellow pilots—and that's bad!
>
> I miss you very much. Wish I could be there so we could talk and talk and talk about books—and about us!

But Mike maintained his distance from Dave, throwing himself into the business of becoming a killer pilot. He lived for those moments when he was in the air and dive bombing was his delight.

They had all learned a maneuver called the split-S. To do this particular stunt, the pilot simply rolled the aircraft over on its back and then let the nose fall toward the ground. The result was a long swooping dive at almost any angle that the pilot wanted to allow his plane to take.

When this maneuver was mastered, the actual dive bombing practice began. The target was a large bull's-eye outlined in a small clearing in the nearby Everglades. It had a solid white center and an outside ring also in white. Stone gave them their final instructions before they took off.

"Line up your target at an altitude of eight thousand feet on a course heading. Fly over the target and at the same time do a split-S. Then as you plunge down on the target, use your sight for aiming and trigger off your bomb."

"That sounds pretty simple," Mike shrugged. "Nobody's going to be shooting back at us."

Stone stared at him. "We'll let you take the first shot, Mr. Hardin," he said, a slight smile on his lips.

Mike welcomed the opportunity, and when he took off in his F24 he was determined to show what he could do.

He approached the target, but the relatively simple exercise suddenly became more complicated. He made his split-S dive, but somehow everything went wrong! He couldn't get his plane under control and had a wild ride in which he hung from his seat belt after a gut-wrenching pullout and a moment of blackout—and the bomb barely missed a Seminole Indian village miles away!

When he landed with the rest of the flight, Mike crawled out of the aircraft, pulled off his flying helmet, and threw it on the ground. The other pilots enjoyed his anger, grinning and calling out, "Hey, hotshot, what you got against Indians?" and "Now I got it, Mike, we'll send you to bomb London, and you'll probably hit Berlin!"

Stone let the ragging go on, then said, "All right, I'll take you one at a time. You first, Mr. Hardin."

For the rest of the day Stone went over the art of hitting the target with Mike. And Mike wanted so badly to get the thing right that he put his animosity aside and soaked up the instructions.

"You've got to be in *control* of the plane in the dive, Mike," Stone stressed. "Do everything you can *before* you dive—set the power, all the flaps and tabs, RPMs—get everything done before you go in. And never go too low—thinking you can get a better hit. Crashing into the ground while pulling out of a dive is a pretty permanent error!"

For several days the practice went on, and Mike mastered the dive perfectly. Once he had it down, he put bomb after bomb right in the center of the target.

Bailey Sutton, one of Mike's closest friends, asked him about it. Sutton was a tall Texan with blond hair and direct blue eyes. "How do you *do* it, Mike?" he demanded. The two of them were ambling down the streets of Miami on one of their rare excursions. "I can hit anything with a rifle or a handgun—but somehow I can't get the hang of this thing."

They were passing a theater with a long line outside, and Mike stopped to look at the poster. Ignoring Sutton for a moment, he nodded at the picture. "Want to see this?" he asked.

Sutton peered at the bill and read the title. *Citizen Kane.* "Naw, it looks like you gotta' *think* to watch it. Let's go back and see that one with John Wayne—*Stagecoach.* You ain't gotta think to watch him!"

"Okay." The two tall officers reversed and headed back down the street. Mike had not forgotten Sutton's question and began to speak of a theory he'd come up with.

"Bailey, you need to start thinking different about bombing," he said. "They talk about 'dropping' bombs, but I don't think that's quite right."

"Well, we do drop them pesky things!"

"That's what they do with bombs from high altitude—open the bomb bay and let the bombs drop out. But that's not what a dive bomber does. What we do is *aim* the whole plane, just like you'd aim a rifle. At least, that's the way I've been thinking," Mike said slowly. "I visualize my plane as a cannon with my sight the same as one on a regular gun. At the instant of release, I think of my bomb as a bullet leaving the muzzle, moving at the velocity of my dive and speeding at the target exactly as a bullet does when fired."

"Hey, that sounds pretty good!"

"Well, it's helped me a lot," Mike shrugged.

"I'll do 'er, Mike!" Bailey exclaimed. "I'll be Big John Wayne up there, and that airplane will be my pistol! Bang!—and that's the end of that ol' Jap carrier!"

Bailey's scores improved dramatically, and the tall Texan was extremely vocal about the reason why. After a day in which he plastered the target, he beamed at the mess hall, saying, "Why, it's easy! Just like shootin' fish in a barrel!" He threw his arm around Mike, grinning broadly. "All you guys got to do is follow 'Doctor Hardin's Method of Droppin' Bombs'! Satisfaction guaranteed." He explained the method to the other pilots, and when Stone got word of it, he merely shrugged.

"If it helps the men hit the target, I don't care what they do."

He even commended Mike for his methods and was gratified to see a little warmth in the big pilot's eyes.

Maybe we'll get our problems out of the way, Stone thought hopefully. *Only a few more days until the training is over—surely we can make it without any more trouble!*

But that was not to be—the Miss Florida contest loomed ahead, and though Dave had no way of knowing it, that meaningless contest would create problems between Mike Hardin and Dave Stone that would make earlier troubles seem minor!

* * *

"Hey, Mike, come on!"

Hardin looked up to see Bailey Sutton and a short, muscular pilot named Sam Devito motioning at him frantically.

"What's up?" he asked lazily. He was sitting beneath a palm tree studying a book on navigation, enjoying the sunshine and the breeze. Graduation was upon them, only four days off, and he was feeling satisfied.

The two pilots hurried up, and Devito stared down at him. He was from New Mexico and could fly a plane better than any of the pilots—except for Mike himself. He was the arm-wrestling champion of the world, he claimed, and could put Mike's hand down as if he had been a teenager. But for some reason Mike didn't resent this, and he smiled up at the beefy pilot. "Go away, Cowboy. I've got studying to do."

Sam shook his head sadly. He'd been a rodeo star in New Mexico, and his face was punched out of shape from collisions with Brahma bulls and other large animals. "We don't want this one, Bailey," he remarked. "Too good looking. He'll make us look ugly."

"A warthog would make you look ugly, Sam," Mike grinned. "Where you two going all dressed up?"

"Why, we've been assigned hard duty," Sutton grinned. "Got to escort some of them ol' girls in the Miss Florida contest." He sighed heavily and shook his head sadly. "It's a rough job—but somebody's got to do it!"

"We need one more, Hardin," Sam nodded. "But I can see you'd rather study navigation."

Mike was on his feet like a cat. "Let's do it, fellows. We volunteered for this war, now let's act like men!"

The three pilots left the base and were soon surrounded by beautiful young girls. The contest went on for three days, and for two of those days the three of them escorted the curvaceous girls and had the time of their lives.

On the third day, they were yanked out of this duty by Stone, who'd been lenient. "Graduation is day after tomorrow; I want every man here for one last flight in the morning," he told the group. "Every man in bed by eight o'clock. This is the big one, and lots of people will be watching you."

Mike groaned, for he'd managed to wrangle a date with one of the runners-up—a statuesque redhead from Tampa. He tried to get permission to miss the flight, claiming that it was good PR for the navy, but he was turned down flat.

"Too bad, Mike," Sam Devito grinned. "You sure had a rope on that little filly!"

"I'll still have that date!" he nodded.

"Yeah? Well, you better cover your tracks," Sutton advised, his eyes serious. "Captain Lassiter's on the warpath. He's givin' all the instructors a rough time. You show up late, and Stone will tie a can to your tail!"

"I'll be there when we takeoff," Mike said with a fixed determination on his face. The three friends enjoyed their day, and when Sutton and Devito left at six o'clock to head back for the base, Mike said, "You guys cover for me."

"Can't fly your plane for you," Devito warned. "Don't be late!"

But Miss Tampa proved to be strong medicine! Every time Mike tried to leave, she'd take his hand and whisper, "Just a *little* longer, Mike honey!"

The next morning Mike woke up with a massive headache. He lifted his head and saw that it was 8:20. With his skull splitting, he dressed and grabbed a cab to the base. But as he got out of the cab, the flight thundered overhead, and he grew even sicker.

He slunk into his room and stayed hidden until the flight came back. When the men came trooping in, he grabbed Devito by the arm, demanding, "Did Stone say anything about me?"

Devito shook his head. "Son, you done messed up good! I remember once when a big red Brahma got away from me up in Montana. I knew I was a goner! And I wasn't wrong, 'cause that big steer walked all over my frame." He stared intently at Mike, adding dolefully, "Bad as that ol' steer was, Mike, I think I'd rather have *him* on me than Stone. He was plenty sore—and Lassiter took a piece of him, I think. You better get ready for a real bad ride!"

Mike knew waiting was no good, so he went at once to Stone's office. He found Dave sitting at his desk staring at the wall. When Hardin entered, Stone's eyes were hot with anger.

"Lieutenant—"

"Hardin, you're no good!"

"Now, wait a minute—!"

"I'm not waiting a minute or a second," Stone said, keeping his voice under stiff control. "I've tried to make allowances for you, Hardin, but no more. You're just not dive bomber quality."

Mike's anger flared. "My scores are the highest in the group!"

"And what good did that do us when we were in the air and you were out chasing women?" Stone demanded.

"It was just a practice flight," Mike said stiffly.

"Oh? So now you're the man who's going to decide *which* flights are important enough for you to join? Well, Mr. Hardin, I'll just make it easy for you. You can chase women full time!"

Mike suddenly felt an emptiness in his stomach. "What—what does that mean, Dave?"

"It means I refuse to qualify you for combat duty."

"You can't do that!"

"You don't think so?" Stone got to his feet and walked around the desk. "You watch and learn then." Disgust scored his face, and he opened the door, nodding at it. "Maybe they'll let you be an instructor—but I'm not risking the lives of other men with you. Get out!"

Hardin's world had suddenly fallen apart. He stood mutely before Stone and knew that he'd brought it on himself. He wanted to beg for another chance, but he wasn't the kind of man who could do that—so he fell into a blind rage.

"You're a coward, Stone!" he said, fury making his face crimson. "You're a gutless wonder! If you were a man, you'd fight like one."

And then Stone made his big mistake. "I'll just take you up on that," he said evenly. "Name the time and the place."

"Behind the hangars at ten tonight."

"I'll be there!"

*   *   *

Mike Hardin stood staring down at the still figure of Dave Stone—feeling as rotten as he'd ever felt in his entire life. He'd had many fights, but something about this one had been degrading. The two of them had met behind the hangar, stripped off their jackets, and without words had plunged toward each other.

It had been a vicious affair, but hopeless for Stone from the start. He weighed no more than 150 pounds, and though trim and in good condition, he was no athlete. His last fight had been in the fifth grade, and he despised the idea of fighting—even in the ring.

Hardin, by contrast, was slightly over six feet tall and weighed 187 pounds, all hard muscle. He'd spent his life in some sort of physical activity, most of it hard contact such as football. He'd also been on a boxing team when he was sixteen, and though he hadn't pursued it, he had learned a great deal about fighting.

Mike had looked forward to the fight with an unholy joy. *He can kick me out of the navy—but I'll pound him to jelly first!* was his attitude.

But when the fight had started, Mike discovered that it was not a fight at all, not in the way he'd expected. Stone had come roaring in, flailing with both fists, and Mike had promptly knocked him flat on his back with a hard right. Stone had come to his feet, blood running down his mouth, and had come right back, his lips pressed tightly together.

Within three minutes, Stone's face was a bloody mask. He'd been down on the hard concrete several times, but he had climbed doggedly to his feet and come right back at Mike.

Mike had been hit in the chest and once on the forehead by wild blows, but he was otherwise undamaged.

He discovered that he was ready to quit; the slaughter of the smaller man was not a pleasure, not as he had anticipated. He hit Stone again, putting all his might into the blow, and the smaller man was driven backward where he lay on the hard concrete, his arms and legs moving spasmodically. But he rolled over and painfully pushed himself to his hands and knees, his head dangling and blood dripping from his nose and mouth.

As Stone struggled to get to his feet, Mike cried out inside, *Stay down, blast you! Stay down!* But as he watched, Stone came upright, discovered that he was facing the wrong direction, and turned slowly to face Hardin. His face was bloody, one eye was completely shut and the other a mere slit.

Mike said, "Let's quit this, Stone. You're whipped."

But Stone shook his head, staggered forward in a lurching gait, and pushed at Mike feebly with his fists. He missed and Mike knew he'd never stop. Hating to cut the man up, he took a firm stance and launched a blow that caught Stone in the jaw. It was a knockout punch and Stone went down in a heap and lay without moving.

Mike stood over him, hating himself. *You really proved something, didn't you, Hardin? You proved what a lowdown skunk you are!* He remembered suddenly the first time he'd met Dave Stone at the airport outside of Liberty. An image flashed through his mind of Stone's cheerful grin as he'd offered to take him up, then later on the ground when he'd said, "If you really want to get into naval aviation, Mike, let me know and I'll help you all I can."

As Mike stood in the dim light of the single bulb that shed a feeble glow over the fallen man, he knew himself, and it was a bitter moment.

Suddenly a voice came from the darkness, startling Mike so badly that he whirled—just in time to see Bailey Sutton and Sam Devito emerge.

"Well, you finished, Hardin?"

Bailey's voice was hard-edged, and as the tall pilot came into the light, Mike saw that his eyes were cold and his lips tight. Switching his gaze, he saw that Sam was grim and unsmiling.

"How—how'd you guys know about this?" Mike stammered. He felt dirty, as if he'd been caught doing something perverted and evil.

"Stone's clerk overheard you two arguing. He told me about it." Devito looked down at the still form, then looked back at Hardin. Devito was a tough fellow with battered features and a set of hard, black eyes. "Get out of here, Hardin," he spoke flatly. He turned and knelt beside Stone, touching the beaten man's face gingerly.

Mike swallowed hard but couldn't find a word to say. He liked Devito as much as any man he knew, but he saw that they were no longer friends.

"Unless you'd like to punch me out." Mike glanced at Bailey, who'd spoken, seeing that the Texan was angry to the bone.

"Look, you guys," he began awkwardly. "I didn't want this to happen."

"That's not the way we heard it," Bailey said. "The way we got it, Stone wasn't going to qualify you and you told him he wasn't enough of a man to fight you in the alley. Wasn't that the way of it?"

"Well, I guess that's right, but—"

"You're a real big man, Hardin," Sutton said, dislike in his twangy voice. "But if you don't get out of here, I'm going to peel your potato—and if I can't do it fair, there's other ways. And take this, too—don't you ever speak to me again, because in my book, you're a coward and a skunk! Now—you git!"

Mike watched as Bailey turned and helped Sam lift the still form of Stone. The cursing had not angered him, which was strange. He turned and left the scene, not looking back. He heard Devito say, "We got to get him patched up, Bailey—he can't go to graduation looking like this—!"

*   *   *

Graduation was at ten o'clock. At ten minutes after nine, Mike was still in his bed and he was half-drunk. After the fight, he'd bought half a pint of gin and swallowed it like water. It had not dimmed his memory enough, however, and all night long he'd lain in bed hating himself for what had happened.

He'd heard the other men shouting with glee as they got ready to get their wings. Now he lay in bed, bitterness and self-loathing tearing at his gut. *It was all right there—right in my hand!* he thought. *And I had to blow it—me, the big man!*

He tried to make plans, but couldn't think. Maybe they'd let him be an instructor; that was a bleak prospect. Later, perhaps they'd let him try again for combat duty—but his group would be gone. They'd be fighting, and he'd be—

Suddenly the door opened—and Dave Stone walked in!

Mike blinked, then rolled out of the bed, feeling foolish in his shorts and T-shirt in front of the immaculately dressed Stone.

Stone's face was puffy and bruised, but his eyes were clear. He stared at Mike and said evenly, "Get your uniform on, Mr. Hardin."

Mike could not think for a moment. "Sir—?" he asked, his mind in a spin. "I don't—"

Stone was looking at him critically. "You're going to get your wings. I signed your papers."

For one moment, Mike Hardin could make no sense out of what Stone said. It was all over in his mind, and now this!

"I—I don't understand," he mumbled. "You said—"

"I know what I said," Stone snapped. His lips were puffy and he was in pain, Mike could see. "I was wrong. I let my pride get in the way—which is always a mistake. You're a good pilot and the navy needs you." He paused, adding, "I think you're a sorry excuse for a human being, Hardin, but that's my private opinion. As an instructor, I have to ignore that and put you into action."

Mike could not believe what he was hearing. "Lieutenant—I got to say this. That fight last night—"

He was about to say that he was wrong and to try and tell Stone how much he hated the whole thing, but Stone spoke up.

"I've got no hard feelings, Mr. Hardin, but Devito and Sutton have. And they made a mistake. When they got me patched up, they told the rest of the men in the group about the fight." He hesitated, then added, "I tried to tell them it was as much my fault as yours—but the men don't see it that way."

"They've got a right to despise me."

"Maybe they do," Stone said. "It'll be rough. You know how it is when the group gets down on a man. I think I'd better get you transferred to another group."

"No! Don't do that, sir!" Mike burst out.

"It'll be easier for you—"

"No, sir, please don't do it," Mike pleaded. "I know what it'll be like—but I've got to stay with my group!"

Stone stared at him. "First time I ever heard you say anything in favor of group integrity."

Mike remembered all his rash statements about that subject, but he shook his head stubbornly. "It's a thing I can't run away from, sir. Please—let me stay with my group."

Stone nodded. "All right, it'll be like that. Now, get dressed and get to the field! And I might as well tell you, after we have a short leave, we'll be joining the *Yorktown*—and she's headed for something big!"

*   *   *

Graduation exercises were simple and to the point. After they were over came the more important moment. There were speeches and then each man was given a set of shiny new gold wings.

After the dismissal, the group came together and replaced their cadet boards with the new ensign boards. The tradition was that a man's best friend pinned his wings over the left breast pocket, and soon the men were paired off, laughing and slapping each other on the back.

Dave Stone watched as Mike Hardin stood alone. Not one of the other pilots came to congratulate him, and the big man turned and walked away, holding his wings clenched tightly in his hand.

He's in for a rough time, Stone thought. He himself had no rancor, but he knew that the men had turned against Hardin. *The rest of the men know the Japs are the enemy—but Mike Hardin will see an enemy every time he wakes up!*

14

REMEMBRANCE OF TEARS

Coming out of the cloud bank, Mike gazed down a mile and a half at the sun-spangled surface of the sea. The Japanese fleet lay below him like a child's toys, plowing steadily through the blue-green waters. To his right, other clouds, soft and white and fleecy—shot through with silver where the sunlight hit them—floated along on their ocean of air. What a beautiful sight, he thought—a perfect day for killing.

Mike recognized the Shokaku, *one of the massive Japanese aircraft carriers, surrounded by escort ships. He dropped his flaps and with a hard throttle, rolled the Dauntless over into a steep dive. With a tremendous roar of his engine, Mike plummeted toward the carrier as it knifed through the rolling swells of the Pacific. He saw the deck of the ship rushing up at him, tiny men running about frantically. With the wind howling in his ear, he released the bomb.*

But it all went wrong! The bomb splashed harmlessly short. Mike yanked back with all his might on the controls, trying desperately to pull out of the dive, but they were frozen as tightly as if they had been welded. The tortured engine screamed like a banshee, the throttle stuck on full. A Japanese sailor ran across the deck and leaped overboard to escape the doomed American aircraft. Mike tried to pray. He saw clearly and precisely the heavy rivets on the steel plating of the conning tower just before . . .

"Uuuhh!" Mike came awake with a start, a cold sweat pouring from his body. Sitting up in bed, he put his hands over his face, took a deep breath, and lay back in the darkness of his room, breathing heavily. The streetlight cast a thin amber glow across the ceiling. Six times the bell tower on the Methodist church rang out across the quiet town. Pots clanked in the kitchen as his mother prepared supper.

Mike had arrived from Miami around three o'clock in the afternoon, finding his mother seated at the kitchen table sorting through his Lone Ranger cap pistols, Buck Rogers ring, Jack Armstrong whistle, and other toys he had collected through the years. They drank coffee and talked for two hours, Darla Hardin taking her son's hand and leading him back down the streets of his childhood. Then, exhausted from the trip and the long hours of training, he had gone to his room, lain down across the bed, and dropped off to sleep.

He got up and walked down the hall to the bathroom. Flipping on the light, he stared at himself in the mirror. A slight redness showed in his eyes. They were beginning to get puffy, with incipient dark circles beneath them. *Too much night life.* He splashed cold water on his face, rubbing it briskly with a thick white towel.

Looking back in the mirror, Mike grimaced. "Ugh!" He still felt groggy. Dropping his uniform on the floor, he took a hot shower. Then he combed his dark hair back, long enough on top now to show a slight curl. After putting on a fresh tan uniform, he took his scrapbook from the dresser and sat down on the bed.

Recalling all his glory years in football, beginning in junior high, Mike thumbed through the scrapbook, lingering on the last page. The headline read, LIBERTY LOSES DISTRICT CHAMPION-SHIP. Below it, he was frozen forever in the harsh glare of the flashbulb, stretched out in midair, reaching for the one shoe that the photograph had captured.

Mike saw again the freckled-faced defensive back pluck the fumble from the air and zip past him, heading for the goal line. As he had done a thousand times before in his mind, Mike sprinted after the skinny little halfback. Taking that last desperate lunge, he crashed headlong onto the field with the cleat slicing the tip of his finger as he clawed for the final tackle, for that elusive victory that was forever lost.

He thought of another victory that had been snatched from him. Remembering how lovely Leah Daniel looked at their last meeting, Mike felt anger smoldering in his chest. *If it wasn't for Stone, I'd have done all right with her. He had to mess things up for me. Tried to wash me out of the navy, too, but I showed him. And I'll show him with Leah Daniel too!*

Closing the scrapbook, Mike tossed it back on the dresser. He sat for a full minute, staring at the half-inch scar, white as bone, on the tip of his forefinger. Then he grabbed his hat from the bedpost and walked out into the hall.

"Mike, is that you?"

"No, it's the friendly neighborhood burglar," he called back, walking toward the kitchen. "Mike said it'd be all right if I helped myself to a few things."

"Oh, you, hush your silliness and get in here and eat your supper." Darla Hardin served Mike's porkchop, field peas, and mashed potatoes onto a plate and set it on the table.

"I'm not very hungry, Mama. I'm gonna try to get ahold of Leah Daniel. Maybe see her tonight."

Darla pulled his chair out. "That's all right. You still need your supper. Now sit down."

Mike shook his head. "Really, Mama, I'm not hungry at all. We eat all the time in the navy."

"You certainly haven't put on any weight," Darla observed, glancing at her son's flat stomach.

"Exercise. But we eat night and day. It's the only thing we have to do for fun," Mike lied.

"Well, all right, but you're going to eat a big breakfast tomorrow morning."

He noticed his mother's blue silk blouse, pleated gray skirt, and high heels. A tiny drop of brown gravy spotted the frilly white apron. It never failed to amuse him, seeing her so dressed up just to cook supper. *I guess we all have to do whatever it takes to make it in this ol' world.* "You look real pretty tonight, Mama."

Darla blushed. "Oh, I bet you say that to all the girls. But thanks anyway."

Glancing at the clock above the stove, Mike's face went somber. "Daddy still stoppin' at Rudy's Tavern every day?"

His mother turned away, stirring the pot of peas on the stove absently. "Sometimes."

"Well, tell him I'll see him tomorrow." Mike stepped into the living room, flopped on the couch, and picked up the phone.

Darla turned from the stove. She couldn't make out the words, but she recognized the tone of her son's voice. She had heard it dozens of times before when he had zeroed in on one special girl for his "Chick of the Week Club."

Mike stepped into the kitchen, beaming. Darla Hardin smiled almost sadly, shaking her head when he gave her the thumbs-up sign. After brushing his teeth and combing his hair, Mike kissed her on the cheek and hurried out the kitchen door.

*   *   *

The Liberty College women's dorm was in its usual weeknight doldrums. Magazines rested in precise stacks on the end tables. Muted lamplight lay in pale gold patterns across the rugs, neatly arranged at right angles with the furniture.

The girl behind the reception desk stared hard at Mike's lean build in his tan uniform with the shiny new wings on his chest. Giving him a bright smile, she tossed her head, the dark brown ponytail flouncing as she rang Leah's room.

Mike smiled back. *This one looks like she might be worth a little followup.*

"You a pilot?" Ponytail grinned.

Mike buffed his wings with the sleeve of his jacket. "How'd you figure that out? You must be the house detective."

Ponytail laughed softly.

As he was about to speak, Mike glanced at the stairs and saw Leah coming down. Her hand trailed gracefully along the dark, polished banister. Then she was walking toward him across the hardwood floor, her hips swinging the long, full skirt softly back and forth like a boat rocking in a gentle swell. Mike forgot all about Ponytail.

Leah's dark blouse matched the auburn color of her hair, which lay softly about her shoulders. "Hello, Mike. You certainly do look fit. But then you always did, didn't you?"

"If you say so, Miss Daniel. How 'bout a bite to eat?" Leah's self-assurance troubled Mike. He preferred girls who fawned over him—he thought! But Leah, becoming more and more of a challenge for him, was proving to be an exception to the rule.

"No thanks. I've already eaten. It was kind of late when you called, remember?"

"I thought we'd go to George's Steak House. You like that place don't you?" Mike jibed, remembering dimly the scene he had caused. He wanted to take her there for precisely that reason. So he could erase the memory of his drunken display—and so he could be with her at the same place David Stone had.

Leah remembered that night. "I'd just as soon go somewhere else, if it's all right with you."

"Sure."

Outside, Mike opened the door of his Ford coupe for her, then walked around and got behind the steering wheel. He sat for a moment, staring at the deserted street. "I made a fool of myself that night, Leah. I'm sorry for offending you."

"We all make mistakes, Mike. There's no reason we can't still be friends."

Friends? Is that what you've come to, Mike? A doll like this just wants to be friends with you. He remembered Leah's religious upbringing. "I think I should tell you something, Leah."

"Certainly."

"It's kind of personal."

Leah turned to gaze into his face. "That's all right. You can trust me. I'd never violate a confidence."

"I've given up drinking," Mike lied.

* * *

"Boy that's good," Mike smacked, taking the last bite of his hamburger. "I forgot what a good hamburger Ollie makes."

Leah enjoyed watching Mike eat. "My mother says you can tell a lot about a man by the way the eats."

"Is that right?" he asked nervously. Then, avoiding the subject, he yelled over to Ollie, who was fixing chocolate malts for a couple at the counter. "My compliments to the chef."

Ollie waved back.

Mike wiped his mouth, left the booth, and walked over to the jukebox. He dropped in two nickels, studied it a moment, and punched in his selections. Dooley Wilson began his relaxed version of "As Time Goes By" as Mike slipped back into the booth.

Leah swallowed a bite of her strawberry sundae. "How's the navy?"

"Couldn't be better," Mike bragged. "I had the highest marks in my training section. I can't wait to get my bomb sight on one of them Jap carriers."

Leah frowned. "That's a dangerous job, isn't it? I couldn't get Dave to talk about it much, but my roommate's boyfriend is in the navy. He told her dive bombers were the worst assignment you could get."

Mike couldn't believe that Leah had opened such a door for him. He hung his head modestly. "Well, it's not for the faint of heart—that's for sure."

"This war's so terrible. People never knowing from day to day when that little green car will drive up to their house with a telegram from the War Department."

Mike bore in. "I don't think combat's gonna be so bad. If you don't make it through a mission—at least it's over with before you know it. One big boom and you're gone."

Leah flinched involuntarily.

"What bothers me is the thought of gettin' captured by the Japs," Mike continued.

Taking a bite of her sundae, Leah listened intently, thinking of all the boys who faced death when they put on their country's uniform.

"You heard what the Japs did to the three pilots they captured during Doolittle's raid on Tokyo, didn't you?"

"No." Leah's eyes widened.

"Killed 'em." Mike stared at her red lips, wet from the ice cream. *I'd sure like to kiss her right now.*

"Oh, my goodness!"

"Yep. Cut their heads off with one of them Samurai swords!" Mike made a slicing movement with his hand. He had no idea how the fliers were executed, but his story had the desired effect on Leah.

She dropped her spoon into the sundae dish. "That's awful. Those poor men."

"They're playing for keeps out there in the South Pacific, Leah," Mike smirked. "No mama's boys allowed."

Back at the dorm, Mike pulled over to the curb behind a huge oak that shielded them from sight and turned the engine off. "Nice night, isn't it?"

Leah felt the soft April breeze touch her face. The smell of jasmine and oleander floated on the night air. "Just beautiful."

"Not as beautiful as you are." Mike turned to Leah, his arm going around her shoulder as he leaned toward her.

"No, Mike!" She pushed against his chest.

He was shocked. He thought she had been softened up perfectly. *You're slippin', boy.*

"What's wrong?" Mike asked, trying to sound properly offended. "I messed up once. I thought you'd forgiven me."

You messed up a lot more than once, Mike Hardin. Leah remembered the scene in the third-floor hallway when he had called her the names, his never writing or coming to see her, his drunkenness at the restaurant, and the way he had treated other girls. "I have forgiven you. We're just friends."

"Friends?" he asked incredulously.

But Leah knew what she felt—what she had always felt for Mike was far stronger than friendship. Even now, with his little boy's pride bruised, she couldn't help wanting to give in to him—to feel his strong arms around her, his lips pressing against hers. "Yes, friends—for now anyway."

Mike immediately saw the chink in her armor. He flashed his best smile. "Well, I guess that'll have to do then—for now!"

Mike lay siege to the fortified city of Leah Daniel, bombarding her with flowers, gifts, and flattery. The perfect gentleman, he opened all doors, pulled out all chairs—did everything but throw his cape across a puddle for her—and would have done that if his navy uniform had come with a cape.

Ten nights later, at his home, Mike peered into the steamy bathroom mirror. He knew from previous sieges that tonight would be the night the walls came tumbling down. He had the roses and reservations for a candlelight dinner. *"Yes sir, Mike, ol' boy. Tonight's the night!"*

Across town, Leah stepped out of the tub and slipped into a white terry-cloth robe to take a call from the front desk. A gentleman awaited her. *I've never known Mike to be this early before. Guess he couldn't stay away any longer.*

Leah dressed hurriedly in a black linen dress that showed a modest amount of creamy shoulder and back, slipped into black heels and brushed her hair. Hurrying down the stairs, she saw David Stone sitting on an overstuffed sofa next to a floor lamp. He wore pleated gray slacks, white button-down shirt, and, when he saw her, a wide smile. A large manila envelope rested on his lap.

"Whatever are you doing here, David?" Leah crossed the room and kissed him on the cheek as he stood up.

"Came to see the prettiest girl in Georgia," he beamed. "Aren't you happy to see me?"

"Of course. But didn't you get a leave? Where have you been all this time?"

"New York City, my dear."

Leah felt a small current of excitement down her spine. "What've you been doing in New York?"

"Guess I'm still an acquisitions editor at heart," David remarked a little too casually. "Anyway, I managed to get a promising writer's manuscript approved for publication."

Leah grew weak in the knees. She felt almost as though this were happening to someone else. The wondrous prospect that loomed before her was more than she could bear. She wanted to ask David the obvious question, but couldn't.

He stood up quickly. "It's yours, Leah! Scribner's wants to do a book of your short stories!"

She put both hands to her throat. "Scribner's! Why that's Hemingway's publisher!"

"You've hit the big time, Leah! When Scribner's does a book, they do it up right."

"Oh, David, thank you so much!" Leah threw her arms around him, kissing him squarely on the mouth.

At that moment Mike Hardin strolled through the door carrying his freshly cut bouquet of red roses. At the sight of David Stone, anger burned in his gut. He took a deep breath, settled himself down, and walked over to the sofa.

"Mike," Leah said excitedly. "Look who's here!"

"David," Mike said coolly, his roses drooping in his left hand.

David extended his hand. "Hello, Mike."

Grudgingly Mike shook his hand.

"Guess what, Mike?" Leah beamed.

Mike glared at Stone in silence.

"David had my book accepted for publication by Scribner's! Isn't that wonderful?"

"Great," Mike mumbled.

Leah took each of them by the hand. "We've just got to celebrate. Where do you want to go, Mike?"

"Uh—I hadn't really planned . . ."

"I don't want to spoil your evening, Leah," Stone apologized. "I'll come back tomorrow."

"Don't be silly, David," Leah protested. "This is the most exciting night of my life—and you've made it all possible!"

Mike felt the banked fires of anger flaring up inside of him, but he didn't want to explode and ruin things with Leah for good. "This is your big night, Leah. It's what you've worked so hard for—and I didn't have a thing to do with it. You two have a good time."

"No, Mike. We have a date." Leah took him by the arm. "We'll all go have a nice dinner."

Mike knew he had to leave before he lost control. In his mind, Stone was responsible for driving a wedge between him and Leah. He handed Leah the roses. "We'll do it another time."

"But Mike . . ."

"It's okay," he assured her, turning and striding across the room. The door slammed behind him.

"I wish he hadn't left," she murmured, staring at the dark red flowers.

"I'm afraid he doesn't like me very much," Stone observed, a solemn expression crossing his face.

"Nonsense," Leah countered. "It's—it's just that this night was supposed to be—special."

Stone smiled knowingly. "Well, it still is, Leah. What could be more special for a writer than having her first book published? You still want that dinner?"

Leah glanced at the door Mike had just disappeared through. "Why not?"

After an elegant dinner, Leah and David sat side by side in rockers on the side porch of the dorm. The pale moon cast moving shadows in the yard from the trees blowing in the night breeze and created a checkerboard of brightness where it shone through the latticework at the end of the porch.

"The stories have to be edited," he commented. "Scribners wants me to do it with you. In fact, they put that clause in the contract. I hope you don't mind."

"You know anybody who could do a better job?"

"Not offhand," Dave laughed. "It's going to take a lot of hard work though."

"When do we start?" she asked eagerly.

"What's your schedule?"

"Classes till noon. Work at the library till five."

"My leave's up Monday. That leaves us three nights and the weekend."

Leah pursed her lips in thought for a moment. "Tell you what. Meet me tomorrow at the library at five. I think I can get us an office. We can work there from five to midnight for three nights and all day on Saturday and Sunday."

"That just might do it."

* * *

When Mike had stormed down the front walk of the dorm, he got in his car and drove straight to Rudy's Tavern. As soon as he walked into the dim, smoke-filled room, he spotted his father perched on a stool at the bar, surrounded by his buddies. "Chattanooga Choo-Choo" blared from the jukebox.

"Mike! Mike! Get yourself over here!" Kyle Hardin rose from his stool, slapping his son on the shoulder and pulling him over to the group of men. "Tell us all about them new-fangled planes you're flying for the navy. Hey, Rudy. Get Mike here a bourbon and water."

Mike protested to no avail. After two drinks, the company of the older men became tolerable. After three more, he thought they were absolutely the funniest bunch of men he had ever been around. They were singing World War I songs at three o'clock in the morning when Rudy pushed them all out the door.

Struggling out of bed at the crack of noon the next day, Mike threw up, showered, and called Leah at the library. "What do you mean you can't see me tonight?"

He listened as she explained about editing her book. "But this means we can't go out at all. I have to leave Monday morning."

"I'll try to work something out so I can see you off, Mike," Leah explained. "I hope you understand."

"Yeah, sure," he mumbled. "See you around." He hung up the receiver and immediately picked it back up.

Darla Hardin stood at the door to the living room, listening to her son speak to someone in that tone of voice she had come to know so well.

"Sure I do." Mike held the phone away from his ear, frowned at it and put it back. "Your ponytail is just as cute as a little speckled puppy. The rest of you ain't half bad either."

* * *

"Well, that's it." David Stone unrolled the sheet of manuscript from the big Underwood typewriter, placing it carefully on the neat stack that lay on the heavy oak table.

Leah glanced at the big schoolhouse clock. "Ten-thirty. You said we'd get it done."

Stone rubbed his eyes with both hands. "And I've enjoyed every minute of it."

"I'll just bet you have, David. You've used your entire leave to work on getting my book published, when you should have been out somewhere having a good time." Leah smiled warmly at him. "You're a very special man, David Stone."

His face colored slightly. "I mean it, Leah. I'd rather *work* with you than *play* with anybody I know."

Leah laughed softly. She stared at his tired brown eyes, a few strands of his chestnut-colored hair hanging over them. "I can never thank you enough for what you've done for me, David. And I'll never forget it."

Stone rubbed the back of his neck and stood up. "I guess it's pretty obvious how I feel about you, Leah."

She glanced up at him, her eyes bright with emotion. "You— you've never said anything."

"I'm good at writing words, Leah," he smiled. "Guess I'm not very good at saying them."

Leah watched him pace slowly back and forth.

Dave stopped, gazing directly into her eyes, more gray than blue in the dim office lights. "I love you very much, Leah. I guess the timing's all wrong telling you this now, but I can't hold it back any longer."

"I—I don't know what to say," she stammered. "We've been very close, but . . ."

"You don't have to say anything right now." He sat wearily on the edge of the table.

Leah rose and took his hands in hers. "I just need some time, David," she smiled. "Have you found out what your assignment is yet?"

"The *Yorktown*." He felt Leah's warm hands on his. They seemed to take away the fear that gnawed at him and the loneliness he knew lay ahead. He wanted to lie down beside her, hold her close to him, and forget about the war.

Leah put her arms around him. "Oh, David, David! I'll write you every day. I'll pray for you every night."

He returned her embrace, feeling her soft cheek against his, her breast pressing firmly against his chest. He willed himself to remember every contour of her body, the smell of her hair, the warm wetness of her tears as they caressed his face.

15

BATTLE OF
THE CORAL SEA

*I*f any of you have any romantic notions," Lieutenant
Commander William Naylor said emphatically, "get rid of them
now!"

Better known among the pilots on the *Yorktown* as "Wild Bill,"
Naylor was a short, burly man of twenty-eight. His piercing black
eyes pinpointed the pilots he'd gathered into the briefing room so
sharply that each man felt he was the sole target. Naylor went at
everything in exactly the same manner as he did to kill a Jap carrier—with every ounce of determination he had!

Mike Hardin leaned forward as Naylor spoke, determined
to prove to this man that he was the best pilot who'd ever flown
off the *Yorktown*. He'd already proven his capability, for in the
week the group had been aboard, he'd stood head and shoulders
above the other pilots. Even Naylor himself had been heard to
say so!

"So far, the Japs have had their own way," Naylor continued.
"They control everything out here. They've got Formosa, the Phil-
ippines, Indochina, Thailand, Burma, Malaya, Sumatra, Borneo, the
Marianas, the Marshalls, the Gilberts, most of New Guinea, and almost all the Solomons." He suddenly grinned, the severity of his
countenance broken by the smile. "And you guys are here to take it
back from them!"

"Why, we ort not to have too much trouble, Commander."
The speaker was a slight pilot from Mississippi named Stan
Collins, known as "Stonewall." He carried a Confederate flag that
he swore he'd plant in the Imperial Palace in Tokyo, and he idol-
ized Stonewall Jackson. He spoke in a lazy drawl replete with

grammatical errors, added purposely—for he had a degree in English literature from Ole Miss.

Naylor studied the Mississippian carefully, then nodded. "You keep on thinking that way, Lieutenant Collins," he said. "Faith is a wonderful thing—and the odds we face will call for every bit of faith we have." He turned and pointed at the map on the wall behind him. "What the Japs have is the largest combined surface area ever under one flag—bigger than Alexander's conquests and the Roman Empire, bigger than the empires of the Great Khans, the Spanish, and the British! And if the Japs hold on to this empire, it's going to be rough going for us."

Dave Stone spoke up from the back of the room. "Looks like they've got a corner on oil and raw materials."

"Exactly!" Naylor slammed his fist against the map. "Unless we can run them out of here, the Allies won't have oil or gas or rubber for tires! You can't fly a Dauntless on R.C. Cola—and you can't land on skis!"

"What's going to happen, Commander?" Mike demanded. "Will we see action soon?"

Naylor turned his sharp black eyes on the speaker. "That's the *one* thing you don't have to worry about, Hardin. The Japs *have to* hold on to this area or they're a goner. And their high command has already learned that carriers are the only way to win. Always before, it was the battleship with its big guns that was the backbone of the fleet. But we all know now that no fleet can control the seas without controlling the air over it."

"But the Japs didn't destroy a single carrier at Pearl Harbor," Stone said. "That was their big mistake."

"Right! And right now we're headed for a shootout that's going to prove that all the old rules are gone," Naylor answered. "You men will be in the history books after it's over. Just try to stay alive is all I ask." A sardonic light fired his black eyes, and he nodded, "Those dive bombers you're flying are expensive and hard to replace—so I'm going to work your tails off to be sure you don't lose them!"

"Aw, we'll wipe them little sons of Nippon out!" Stonewall asserted.

"You didn't do so good wiping out the Yankees in the Civil War," Leon Hamnett, a rangy pilot from Michigan spoke up.

Stonewall gave him a dark glance and muttered, "It ain't over *yet!*"

* * *

As a junior ensign in a new squadron, Mike knew that his chance to fight in the oncoming battle was limited. There were eighteen aircraft in the squadron, of which only fifteen or sixteen were flyable at any one time, with twenty-one pilots on the personnel roster. His chance to fly a strike would come only after all the others had made their first strike, and only if the squadron commander would let him go. His first duties consisted of manning standby planes for launch on deck, engine warmups, and striking below.

Burning to show what he could do, Mike's ego was bruised by this, but he was wise enough to know that if he ever wanted a chance to hit the enemy, he had to endure it. Dave Stone was surprised at the enthusiasm with which Mike threw himself into these rather unromantic duties, and he said so.

"Mike, you're doing a good job," he said one morning after returning from a training flight.

Mike forced a grin. "Well, I'll do just about anything to get a shot at the Nips."

"You'll get your chance," Dave nodded. "I'll talk to Naylor. Be a shame to waste your talent warming up engines."

Mike shot a quick glance at the smaller man. He had never believed that Dave held no grudges after the beating he'd given him. Now he said carefully, "I'd appreciate that." It seemed a bare statement, and he added with some embarrassment, "I—I feel pretty bad about that fight, Dave."

Stone shook his head briefly. "Forget it, Mike. We've got too much to do to nurse grudges."

Mike was impressed with Dave's attitude, but a thought came to him. "I wish the other guys would feel that way about it."

"They'll come around," Dave assured him. He looked over to where several of the other pilots were engaged in animated conversation, Bailey Sutton and Sam Devito among them. He wanted to join them but knew that he couldn't force Devito and Sutton to forgive Mike. Instead he said, "Come on, let's have some coffee—and I've got something to show you."

Eager to have someone to talk to, Mike accompanied Dave, and soon the two of them were drinking coffee in the mess hall.

Dave pulled out an envelope, saying, "Big news from Leah—but you may have heard it."

"No. I haven't heard from her."

Dave caught a note of regret in Mike's voice and said quickly, "Yes, well—mail's slow out here. You'll be hearing from her, but let me give you just a little bit of news."

Unfolding the single sheet of paper, he read,

> "The book is out! I feel like an impostor though. As if someone else had written it and put my name on it. Actually! I carry a copy with me all the time, and about fifty times a day I take it out, read the name on the cover, and try to believe that it's my book. And when I read the stories, it's with a detachment I can't believe, David! I sometimes think, *What awful writing*—but with no shame. And sometimes I think, *What a wonderful sentence!* but with no pride. It's as if I were reading someone else's book!"

Dave grinned at Mike, saying, "She's the only truly *humble* writer I know. Most writers are egotists. I always think of what Logan Pearsall Smith said about that—'Every author, however modest, keeps a most outrageous vanity chained like a madman in the padded cell of his breast.' But Leah is the same always."

Mike listened as Dave read the letter, then asked, "She's going on a tour promoting her book? That's big time, isn't it?"

"Yes, in a way. The publishers don't ask a writer to do that unless they feel sales are going to be high."

Mike took a sip of his coffee, his face a study. He'd always thought of Leah as a nobody—sweet, but not a girl who'd ever attract much notice. Now he asked, "Dave, is there a chance she could ever become famous—I mean like Hemingway or some of those people?"

Dave thought for a moment, then shrugged. "Not that big, maybe. But she's got the talent to wind up in the lit books. She's got a fresh voice, and the world is looking for that. Harper Lee wrote one book, but people will be reading it for a long time. I think Leah's good enough to make it."

Mike shook his head. "She'll change, then. People don't stay the same when they get famous."

"Wouldn't be so sure about that—although you're right in a general way. But Leah's not your typical writer, Mike. She's known the Lord for a long time."

A sudden wave of discontent and regret swept through Mike. He slumped forward, putting his elbows on the table. Memories surfaced, bringing a pang he'd seldom known, and he spoke in a tight voice. "I gave her a hard time. Wish I could change things."

Dave shook his head firmly. "Don't start down that road, Mike. None of us can go back and change what we've done. But we can change what we *are*—or I guess I'd say, God can change us."

Not wanting to hear a sermon, Mike drank the last of his coffee and rose quickly. "Guess I'd better get back to work. Thanks for sharing the letter."

Dave sat at the table and the thought came to him: *Shouldn't have preached at him. He's having a bad enough time as it is.*

All afternoon Dave thought about Mike and finally paid a visit to Commander Naylor. "I'd like to have Hardin fly with me, sir."

Naylor was surprised, for he knew a little about Mike's problems. "You sure, Stone?"

"Yes, sir, I am."

"All right. I like to let my flight leaders make their own decisions."

Dave knew that Naylor disagreed with his choice, but when he told Mike about his new assignment, he was glad to see the excitement that sprang to Mike's eyes.

"That's great, Dave!" Mike said. "I'll stick to you like a leech!"

To a dive bomber section or division leader in combat, good wing men were more precious than diamonds. Mike soon found out that Dave was one of the great ones. He flew his airplane in a rough, aggressive manner that might have confused many pilots, for it was their job to stay in formation no matter what happened. Mike set out to prove that he could fly the tightest formation in the U.S. Navy, and in the days of intense training that followed, not once was he ever shaken off by anything Dave did.

For days the training went on, and much time was spent eliminating problems. The SBD telescope sights and windshields fogged over, starting at about seven thousand feet, causing many of the pilots to lose sight of targets and release high. By trial and error, the squadron leaders discovered that approaches at about fifteen thousand feet produced no fogging, and that became the maximum altitude used for attack.

Learning to hit the target was a constant theme. "If you don't put the bomb on the target," Naylor drilled into the pilots, "everything's lost."

Many of the pilots missed because of a last-minute attempt to correct a dive. But Mike had learned that it was essential for the aircraft to remain in the dive as the bomb separated from its carrying shackles on the plane, and his average was the best in the squadron. This was the factor that made Commander Naylor say privately to Dave, "Hardin may have a sackful of problems—but he can put a bomb on the target. I wish we had some more with his eye!"

*   *   *

On the morning of May 7, 1942, Vice Admiral Takeo Takagi, commanding Carrier Division 5 and in charge of Operation MO, the invasion of Port Moresby, was concerned. He knew that American aircraft carriers were somewhere near him in the Coral Sea and had been for several days, as evidenced by the raids of May 4 against the Japanese land and sea forces at Tulagi. While continuing search efforts, his invasion force of eleven transports, four heavy cruisers, the escort carrier *Shoho*, and escorting destroyers proceeded on a direct course toward the invasion site.

So it was with some elation that Takagi received an early morning report from the pilot of a cruiser-based floatplane that he had sighted a carrier and escorting cruiser. In reality the scout had found and misreported the U.S. oiler *Neosho* and its escort, the destroyer *Sims*. The admiral hastily ordered his two big carriers, *Zuikaku* and *Shokaku*, to launch an all-out attack. By 0830 thirty-six Val dive bombers, twenty-four Kate torpedo planes, and eighteen Zero fighters were on their way to the scene of the contact.

When this seventy-eight-plane group arrived at the target and found two unprotected ships and no U.S. carriers, they attacked and sank the unfortunate quarry using only bombs. After an easy victory, the Japanese aircraft returned to their carriers.

Meanwhile Rear Admiral Frank Jack Fletcher on the *Yorktown* was as concerned about locating the Japanese carrier force as Takagi was about finding his. The morning watch soon made a contact:

Lieutenant John Nielsen, after shooting down a Japanese reconnaissance floatplane, sent a report to *Yorktown* about the location of six ships.

Mike Hardin knew nothing of all this, but when he was awakened out of a sound sleep by a loudspeaker blaring out, "All pilots to the briefing room at once!" he knew something was up. He came out of his bed like a cat and joined the scramble to get to the briefing.

Commander Naylor's black eyes were glittering with excitement as he said, "We have located a Japanese force and will attack at once. This will be a maximum strike; every available plane will be employed."

Mike's heart was racing as he joined the others, and soon the squadron made a perfect launch—seventeen SBD-3 Dauntlesses airborne, each with a thousand-pound bomb and a one-hundredth-of-a-second delay fuse. It was truly a maximum effort, with every pilot in the squadron headed for the enemy. Only four pilots remained behind in a deserted ready room.

The sky was blue and the sea beneath was green as Naylor led the flight on a slow climb toward the position. Mike hugged Dave's wing as they kept their places in the formation, and when his rear gunner, a thin redhead named Wally Jones from North Dakota, yelled, "There they are, sir!" it came as a shock to him.

Looking down he saw the ships, looking like toys on the surface. "I see them, Wally," Mike said. Glancing around he caught Stone's eye and saw that his wing man was aware of the target. "Here we go," Mike said to the gunner. "There'll be some Zeroes, so don't let them get away."

"Right!"

But to Mike's disappointment, Naylor's voice crackled over the radio: "We will attack. Lieutenant Stone—you will remain as observer and reserve."

Mike glanced quickly toward Stone and saw that the other pilot was as disappointed as he was. They watched as the rest of the flight threw itself into a steep dive. At the same time a flight of lumbering TBDs of Torpedo Squadron 5 bored in at the targets. Mike saw for the first time the flowering of flak as it burst around the planes in a strange, deadly beauty and flinched when two of the torpedo bombers exploded in a burst of orange flame.

I don't know if I'd have the nerve to fly one of those things or not, Mike thought. The TBDs were slow and couldn't take evasive action. And every gun on the enemy ship they attacked was aimed at them. Then the Dauntlesses screamed down on the ships and he saw several of the bombs make hits. Others fell into the water, sending up white geysers.

As the bombs and torpedoes exploded on the small carrier—actually a baby flattop, Wally Jones was screaming and Mike wanted to do the same. Five minutes after the *Yorktown's* planes had begun their attack, *Shoho* was a mass of flames. Five minutes later it sank.

Mike watched as the ship plowed itself under and said to Wally, "Scratch one flattop."

The flight came up, all bombs gone, and Mike heard Naylor say, "Stone—put your bombs on that heavy cruiser!"

"Yes, sir!"

Mike grinned at Dave, who waved down, and the two of them put their planes into steep dives.

Far below, Mike saw the slim shape of the cruiser, and flak began to explode around the planes. Mike watched as the four planes went in. He was last in line and had a glimpse of Sam Devito's plane as it took hits on its port wing and had to break off the attack. Dave led the group, but his bomb missed narrowly, falling just behind the cruiser. Bailey Sutton's bomb struck the ship on the fantail doing no great damage. Dave's voice came over the radio, "It's up to you, Mike!"

Hardin's world narrowed to the long, thin shape of the cruiser below. Tiny flashes from the machine guns and antiaircraft guns winked all along the length of the ship. The air seemed full of shells, and Mike remembered what a soldier had said about Gettysburg during the Civil War: "The air was so full of bullets you could have put your hat out and filled it with them!"

When he looked through his bomb sight, a strange sense of peace came over Mike that did not even seem strange at the time. The puffing explosions of the flak, the screaming of the wings of the Dauntless, all seemed to fade away so that he dove into a world of silence.

The cruiser that had moments before seemed like a toy swelled suddenly in size, and he saw the tiny forms of sailors running across the deck. A Zero appeared on his left, guns winking like sparklers, but he hardly heard the sound of the slugs tearing into the side of his plane.

And then he saw the black hole of the stack of the cruiser, belching ebony smoke. Fixing his eyes on this, he held the Dauntless steady. Dimly he heard Wally's guns crackling; his entire focus was glued to the black hole. The cruiser turned in a belated evasive tactic, but Mike adjusted his dive accordingly.

The details of the ship leaped into even sharper focus—he could see the tiny flags fluttering from the bridge. His hand rested on the bomb release and for a moment he thought, *I'm about to kill hundreds of men!*

He released the bomb, careful not to come out of his dive too soon. When the bomb was clear, he pulled up, and the wrenching of the Dauntless pulled him back against his seat. He heard no explosion and a dull sense of defeat began to well within him.

Then Wally yelled, "Right down the stack, Lieutenant! Right down the stack!"

Mike pulled the Dauntless to one side just in time to see the cruiser shudder and lift out of the water. It seemed to explode from within as the thousand-pound bomb detonated, and he found himself yelling wildly. Over the radio he heard Naylor's voice. "You got him! You got him, Hardin!"

Even as Naylor was shouting, the sound of bullets hammering into the plane shook Mike, and he knew a Zero was on him. He threw the ship into a steep turn, wondering why Wally didn't return the fire. Turning, he saw the small gunner slumped over, his shoulder a bloody ruin.

The Zero was turning, and Mike knew he had only one chance. Instead of fleeing, he turned straight toward his opponent and as the two met he squeezed the trigger on Dauntless's forward cannons.

For a few seconds the two planes spat death at one another, but then the Zero exploded violently, filling the air with smoke and fire. Mike pulled up and half an hour later landed aboard the *Yorktown.*

He was the last to land and found himself surrounded by a bunch of yelling pilots—including Sutton and Devito.

"You did it, you son of a gun!" Devito grinned. "Sunk a cruiser with one bomb!"

Sutton was beating Hardin on the back, his face wreathed in a sunny smile. "You ol' hardhead!" he yelled. "Always a show-off!"

Mike felt lightheaded and said, "Let's get Wally to sick bay, then we can talk." He accompanied the stretcher crew and knew that it would be a long time before Jones would see action again. Then as they all went to the ready room for their debriefing, Mike knew that his world had changed. He knew it even more clearly when Admiral Fletcher said in front of the entire squadron, "I'm putting you in for the Navy Cross, Lieutenant Hardin."

The experts said that the Battle of the Coral Sea was a tactical victory for the Japanese with the sinking of the *Neosho*, the *Sims*, and the carrier *Lexington*, but it was a strategic victory for the Allies—their first—who had circumvented the capture of Port Moresby.

Mike Hardin found it difficult to look at the big picture though. He was subjected to such high praise from his fellow pilots and from his superior officers that he slipped into some of the arrogance that had been his during his days of athletic fame.

He was not conscious of this—but Dave was. He tried to talk to him about it one night. He came to sit beside Mike at the movie being shown on deck—*The Maltese Falcon*, starring Humphrey Bogart.

"Mike, I've been thinking about how we can get a little more snap into our attacks," Dave said and began to go into some details of the plan he'd been working on.

Mike looked at him tolerantly, but he shook his head. "We're doing pretty good, Dave. If it ain't broke, don't fix it."

Dave stared at Mike silently. He knew it was hopeless to warn the big man of the danger of overconfidence. He turned to leave, and Mike's voice followed him.

"Tell Leah about the Navy Cross, Dave. I think she might be impressed."

16

MIDWAY

*H*ey—Lieutenant!"

Mike turned from the side of his Dauntless and was shocked to see Lennie Leslie, one of his classmates from Liberty High, approaching along the deck. He would have been little more surprised to have seen Coach Bonner Ridgeway himself on board the *Yorktown!*

"Lennie!" he exclaimed, and forgetting regulations, he reached out and hugged the slight man. "What in the world are you doing out here?"

Lennie's black hair was falling over his forehead and he brushed it back with an automatic gesture. He was grinning broadly and when Hardin stepped back, he saluted smartly, saying, "Petty Officer Leonard Leslie, gunner and radioman, sir—reporting for duty!"

Since Mike had lost Wally Jones, he'd been accompanied on his flights by various men drawn from the pool of available talent. He disliked this method, feeling that the two men in a Dauntless needed an established rapport to make their attacks more efficient. But somehow he couldn't see Lennie as the right man to ride behind him. Then he realized that he was still thinking of Leslie as a high school sophomore.

"I joined up and made up my mind to get in the air," Lennie said. "I know you could have any of the replacements you want, Mike—I mean, Lieutenant—but I graduated at the top of my class." A wistful look came into the young man's mild blue eyes. "I sure would like to be your gunner!"

"Well, you'll sure get a shot at it, Lennie," Mike smiled. "Let's go up and I'll check you out."

"Yes, *sir!*"

177

The two men climbed inside the Dauntless and Mike took off. As he cleared the deck, he marveled at how quickly the *Yorktown* had been repaired. The ship had taken a big hit at the Battle of the Coral Sea and been sent to Tongatapu for repairs. She had limped into port on May 15. The word from the refitters was that the repair would be a three-month job. But as the ship stood high in the dry dock, Admiral Chester Nimitz appeared in rubber boots and waded beneath the giant carrier to see the damage for himself. Sprung seams along the hull could be welded closed and a huge steel plate could be patched to her skin quickly.

Fifteen hundred workers poured aboard; huge lights were rigged around the dry dock to begin the patch job. More than 150 welders and shipbuilders began round-the-clock work. The ship's crew also helped to heal the wounds and brought stores, food, and ammunition aboard.

The *Yorktown* came out of dry dock on the twenty-ninth. She had sailed at 0930 on May 30 with a hastily gathered new air group. Now as Mike looked down, he remembered Admiral Nimitz's appearance to the officers and men of the ship. He'd apologized for sending them back into action immediately, but he pledged that after the battle he'd send the ship to her home port in Bremerton, Washington, for a long liberty.

Mike checked Lennie out and was pleased with the young man. When they had landed, he said, "You did fine, Lennie. I'll be glad to have you with me."

Lennie beamed, his thin face split in a toothy smile. "Thank you, sir! I won't let you down!"

The two men worked well together, and Mike was pleased to see that Lennie did not presume on their old acquaintanceship. The gunner never approached him when off duty and in the air was all business.

Mike found him one day sitting on a coil of rope on the fantail reading a book. As he approached, Lennie leaped to attention, but Mike said, "At ease." He leaned on the rail and gazed out over the sea. "Good book?" he asked idly.

"Well, I'm in it," Lennie spoke up. When Mike turned to stare at him with surprise, he held the book out. "You might be too, Mike."

Mike took the book and a shock ran along his nerves as he read aloud the title and the name of the author. *"The Wayward*

Heart—by Leah Daniel." He stared at the cover for a long time, then looked up at the young man watching him. "You're in it?"

"Sure am!" Lennie nodded emphatically. "Oh, not my name—but the third story—it's all about me!"

Mike smiled. "I'd like to read that."

"Oh, take it along!" Lennie said quickly. "It's just out, so I brought some extra copies."

"You sure?"

"Why, yes sir," Lennie nodded, adding, "we graduates of Liberty High got to stick together, don't we?"

"Sure do," Mike nodded. He stood there on the rail, holding the book and talking quietly to Lennie—or more accurately, listening as the gunner spoke. His mind was not on the coming battle, for he was thinking that the gray-blue of the sea was much the same color as Leah's eyes.

He left after a time and went to his bunk. Stretching out, he opened the book to the dedication page. "To David Stone—my teacher," he read aloud. There was something in the simple words that gave him pause, and he lay quietly for a time thinking of the history of the three of them—Leah, Dave, and himself.

He began to read and was shocked at how much of the book was a reflection of his world—of Liberty, Georgia. Leah had changed the names—but the people he knew were all there. Alvin Ditweiler, Bonner Ridgeway, Ben Logan, Leslie Gifford.

He had never been a reader—especially of fiction, which he had frequently dismissed as "something that's not true." But as he read, he saw that the stories *were* true. Leah had taken her world, small as it was, and had made it come alive. And the truths that had mattered to her were dramatized so vividly that any reader could say, "Yes, life *is* like that!"

Mike read steadily, unaware of the time. He skipped the evening meal, and after the rest of the ship was asleep, still he read. Leslie had been right—he had been in the third story. The story dealt with a small incident that Mike remembered well—of a young boy who'd been run down by a drunken driver. The boy's name had been Phil Lattimore, and he'd been Lennie's best friend. Not much happened in the story—but the terrible grief that had been Lennie's was set forth with bold strokes. It was not a sermon on the evils of drink—yet it made Mike feel a streak of raw anger at the callousness of the driver such as he had never felt at a story in a newspaper.

The last story was about him.

The name was different, but it was the story about a football player who used a shy young girl badly—in fact, in exactly the same way that he had used Leah. Mike clenched the book so tightly that his wrists ached, and he expected to find hatred in the young girl—but he didn't.

He felt a wave of shame wash though him as the girl in the story was used—then put aside. Blindly he shut the book and turned out the light. But he couldn't blot out the words—or ignore the rotten feeling that had come to him. As he lay in his bunk, staring into the darkness, he wished he could see Leah, that he could tell her so many things!

But the *Yorktown* was headed toward Midway—and he well knew that many of the men who lay sleeping in their bunks would never see home again.

Sunset found the gallant ship steaming with a bone in her teeth toward a rendezvous with the enemy. One patched-up aircraft carrier, flying a maverick air group, was headed toward defeat or victory in the greatest carrier naval battle of the Pacific war with Japan.

* * *

The Battle of Midway may have been the greatest sea battle of all time. Certainly it was the most significant one in U.S. naval history. Historian Gordon W. Prane named it the "miracle at Midway," and Walter Lord entitled it the "incredible victory." Samuel Eliot Morison called Midway, "Six minutes that changed the world."

The date was June 4, 1942, and the six minutes were from 1024 to 1030. The place was the open sea, a little more than a hundred miles northwest of Midway Island. Here, steaming in a box formation, were four of Japan's finest flattops—*Akagi, Kaga, Soryu,* and *Hiryu*—under the command of Vice Admiral Chuichi Nagumo.

Admiral Yamamoto, Japanese fleet commander, had convinced the high command that the empire would never be safe until the American fleet was destroyed. The specific step he proposed was the occupation of Midway Island. It was within bombing range of

Hawaii, and once it was taken, the United States would have to commit all its ships to retake it.

The entire combat force of the Imperial Navy was thrown into the attack—eleven battleships, their four biggest carriers, and heavy cruisers—plus an invasion group to follow and a diversionary attack group to strike in the Aleutians. Yamamoto's plan was to destroy the local Midway defenses by an overwhelming air attack, then take over the island.

And it would probably have worked—except for a case of hives.

Admiral Bull Halsey had the hives, and in his place Nimitz appointed Admiral Raymond A. Spruance to command the American carrier force. It was one of the best choices Nimitz ever made—or anyone else. Spruance had no experience in carrier war, but he submitted everything to a process of cold, remorseless logic and was known in the fleet as "the thinking machine."

The grand assault opened on June 3 when carrier planes attacked Dutch Harbor. This was supposed to draw off part of the carrier fleet from the Pacific—but it did not, for army pursuit planes appeared and drove the carrier planes away. Not one ship or plane was diverted from the American defense.

Early on June 4, a Thursday, with light winds and small clouds over the American carrier force, the Japanese admiral launched his strike against Midway—108 planes, with another 108 following half an hour later. The attack did not succeed, and Japanese flight leaders radioed that another strike would be necessary. Admiral Nagumo turned north under the cloud cover to refuel and rearm his planes.

At this moment there entered a force of whose very existence the Japanese were ignorant—Spruance and the American carriers. *Yorktown* had flown early morning search missions and located the Japanese carriers. The two carriers *Hornet* and *Enterprise* ran to within 175 miles of the Japanese position and launched full strikes —every plane on both carriers—in the hope of catching the enemy planes while they were refueling on the carrier deck. Two hours later the *Yorktown* launched its planes.

Spruance's was one of the key command decisions of the war, but it was a close thing. The American planes had to hunt for the Japanese carriers, and the fighters, dive bombers and torpedo planes became separated. The result was that the torpedo planes, low over the water, reached the Japanese first and without fighter cover, received the undivided attention of the enemy combat air patrol. They were shot to pieces. Only four of them ever got back to their carriers. There was a single survivor from *Hornet's* Torpedo 8 squadron, Ensign George Gay, who floated on a rubber seat cushion, settling himself just in time to see the most tremendous spectacle of the war.

But the deaths of the men in the torpedo planes were not in vain, for the Japanese carriers, maneuvering desperately, had to concentrate their fighter and firepower on them—with the result that the fighters were at a low altitude when the incoming Dauntless dive bombers came screaming down to attack the carriers virtually unopposed. They also found the carrier decks loaded with refueling planes.

Mike's squadron flew in six wedge-shaped sections, inverted V's, three planes in a section, two sections in a division. The gunners, facing the rear, were splayed as men would be sitting on a flight of steps. Any enemy fighters making runs on the squadron from the rear would be confronted with the muzzles of thirty-six .30 caliber machine guns.

Mike looked down and saw the Japanese striking force—a huge fleet, so many ships it had to be the main body. He was jumpy, expecting fighter planes at any second, but they did not appear. He stared at Bailey on his left, who shrugged, then back at the sea. Among the ships he could see two long, narrow, yellow rectangles, the flight decks of the carriers. The yellow stood out dramatically on the blue sea. Then farther off he saw a third carrier—and suddenly another long yellow rectangle came sliding out of the obscurity of the storm area.

Four Jap carriers!

"Stone—stand by. There ought to be fighters coming in."

"I've got it under control, sir," Stone answered. He looked out, checked his flight, then stared down at the fleet beneath.

Every ship in the fleet advertised itself as Japanese, with markings painted on its forward turret. The turret top appeared as a square of white with a round, blood-red center. But on the deck of each carrier, bow or stern, the marking was exactly like that which appeared on their planes. On the nearest carrier the symbol measured at least sixty feet across—a five-foot band of white enclosing a fifty-foot disk of red.

"What a target!" Dave whispered. He had often stood on a chair staring down at models, but now he was seeing the real thing.

Naylor's voice came over the headphones. "Gallagher, you take the carrier on the left; Best, you take the carrier on the right; Stone, you follow me."

Dave kicked his rudders back and forth to cause a ducklike twitching of his tail. This was the signal to attack, and he pulled his nose up and, in the stalled position, opened his flaps.

Mike was watching carefully and put his nose down at once. He picked up the carrier target below and made the best dive he'd ever made. As he went down he saw the first bombs land on the yellow deck. He recognized her as the *Kaga* and she was enormous. The *Kaga* and the *Akagi* were the big names in the Japanese fleet. She was racing along at thirty knots into the wind and made no attempt to change course. Mike came at her a little astern on the left-hand side. By the time he was at twelve thousand feet he could see all the planes ahead of him.

Hardin saw the bombs from the group commander's section drop. They struck the water on either side of the carrier. He had picked the big red disk with its band of white as his target, and when he was almost at the dropping point, he saw a bomb hit just behind where he was aiming. The deck rippled and curved back in all directions, exposing a great section of the hangar below. He knew the last plane had taken off from that deck for a long time!

He readjusted his aim for a point just ahead of the bridge and dropped his bomb. After the drop he kept his position for a second before pulling out of the dive to make sure he didn't "throw" the bomb.

Mike was determined to see the bomb hit. After release, he kicked his rudder to get his tail out of the way and put his plane into a stall. He was simply standing there to watch it. He saw the five-hundred-pound bomb hit abreast of the carrier's island. The two one-hundred-pound bombs struck in the forward area of the parked planes on the yellow flight deck.

Got to get out of here! he thought and suddenly realized that three Zero fighters had taken off during his dive. But he found that the three Zeroes were climbing after a group of Dauntlesses already retiring from the action.

Mike started to pull away but noticed that a group of Dauntlesses were just beginning a dive on another carrier. The ship's guns were firing tremendously, and without thinking, he turned his plane toward the carrier. He was carried away with battle madness, and his one desire was to rake the carrier with his forward guns to take the pressure off the incoming dive bombers.

Dave saw him turn—and knew exactly what he was doing. He willed Mike to turn away, but that was all he could do. To his horror, he saw Bailey Sutton follow Mike! Both of them flew at the carriers, turned, and raked the huge ship with their forward cannon. Desperately, Dave waved Devito in, and the two of them followed Hardin and Sutton.

It was a foolish move for all of them; the Japanese gunners began to get their range at once.

Mike completed his run, made a sharp turn, then heard the bullets striking his plane. He turned to see Lennie raking the enemy gun turrets in short bursts. "Give it to 'em, Lennie!" he shouted.

Lennie turned and grinned—and at that moment a bullet struck him in the temple. He fell back, the smile still on his face, his eyes staring blindly at the bright blue sky.

Mike cried out. At the same moment an explosion rocked his plane. He knew it was Sutton's plane. He looked to see the shattered fragments filling the air. He watched as the craft struck the water and sunk at once.

Then he was clear, and as he pulled up, he saw that Stone and Devito had followed him. They were both hit, their planes shaking with the violence of the enemy fire—but they managed to drop down close enough to the water that they escaped. Mike followed them, and the three made their way back to the *Yorktown.*

After Mike put his plane down, he sat there in the cockpit, not wanting to see the body behind him. Finally he crawled out and saw the sightless eyes of Lennie Leslie—and beside him a copy of Leah's book, now spattered with crimson. He stood there woodenly as they removed the shattered body; then, after a few minutes, he staggered blindly away. He went to his quarters and vomited, then lay on his bunk, trembling and fighting the hysteria that rose in his throat.

The door opened and Stone stepped in. He stood over Mike staring down at him, his eyes hard.

"I wouldn't care so much if you'd killed yourself, Hardin," he whispered, controlling himself with difficulty. "But you killed three good men—better men than you'll ever be!"

Mike couldn't say a word, and finally Stone said bitterly, "You'll never fly a plane again in this navy," and then he turned and walked away.

The battle ended soon afterward, with four Japanese carriers sunk—and with the *Yorktown* sunk as well. She took three bombs in her engine room, then a torpedo attack finished her off.

Mike and the rest of the crew were transferred to other ships; although the loss of life on board was not heavy, there were empty places at the mess. Bailey Sutton had been a favorite, and Devito had let it be known that it was "the hot-shot pilot who got Bailey killed!"

Mike kept to himself and was glad when he was shipped back to the States. Anything to get away from the eyes of the men who blamed him for the deaths of three good men!

Death had come, and one pilot wrote:

> To some extent they transferred their normal daily affection for their families to the companions in adventure who shared their meals and staterooms and bull sessions and ready rooms, their acey-deucey games and knowledge of their planes, the sky over the sea, the pride in the neat and deadly formations and the unspoken imminence of death.
>
> Then at the end of a certain day, half had died or were lost, and to each one of the other half perhaps none of his close friends was left. It was sudden, unexpected, and devastating.

More Japanese died that day than on both sides in any naval battle of World War I. And after the Battle of Midway, even Admiral Yamamoto was aware that he had lost the initiative.

But this was nothing to Mike Hardin—for something in him had died when Lennie Leslie and two other good men had died.

17

WHEN A MAN IS DOWN

After reporting to the commanding officer, Mike stepped out the jalousied glass door of the two-story stucco building. The sweltering July heat hit him like a living thing—one designed for torment. Drops of sweat popped out on his face. *This is worse than the South Pacific. At least there's usually a breeze on the sea.*

A flight of F24's, parked in echelon on the tarmac, revved their engines in preparation for bombing practice. They fanned out slowly from the ramp, propellers spinning in a mirage of slowness, as they headed for the runway. Forgetting the heat, Mike watched them roar down the runway and lift off, climbing gracefully against a cobalt sky.

He went over in his mind the few words that were spoken when he had reported in:

"So—you've been reassigned as an instructor." Captain Bledsoe sat *at his ugly gray desk, utilitarian like everything else in the room, except for the picture of his smiling wife. He brushed a wisp of sandy hair back from his forehead and gazed steadily at Mike, closed the personnel file, and dropped it on his desk. "Looks to me like your emotional development is lagging way behind your physical skills, Lieutenant."*

Mike glanced at the door as if planning a getaway, turning his hat around and around in his hands.

"Well, I'll keep you under close scrutiny, Hardin." Bledsoe clasped *his hands in front of him. "You'll adhere strictly to the rules this time or find yourself swabbing a deck. I'll not have my instructors graduating a bunch of prima donnas from this base."*

Mike stared at the floor.

"Is that clear enough for you, Lieutenant?"

"Yes sir," Mike mumbled.

"Dismissed."

Standing up quickly, Mike saluted, did an about-face and left the office.

He watched the last F24 melt into a cloud bank. Bledsoe knows I'm responsible for what happened at Midway.

In his mind, Mike stood on the flight deck of the *Yorktown* watching a seaman wash what was left of Lennie Leslie out of the cockpit with a hose. He remembered the time in the third-floor hallway of Liberty High when Lennie had bristled in anger at him for the way he had treated Leah. The words came back to him as clearly as the day he had spoken them: *You may be a big man in this school, Mike Hardin, but you're just a dwarf in my book!*

Mike saw again the black column of smoke billowing upward from Bailey Sutton's Dauntless as it plummeted into the heaving, slate gray Pacific. Thinking back to his fight with Stone, Mike recalled how it had cost him Sutton's friendship. *What's wrong with me? Why do I always end up hurting other people—losing friends?*

Climbing into the Ford, Mike drove slowly along the streets of the base, the tires hissing on the hot blacktop. A company of seamen dressed in bell-bottomed denims and light blue shirts, their heavy brogans thudding in unison, crossed in front of him. A grizzled old chief, his voice sounding like brass and gravel, called a cadence laced liberally with obscenities.

The freckled-faced gate guard, dressed in summer whites and looking about fourteen years old, gave Mike a snappy salute as he left the base. *He looks like that skinny little halfback who took my fumble in for the winning touchdown. Just like him!*

Spinning across the Pensacola Bay Bridge to Gulf Breeze, Mike took no notice of the sunlight glinting on the surface of the bay as it blossomed with whitecaps in the stiff breeze off the gulf. Where the bridge joined the island, palm trees swayed like slender dancers, accompanied by the high, soft rustling of their fronds.

COOTER'S BA —DRAUGHT BEER—TEN CENTS TILL 5 P.M. Mike noticed the sign banging against its frame in front of a weathered clapboard building at the water's edge. He wheeled the Ford into the parking lot, spraying shells onto the side of a ten-year-old Chevrolet convertible. An especially heavy oyster shell thudded against its dull black finish, next to the right front wheel well.

Turning the engine off, Mike pulled the parking brake and slid out of the Ford. He could already taste the cold draft beer going down. As he sauntered across the shells toward the front screen door that hung on one rusty hinge, a voice pulled him up short.

"Where you goin', flyboy?"

Mike turned abruptly. No one in sight. Then a tall man dressed in marine utilities, his beefy face the color of a day-old sunburn, stood up behind the Ford where he had been inspecting the dent in his Chevrolet. Mike bristled at the man's tone but tried to hold back the rage that had been building in him since his meeting with Bledsoe. "Get a beer. Cool off a little."

"Not now you ain't!"

The smoldering coals in Mike's chest burst into flame, crackling and popping as if he could actually hear them. "You with the local temperance society?"

The man's red face glowed brighter. "You put a dent in my car. You're gonna get it fixed."

Mike turned, stalked over to where the man stood and glanced down at the man's fender. Then he looked up at the marine who was easily four inches taller and forty pounds heavier. "How can you tell which dent is mine? You must have names for all of 'em. I'll bet your friends call *you* Mr. Dents, don't they?"

The marine spoke between clenched teeth. "You're gonna pay for that, flyboy."

"No, I don't think so," Mike said politely. "Tell you what though," he continued, pointing to the dent. "I'll help you name it. We'll call this one *Jarhead*."

Mike got the reaction he had anticipated, and he was prepared for it. The marine's big fist whiffed past his head as Mike ducked beneath it. He came up on the balls of his feet, turning his shoulders and leaning into the punch with his powerful legs. Mr. Dents tried to recover but found himself off balance from the force of his own missed blow. His eyes widened as he saw Mike's right fist rocketing toward his chin. It connected with a sickening thud. His head snapped back, the eyes rolling upward in their sockets. At the same instant, his knees buckled under him and he hit the shell parking lot like a sack of feed.

Mr. Dents lay on the shells, his head to one side, mouth slightly open, breathing nasally. Mike stared at him a few seconds, turned and entered the bar through the dangling screen door.

The jukebox was an amber-and-red glow against the far wall. To the left, a rough wooden bar ran the length of the wall. An alcove to the right held a single pool table in the glare of a green-shaded bulb. A sailor in whites sat with a bleached blonde at one of the tables scattered randomly about the bar. The cement floor was covered with white chalk from the shells in the parking lot.

Mike walked to the far end of the bar next to the jukebox, plopping down on the torn cushion of a metal stool. "Two drafts."

The pale-skinned bartender, whose dark hair gleamed with oil, finished drying a mug and set it on the counter. "Two?" He glanced at the door as though expecting someone else to come in.

"One's for thirst—the other for taste," Mike smiled.

The bartender filled two mugs, setting them in front of Mike. Beer sloshed onto the linoleum-covered bar.

Dropping a quarter next to the mugs, Mike ventured, "How you doin' today? My name's Mike Hardin."

"That's fine with me." The bartender picked up the quarter and walked off.

At least he didn't lecture me. Mike drank the first beer without taking it down from his lips. Walking to the jukebox, he took a quarter from his trouser pocket and dropped it into the slot. After staring at the selections, he called out to the bartender, "Hey, you sure these labels are right? There aren't any *new* songs on this thing."

The bartender glanced over at Mike, shrugged, and continued wiping mugs with his dirty hand towel.

Mike punched in his selections and returned to his stool. He drank half of his remaining beer, staring blankly at the jukebox while Frances Langford sang, "I'm in the Mood for Love."

The screen door banged in the wind. A fly buzzed around Mike's head, landed on the bar five feet away, and stuck his head into a puddle of beer next to a half-empty mug. The blonde, her lips bright against her chalky face, reached across the table and took the young sailor's hand in hers. Billie Holiday's version of "No Regrets" drifted on the stale, smoky air of the bar.

"No regrets." That's about all I do have. How did things go so wrong? What am I gonna do now? I can't go back to Liberty—face Daddy and all the rest of 'em. And Leah—what's she gonna think about me? I could have had everything! And I blew it!

The screen door slammed behind him. Mike glanced at the bartender, who squinted in that direction. Then he turned and saw the three men—all in their marine green utilities. Mr. Dents stood in the middle, flanked by Mutt and Jeff. Mutt's head was shaved and glinted in the light flooding in the doorway behind him. He was built like a fireplug. Jeff was pale and wiry.

The three men spread out and moved slowly across the chalk-covered cement toward Mike, threading their way through the maze of tables and chairs. The blonde let go of her target's hand and scurried off to the ladies room.

Wham!

Five heads jerked around toward the bartender. A double-barreled twelve-gauge lay on the bar in front of him. The barrels were sawed off almost even with the end of the stock. The bartender rested both hands near the lethal-looking weapon. Staring at the three marines, he shook his head slowly.

Mr. Dents motioned with his head for Mike to follow them outside. Mike nodded.

When they were gone, Mike walked over to the bartender, tossing a five-dollar bill on the bar. "Sometime in the next hour, would you put a bottle of that Jim Beam on the front seat of a black Ford coupe in your parking lot?"

The bartender nodded, placing his shotgun back on its rack under the counter.

"How 'bout one for the road?"

"You'll need it." The bartender took a shot glass from under the bar, poured it full of Jim Beam and clunked it down next to Mike. "Sure you wanna go out there?"

"Here's to you." Mike gulped the bourbon. It burned all the way down. He thought of the three men who waited for him outside—and what they had planned for him. It surprised him when he discovered that he no longer cared. It just didn't seem to matter. He suddenly realized that nothing really mattered to him anymore. Something worse than fear—worse than dread—had taken him. He had no name for it, but he knew that if it stayed with him for very long it would destroy him.

Mike stepped into the afternoon glare. They stood with their backs to the sun, waiting for him. It wasn't as bad as it could have been. With his back against the wall of the saloon, he landed three punches before Mutt and Jeff pinned his arms at his sides, holding him upright for Mr. Dents. His first punch caught Mike solidly on the jaw and the lights went out.

* * *

The pale disk hovered far away against the blackness. It wavered slightly, then became a still, round brightness. Mike felt a slight prickling on his left cheek, something skittered across his chest. Sitting upright, he brushed the sand crabs away. The full moon painted a shining path across the dark surface of the bay. Someone had dragged him around behind the saloon. He could see his own heel marks in the sand. He felt the jukebox thumping through the thin wall and heard the sounds of "Begin the Beguine" by Artie Shaw.

Mike rubbed his jaw where Mr. Dents had decked him with a big right, felt the tenderness in his ribs where they had kicked him after he was down. *Could've been a whole lot worse. Hope that bartender remembered to put the painkiller in my car.*

The breeze off the bay helped to clear Mike's head. He heard cars pulling into the parking lot around front. Doors slammed, the sounds of women's laughter and the rasp of men's voices came faintly to him around the corner of the building. The screen door banged happily against its door frame like a child with a new drum.

Mike got painfully to his feet, made sure all his parts were in working order, and limped along the side of the building to the parking lot. The bottle of Jim Beam lay on the front seat of the Ford. He got in, popped the cork, and took a long swallow. "Brrrrr," he sputtered, shaking his head back and forth..

"Rough night, huh?" A woman of indeterminate age with hair the color of black shoe polish leaned against the window of the coupe. An abundance of white flesh gleamed in the dim light.

"No worse than usual, I guess," Mike muttered.

"I could show you a good time." The woman smiled, trying to hide a broken tooth by drooping the right side of her top lip.

"Sounds good to me."

The woman gave him a coy smile. "What did you have in mind, Sailor?"

Mike stared up at her solemnly. "Could we go to the pony rides? I've never done that before."

A stunned look crossed her face for two seconds. Then she spoke harshly of Mike's ancestry and suggested some impossible things regarding his anatomy. With a final oath, she spun around and headed toward the bar, the shells in the parking lot playing havoc with her high heels.

Mike took another long pull at the bottle, corked it, and drove through the little town of Gulf Breeze. Crossing the bridge over Santa Rosa Sound, he flicked on the radio. The announcer's nasal voice irritated Mike unreasonably: *Officials at RCA Victor sprayed a recording of Glenn Miller's "Chattanooga Choo Choo" with gold paint for having sold more than one million copies. They dubbed it the first "Gold Record" . . . Now for the war news. Navy officials have . . .*

Grabbing the knob, Mike changed stations in a blurb of static and broken voices. He stopped when he heard the beginning of the "Fibber McGee and Molly Show." When he reached Santa Rosa Island, he turned west on the coastal road toward Fort Pickens, the Civil War fort that guarded the entrance to Florida's inland waters. Twenty minutes later he spotted the shadowy bulk of the fort in dim silhouette against the starlit sky.

* * *

> Holy, Holy, Holy, Lord God Almighty!
> Early in the morning our song shall rise to Thee;
> Holy, Holy, Holy, Merciful and Mighty!
> God in Three persons, blessed Trinity!

Mike heard the song as though it came from some empyreal distance, carrying on the morning wind. His head throbbed with each beat of his heart. Opening his eyes slowly, he saw the red glow at the base of the eastern sky where it slipped down into the sea. White gulls sailed above him, their cries harsh in his ears. He sat up slowly, peering down at the beach from where he had spent the night atop the seaward wall of Fort Pickens.

The white sand dunes were bathed with a pink light from the sunrise. Sea oats moved gracefully in time to the music. Several people stood around a white cross planted in the sand—austere against the pale sky and the shimmering sea.

Mike rubbed his eyes with both hands, stretched himself, and walked down the brick stairs, through the tall-arched entrance, and out onto the beach. A man in his thirties with light brown hair and a reddish beard stood at the foot of the cross, leading his congregation in song. He wore khakis, a white, short-sleeved shirt, and a red tie. The dozen or so people gathered before him included a boy and girl in their late teens, a vagrant in a long coat clutching a brown paper bag, and a middle-aged couple dressed for church, who had taken their shoes off for the walk down to the sandy service.

Sitting on a dune among the sea oats twenty feet away, Mike listened as the preacher lifted his arms and led his small flock in the next hymn.

> All hail the power of Jesus' name!
> Let angels prostrate fall;
> Bring forth the royal diadem,
> And crown Him Lord of All.

Mike remembered the song from long ago, stood again between his mother and father in their Sunday best and sang along.

> Ye chosen seed of Israel's race,
> Ye ransomed from the fall,
> Hail Him who saves you by His grace
> And crown Him Lord of all.
> Hail Him who saves you by His grace
> And crown Him Lord of all.

The preacher picked up his black leather Bible from the sand and opened it, the pages fluttering. "Who can praise Him for His grace and mercy on this beautiful Sunday morning?"

A few amens and hallelujahs rose against the sound of the wind and the surf.

"Thank You, Jesus." The preacher raised one hand toward the sky, then found his text in the Bible and closed it, marking his place with one finger. "There is freedom in Christ Jesus, brothers and sisters. And only in Him are we truly free."

"Amen, preacher." The barefoot woman in her Sunday finery held her white Bible above her head.

The preacher opened his Bible again. "'There is therefore now no condemnation to them which are in Christ Jesus, who walk not after the flesh, but after the Spirit. For the law of the Spirit of life in Christ Jesus hath made me free from the law of sin and death.'"

Mike rested his chin on both hands, listening intently for the next thirty minutes to the bearded man preach from the writings of another man who had lived almost two thousand years before. A man who had written about freedom—while he was in a dungeon chained to a Roman soldier.

"And we can have that same freedom today, my friends." The preacher turned the pages of his Bible. "God's Word tells us that we 'shall be delivered from the bondage of corruption into the glorious liberty of the children of God.'"

Mike thought the sun had gone behind a cloud. A darkness seemed to fall over him. He trembled with cold. The preacher looked so far away, sunlight forming a bright corona about him. His voice carried on a rushing wind. "'If thou shalt confess with thy mouth the Lord Jesus, and shalt believe in thine heart that God hath raised him from the dead, thou shalt be saved.'"

Mike stood to his feet and the small crowd stared at his sudden appearance. Shading his eyes against the sunlight streaming across the sea. The words echoed in his mind: "Thou shalt be saved."

"Come my friends. Come to the 'unsearchable riches of Christ.'"

The shadow of the cross stretched out until it lay only one step from where Mike stood. He hesitated on the brink of eternity, then stepped onto the shadow, following it to the foot of the cross. *I'm so tired of this world. So sick of myself and everything I am. Lord Jesus, I'm coming to You. I've done so many terrible things, I don't know how You could love me, but You do. Somehow, I just know that You do.*

Mike knelt in the sand beneath the cross. The preacher got down on one knee beside him, lay his hand on Mike's shoulder, and lifted the other, holding his Bible, toward the heavens.

The vagrant wiped his face with one hand and dropped his paper sack onto the beach, walking unsteadily across the sand. He knelt down next to Mike. The woman with the white Bible and the young girl followed him, stood next to him, and placed their hands on his shoulders.

The gulls wheeled overhead, their cries rising upward above the wind and the pounding waves. They sounded to Mike like a choir, singing hymns of praise.

* * *

"Do you agree with me, Lieutenant?" Captain Bledsoe brushed a wisp of sandy hair back from his forehead and leaned back in his chair, placing his hands across a belt that he had let out two inches since taking his desk job.

Lieutenant Mark Holden's lean face held an approving smile. "Yes sir, I do. I never thought he'd change after what I read in his file, but I guess miracles still happen. These last two months we've seen a different Mike Hardin. I was a little skeptical about this religion kick he's on—but it's made a difference."

Bledsoe nodded, then dropped the personnel file on his desk. "We've got to have some experienced pilots in the Solomons to stop that 'Tokyo Express.' The Marines on Guadalcanal will never hold out if the Japs keep bringing in fresh troops and supplies. And those battleships have to be sunk before they shell those poor boys into oblivion."

"Well, Hardin's not only the best pilot on this base, but he's pounded group integrity into his men until it's second nature with them. You'll never see any tighter formations."

"Nothing left but to cut the orders putting him back on sea duty then." Bledsoe handed the file to Holden.

"Yes sir." Holden stood up, saluted, and did an about-face.

"Oh, one more thing, Lieutenant."

"Yes sir?" Holden stood with his hand on the doorknob.

"See that Hardin's sent back to his old squadron."

"Yes sir!"

18

GUADALCANAL

At 0545 on August 7 a flight of ten Douglass SBD's raced down the deck of the USS *Enterprise* and into dark Pacific skies. They had been transferred from the wounded *Yorktown* at Pearl Harbor and were flying a support mission for the invasions of Tulagi, Gavatu, and Guadalcanal. Their targets were the antiaircraft gun positions and radio installations on the south shore of Tulagi.

After they had dropped their bombs, Dave Stone led the flight back to the *Enterprise* to rearm. High above Sealark Channel (later renamed Iron Bottom Sound because of the tremendous number of ships sunk there) he saw the landing barges streaming from the transports, carrying marines toward the long curve of Lunga Bay on Guadalcanal. There appeared to be no resistance on the beaches.

Suddenly, "Tallyho, flight of bogey bombers," crackled over Dave's headset. He recognized the voice of Stonewall Collins and glanced to the right where Collins was flying slot.

From the north, eight Japanese "Betty" bombers roared in to attack the unloading transports. As the F4F escort fighters took off after the bombers, Dave barked a warning into his headset. "Look out for Zeroes coming in with the bombers."

The pilots tightened their formation without thinking, a lesson learned at the battles of Coral Sea and Midway. A straggler, especially one of the much slower SBD's, was a prime target for the swift Zeroes. The rear gunners were alert and ready for action with their twin-mounted .30 caliber machine guns. Pilots and gunners scanned the skies, their heads swiveling like turrets. Discipline provided the best defense, with the close formation allowing the combined firepower of all aircraft to be brought to bear on any enemy pilot who made a run on them.

Ten minutes out from Sealark Channel, Dave spotted it. "Bogey at ten o'clock." His voice snapped the flight to immediate attention, their heads pointing in the same direction.

The Japanese pilot quickly closed the distance. At three hundred yards he opened up with his 7.7millimeter guns. He gave no sign of veering off when the ten gunners of the SBD's returned fire as a single man. The firepower of the twenty .30 caliber machine guns concentrated on the light fighter caused it to shudder as if a giant hand had grabbed it. The cockpit disintegrated and the left wing flew off. Enveloped in orange flames and black smoke, it rolled over and began a ragged, twisting spiral toward the choppy surface a mile below.

"That ol' boy had guts. I'll give him that." The slow drawl of Stonewall Collins came through the headsets.

"Maybe so," Sam Devito twanged in hard counterpoint to Collins's soft speech, "but he sure was lacking in the brains department. I hope they ain't all that crazy."

"Wild Bill" Naylor spoke solemnly. "Don't count on it, Devito. The Japs' creed is death before dishonor. We'll see a lot more like that one—or worse—before this war's over."

Three missions later, the pilots and gunners sprawled in the briefing room, drinking coffee, smoking cigarettes, and swapping yarns about all the kills they had made that day. This was to be their pattern for three more days, at which time the islands were thought to be secured by the marines. Then the carrier task force moved to the south, flying sorties against submarines and surface ships for more than a month, keeping as few Japanese supplies and troops from reaching Guadalcanal as possible.

Late one August afternoon, Lieutenant Commander William Naylor entered the briefing room. The men sat up straighter in their chairs, finishing their coffee and cigarettes.

His black eyes searched their faces earnestly. "We've got some unusual orders, boys."

Conversations ended as they gave him their complete attention, a slight murmuring dying out in the room.

"We're going to be part of the 'Cactus Air Force.'" A rumor of a smile crossed Naylor's dark face.

"Cactus? 'At's the code name the marines give to the invasion of Guadalcanal." Collins spoke from the back of the room. "We gonna leave the *Enterprise?*"

"That's right, Lieutenant," Naylor replied, turning to his maps on the wall.

Some of the men lit cigarettes.

Naylor pulled down a map. "You can see why the 'Canal is so important, because of its strategic location. Henderson Field is the most important piece of real estate in this part of the world. That's why twenty transports full of marines and our carrier task force were committed to taking it. Now we're gonna hold it. That strip of coral and gravel 130 feet wide and 3,800 feet long could change the course of the war in the South Pacific."

"Can't we do just as well from the *Enterprise?*" Leon Hammett asked thoughtfully.

"It's going to remain in the area, along with the rest of the force," Naylor replied. "But we've got to have a physical presence on the island, and right now the army hasn't got enough aircraft to do it. So Flight 303 is going to fill in till they do."

The next day at dusk all the men sat outside their tents, pitched between the runway and the dense jungle at Henderson Field. They had just landed and taxied onto the ramp space when the marines, glad for the additional firepower, met them with supper.

"What's this stuff?" Collins asked, spearing a piece of meat on his tin plate and holding it aloft.

Dave took a bite of captured Japanese rice, moldy and bitter tasting. "Australian sheep's tongue."

Collins laughed uneasily. "No, really. What is it?"

"That's the truth." Dave made a face as he sliced a piece off for himself. "One of the marines told me."

"Well, look on the bright side," Sam Devito offered. "For breakfast we get powered eggs."

"Incoming mail!" someone yelled from down the field.

Everyone dumped his supper in a scramble for the L-shaped slit trench near the tents. The freight-train roar overhead caused them to flatten in the bottom of the damp trench. The shell from a warship out in the channel exploded beyond them in the jungle with a flash of white and a concussion that shook the earth. For

thirty minutes the thunderous explosions ripped the night apart.
Then a breathless silence settled over the airfield.

"That's some greeting the Japs give us." Collins broke the silence for all of them.

Devito asked cautiously, "You don't think this happens every
night, do you?"

"Naw," Collins replied. "I hear they mix it up a little."

"What do you mean?"

"Every day at noon the bombers take over," Collins continued.
"You know, just to put a little variety in the game. Give the boys on
the battleships a rest."

Around midnight the whump of heavy mortars and the clattering of heavy machine guns sounded off in the jungle. Seventy-five-millimeter howitzers roared their destructive power, punctuated
by the sharp crackling of small-arms fire.

"Sounds like it's down by the Teneru River." Dave spoke to
Collins who huddled in the trench next to him.

"Them poor Marines," Collins almost whispered. "Must be
one of them Banzai attacks. I'll take my chances up in the skies any
day. I'd rather go out in a big bang than end up on a Jap bayonet."

The next morning, a haggard marine stumbled out of the
jungle. His face was smoke blackened, the eyes wide and dark and
hollow looking. "You boys got somethin' to eat?"

Dave handed him a plateful of powdered eggs. "Where'd you
come from?"

The man spoke through a mouthful of eggs. "Looking for
stragglers. The Japs attacked down at the Teneru last night. We're
just mopping up. Got separated from my squad."

"How'd it go?"

"We whipped 'em pretty bad." The marine scraped at the
tin plate. "They knocked out a machine gun pit on our flank.
Almost broke through the land bridge down by the ocean, but a
couple of guys got the gun going and held them back. We got a
river and ocean full of dead Japs now, but if it hadn't been for
them two boys it mighta been dead marines instead. They saved
our hides."

The marine thanked Dave for the breakfast, and the men of
Flight 303 trudged across the airfield toward the pagoda on the
knoll overlooking the runway. The Japanese craftsmen had

fashioned the building by hand and the joints were held together with wooden pegs. Intended for worship, it was now used for air operations.

Dave heard the distant drone of an engine. The distinctive sound had become a part of his being. It was a Dauntless. He saw it make one pass overhead, breaking off in a graceful turn as it came in for a landing. All the men stood outside the pagoda as the SBD taxied toward them. The cockpit slid back, and the flyer climbed out and dropped to the ground. Dave recognized the distinctive gait at once. *Mike Hardin!*

When he got closer, the rest of the men recognized him, too, turned their backs on him, and filed into the pagoda.

"Hello, Mike," Dave smiled, walking over to greet him. "Glad to have you back."

Mike glanced at the last of the men entering the pagoda. "Looks like you're the only one."

Dave shook his hand. "They'll come around. We need all the help we can get in this place. Hope you didn't forget how to unload a five-hundred pounder."

"I tried to keep my hand in," Mike grinned.

"Well, I guess you might as well get back in the saddle right now. Briefing's in five minutes." As Dave walked toward the pagoda with Mike, he sensed that something was different about him. *Maybe he's growing up. Takes some men longer than others.*

An hour later the flight of SBD's headed up the "slot" where the Japanese convoys came down through the Solomons. They spotted a small force of destroyers far below. Swooping down on them like falcons, the men of Flight 303 released their five-hundred-pound bombs, sinking one and crippling two others. As they reformed for the return to Henderson, five Zeroes swarmed out of a cloud bank toward them. Raking them with fire from their twenty-millimeter cannons, the Zeroes zipped by so quickly the gunners only had time for a few short bursts.

One of the Zeroes billowed smoke from its engine, an easy prey now for the Americans as he limped back north. The other four had disappeared. No one in Flight 303 broke formation. Mike Hardin had begun the long road back.

* * *

"You got more guts than most men I know, Mike." Dave walked next to Mike along the beach west of Koli Point. "It's taken you a long time, but you've got the confidence of all the men. I doubt I could have lasted if they'd treated me the way they treated you."

Mike gazed out at the blue-green surface of Iron Bottom Sound, its rippling waters taking on a pinkish tint as the huge orange sun was swallowed up by the sea. "I guess I deserved more than they gave me. My pride cost us some good men. I'll have to live with that the rest of my life."

Dave saw the pain in Mike's face. "'Forgetting those things which are behind, and reaching forth unto those things which are before, I press toward the mark. . . .'"

Glancing over at Dave, Mike smiled. "That's good advice, even after two thousand years."

"We can't keep beating ourselves with the things we do wrong in this world, Mike. If we do, we're no good to ourselves or anyone else. We can't help remembering sometimes, but we can still put it behind us." Dave stared across the sound at the dark bulk of Florida Island, remembering the tales of the marine raiders who had taken it.

They came to the marine cemetery, located between the sea and the green hills. High above the beach, the evening wind rustled through the palm fronds.

Mike stared out across the cemetery. Rough crosses made from packing crates leaned above a few of the graves. "How many men you think are buried here?"

"Don't guess there's any way to know. So many of the graves aren't even marked."

Mike walked on into the cemetery where the wide coastal plain swept up into the hills. Dave followed him, glancing about at the graves marked with tin plates from mess kits, scratched with brief reminders of who lay beneath the volcanic ash of this remote island. He heard the distant thunder of artillery fire in the hills.

Stopping at a fresh grave, Mike knelt down and stared at the dog tag nailed to a cross planted firmly in the ground. He leaned forward and touched it, running his fingers over the name, serial number, blood type, and religion.

Stone knelt beside him. "Someone you know?"

"A boy from Liberty—Marcell Duke. He was two years behind me. Made first string as a sophomore fullback when I played left half. Made me look good with his blocking." Mike sat down, staring at the dog tag. "Seems so strange to run across someone like this halfway round the world from Liberty. Someone I knew all my life, dead and buried on this terrible island."

Dave sat on the dusty ground beside him. Behind them, on the beach, a drunken marine staggered along singing "Don't Sit Under the Apple Tree."

After a few minutes, Dave spoke. "We'll be leaving here in a few days."

Mike glanced up at him. "How do you know?"

"Word just came in. It'll be announced at the briefing tomorrow morning." Dave smiled. "Guess it won't hurt to tell you now though. You look like you could use some good news."

"How long?"

"Few days. A week at the most." Dave turned, watching the marine till he vanished down the beach behind a stand of coconut palms, his voice lost in the wind.

"Guess he deserves to celebrate a little." Mike spoke Dave's thoughts for him.

"Yeah," Dave added. "The worst is over for them now. That last battle off Savo Island broke the back of the Jap navy in this area. I hear they're calling it the Battle of Guadalcanal."

"The army's moving in now," Mike continued. "That means the marines will be pulling out."

Dave stood up, brushing the dust from his borrowed utilities. "Guess we'll all be heading north. Marines, army, navy. It's still a long way to Tokyo."

*   *   *

In the perpetual twilight of the jungle, a trail ran north from Henderson Field to the Lunga River. It was here that the men of Flight 303 washed their clothes and their bodies, combining the two into a single operation.

"You ever hear from Leah?" Dave walked next to Mike, his extra set of clothes hung over his shoulder.

Mike looked up at the green-gold light filtering down through the high canopy of the trees. "I got a few letters. She still doesn't talk much about making the big time with her book."

"She wouldn't." Dave thought of the times he had spent on the Farm with Leah, strolling the fields, sitting by the pond. "I think she's so absorbed with her writing, with trying to tell an honest story, she doesn't think much about the profit side of writing. She was excited at first, but it got lost in the effort to improve her work."

"Leah's a fine girl," Mike said flatly, remembering the silky touch of her hair.

"Yes, she is."

They came to the river, flowing cool and clear between the towering trees. After hanging their gun belts on a limb, they stripped off their clothes and scrubbed them on stones out in the river.

Mike hung his clothes on a limb that grew out over the water. As he turned, something hit his chest. He grabbed at it frantically, catching it before it hit the water. "Soap? Where in the world did you get this? I ain't seen a bar in days."

"Connections," Dave grinned. "You go ahead and bathe. I'll use it after I hang these clothes up."

Mike waded out into the middle of the shallow river where, over the years, the current had dug out a basin in the rock. Six feet long and three feet deep, it formed a perfect bathtub. He soaped all over, washed his hair, and tossed the soap to Dave, who was wading out from the shore.

"Think I'll go lie down on that big rock and dry out." Mike pointed to a large flat rock downriver next to the bank.

"Take your time," Dave said, lying down in the basin for a leisurely bath.

*   *   *

Mitsuru Kondo crept along the shadowy forest floor in search of death. It was the only thing on his mind. Naked except for a loincloth and a white headband, eyes blazing with madness, he had slipped past the Japanese sentries in the dead of night. He knew they would send a patrol after him, thinking him to be a deserter. *I will not wait in some den like an animal to starve or have the Americans burn me alive with their flamethrowers. I will find an honorable death.*

Coming to the river, Kondo pushed the dense growth aside with the Samurai sword that had been in his family for twelve generations. The afternoon sunlight glinted on the razor sharp blade. Hearing a noise, Kondo looked upstream where an American lay in the middle of the river, his body underwater, his head resting on a rock. He was singing loudly, his harsh American voice intensifying the hatred already burning in Kondo's chest. *Yours is the death I seek, American. In your death, I will find my own.*

Gripping the sword tightly in both hands, Kondo leaped into the shallow river and charged toward the American, screaming his Samurai death cry.

Mike had been lying on the flat boulder near the opposite side of the river. Hearing the maniacal scream, he sprang to his feet. Dave was scrambling out of the shallow basin, trying to make it to the bank where the .45's hung on their cartridge belts. Mike saw that the Japanese had the angle on Dave and would reach him before he could make it to their pistols.

Without a conscious thought, Mike leaped off the boulder and sprinted upstream. Legs churning, his breath coming in great gasps, he willed his body to reach the Japanese before he could bring his sword down across Dave's neck. Mike's vision narrowed. All he saw was the small yellow man splashing through the river, the deadly sword held in front of him. The man changed suddenly into a freckled-faced halfback carrying a football. *Not this time you don't!* Mike thought.

As the Japanese raised his sword over his head to deliver the killing blow, Mike unleashed all the power left in his legs and leaped high into the air. Landing on the back of the Japanese, he drove him into the soft mud of the riverbank. Cat-quick and agile, the Japanese rolled onto his feet. Mike saw the sword flashing toward his head when the man suddenly jerked backward into the air like a rag doll. The thunderous reports of the .45 shattered the silence of the forest as the man's chest exploded in a burst of crimson.

Dave walked over and stood next to Mike, breathing heavily, the .45 pointing down at the dead Japanese.

"Thanks, partner. You saved my life," Mike smiled.

Dave would always remember Mike that way. The athlete in victory, having won his race. At that instant, Mike's head snapped forward—the sharp crack of a rifle sounded from across the river. A second shot hit Dave in the back of his leg, shattering the knee-cap. As he fell, Stone spun and saw the Japanese patrol at the edge of the woods. His face twisted in pain, he emptied his pistol at them.

Hearing the heavy thudding of boots on the trail, Dave saw a dozen heavily armed marines burst out of the jungle and open fire with M1's and Thompson submachine guns. The Japanese disappeared, with the marines blazing into the jungle after them.

Mike lay in the shallow water, his head resting on his right arm as though he were asleep. Dave sat down in the river, holding Mike's body in his arms. He held him there until the marines returned and found him, moaning deep in his chest, rocking back and forth as a mother would rock her child. And the blood of Mike Hardin flowed into the river and down past the marine graveyard where Marcell Duke lay beneath the shadow of the cross.

19

A GENTLE LIFE

*T*he train huffed to a stop, the sibilant sound of escaping steam drowning out the barking of a brown-and-white mutt on the depot platform. Clouds, like white brush strokes across the pale December sky, picked up a soft rose color from the setting sun.

Inside the building, the stationmaster, a short plump man with wire spectacles, waddled over from behind the iron grillwork of the ticket counter and plugged in the Christmas tree. The red and blue and green lights winked through the long window that looked out on the tracks. A serene angel in a shining robe surveyed the scene from the top of the tree.

Leah got up from her seat and walked over to the window. Her tan overcoat hung open revealing a tailored wool suit of forest green worn over a white silk blouse. She glanced over at the ticket counter. "You think he'll be on this one, Mr. Adams?"

"Can't never tell," Adams replied, adjusting his spectacles. "There's so many soldier boys comin' and goin' these days, you just can't never tell." He returned to his paperwork.

At the far end of the platform, a lean man in a navy dress uniform stepped awkwardly off the train, unable to bend his right leg at the knee. He carried a musette bag over his left shoulder. Holding a cane in his right hand, he limped toward the station.

He had written Leah about his leg, but seeing him hobbling painfully across the platform brought quick, bright tears to her eyes. She burst through the station door, flying across the platform toward him. "Oh, David, David! You're home!" As she threw her arms around him, they both nearly collapsed on the wooden planking.

"I thought the Japs were rough," Dave laughed. "Looks like I'm going to have to go back to Guadalcanal to be safe."

"I'm so sorry," she apologized profusely. "You aren't really hurt, are you?"

Dave grinned. "Indeed not. I merely carry this cane around so old ladies will give up their seats for me."

"I—I didn't mean that," Leah stammered. "I just meant that—oh, I don't know what I meant! I'm just so glad to see you! So glad you're home safe!"

Dave looked into Leah's blue-gray eyes. He had seen them so many times in his thoughts in those faraway Pacific islands that seemed unreal now. He ran his fingers through her soft dark hair, gleaming with streaks of deep red color in the depot lights. "I've missed you so much, Leah! I didn't think it possible to miss anyone that badly."

Leah threw her arms around him as he held her tightly. He smelled her hair, her perfume, felt the rounded firm softness of her against him through his heavy wool coat.

They stood together on the platform with people brushing past them, bumping them in their hurry to reach loved ones and return to their homes full of shining trees and bright presents and the sharing of a holiday meal. The winter darkness settled quickly about Dave and Leah as the sun dropped behind the dark hills in the west, but they were lost in each other.

In a few minutes, she trembled. "Goodness, it's freezing out here! Let's go inside."

"Come on over here, kids." Mr. Adams had pulled two of the straight-backed depot chairs over next to the gas heater at the end of the ticket counter. "Hi, young feller. You must be Dave Stone. Leah's told me all about you." He extended his hand.

"This is Mr. Adams, Dave," Leah offered. "He's been the stationmaster here since John Adams was president."

"Actually it was Jefferson," Adams smiled.

He looks like a beardless Kris Kringle. "Glad to meet you." Dave shook Adams's hand and sat down stiffly in the chair. "Nice place you got here."

"We try to keep it that way for all our boys in uniform," Adams said with obvious pride. "It's stays awfully busy around here since this war started."

"Since his wife died, Mr. Adams has practically lived here in the station." Leah showed obvious affection for the man.

"You folks sit here while I get you some coffee."

"We really have to be going, Mr. Adams," Leah objected gently, but remained seated.

"Nonsense! People are always in such a hurry. Make yourself comfortable. I'll be right back."

Adams returned with two steaming white mugs of coffee, handing them to Leah and Dave. "I put plenty of sugar and cream in them. That all right?"

"Fine," Dave replied.

"Now," Adams began, pulling up a chair. "Tell me how we're *really* doing against them sneaky Japs."

* * *

"This is some fancy car you got here, Lady. Your books must be selling better than I thought." Dave sat next to Leah, running his hands over the plush interior of the year-old Chrysler.

She laughed softly. "It's not mine. I don't think I'd ever buy anything as—pretentious as this. It belongs to Scribner's. They let me use it to drive to book signings—things like that. The trains are so crowded these days it's almost impossible to get tickets."

As they rode through the quiet streets of Liberty a light snow began to fall, the tiny flakes drifting like white motes in the glare of the headlights. The winter evening settled down quietly on the little town. Christmas trees gleamed merrily in the windows of the old white frame houses with their high wraparound porches. Trees stood rigid and stark, their bare limbs standing out like filigree against the amber streetlights. Christmas carols rang out on the still air from the chimes in the courthouse tower.

Dave glanced over at Leah, who had both hands firmly planted on the steering wheel. She stared straight ahead. "You look like you're driving in the Indianapolis 500."

She kept her eyes on the road. "This is all so new to me, Dave. I never even saw a car when I was growing up, except the occasional one that happened down our road. If you want to know the truth, I'm scared to death driving this big monster."

"Want me to take over?"

"No." Leah set her jaw. "I'm going to learn to manage this bucket of bolts if it kills me."

"I thought you'd feel that way," he smiled. "By the way, while you're in a managing mood, did you manage to get a room for me at the hotel?"

Leah made a wide turn in front of the courthouse, the right front tire jarring over the curb. "Oops!"

Dave looked behind him. "Maybe you'd better go back. I think we lost the oil pan that time."

Leah frowned at him. "Yes, I did get you a room. And Josephine said to tell you she'd have the biggest and best meal you ever ate waiting for you. Chicken and dumplings I believe."

"And blackberry pie?" Dave smiled, remembering the plump, jolly cook from the hotel.

"Yep," Leah answered, veering toward the center of the street. "Said she only had three jars of canned blackberries left, but one of them was going in your pie."

"*That* Josephine," Dave smiled. "She sure made me a believer in southern cooking."

Leah screeched to a halt at a red light. "Almost didn't see it," she grinned apologetically.

Dave's eyes narrowed in thought. He quickly made a decision. "I have to go see the Hardins, Leah. I wrote them about Mike's death. I was there when . . . Anyway, Darla Hardin made me promise to come see them when I got to town."

Looking at his troubled face, Leah knew it would be difficult for him to face Mike's parents, to have to recall the brutality and horror of war. "We'll do it now then," she said cheerfully. "Then we'll go have dinner."

*   *   *

Kyle Hardin walked down his front sidewalk toward the street. He wore a blue-and-white Liberty letter jacket over his white shirt. His brown tie was loose at the collar, hanging at an angle outside the coat. "Hello, folks. Merry Christmas." He smiled at Leah and Dave as they got out of the car.

They returned his greetings, Dave holding onto the roof of the car to keep the weight off his bad leg. As he stood up, bracing himself on his cane, he glanced at the front window of the house. A white banner bordered in red hung showed proudly through the frosty panes. In its center, a star shone like fine gold.

Kyle looked at the shiny black Chrysler, parked with its right front tire up on the curb, the rear angling out into the street. "Would you like me to straighten that thing out for you, Leah? Somebody might rear-end you like that."

"No, it's fine," Leah frowned. "Not much traffic now."

"Nice jacket." Dave nodded toward the letter jacket.

Kyle tried to suck his stomach in discreetly. "Ain't it though? Mike got it his senior year. Fits me better than my own. I played a little ball myself."

"Guess that's where Mike got his talent."

Kyle's eyes grew suddenly bright. "He was a whole lot better than me." He stared into the distance, a trace of a smile on his face, then snapped out of it. "Hey, what am I thinkin' about! Y'all come on in the house. Darla's been fidgety as a cat all day waitin' for you to show up, Dave."

As they entered the house the warm and spicy aroma of fresh-baked pastries washed over them from the kitchen. Darla wore a red dress and white apron as she bustled about her kitchen, doing her Christmas cooking. The cabinets were laden with pecan, coconut, and pumpkin pies; chocolate and spice cakes; cookies of every shape and size; and a huge bowl of homemade egg nog.

"Come in! Come in!" Darla placed a chocolate pie on the counter and pulled off her oven mitts. She shook hands with Leah and Dave. "It's so nice to meet you, Dave. And Leah, you look just lovely. I finally read your book—cried four or five times. Have a seat. I'll pour us some coffee. Y'all look half-frozen. Excuse this mess. Christmas was always Mike's favorite time of year, and here I am cooking like he was going to be here."

Kyle walked over to his wife while Leah and Dave sat down. Kissing her gently on the cheek, he whispered something in her ear, then took his place at the table.

Darla set the table with delicate china cups decorated with tiny purple violets. Pouring rich, dark coffee into the cups, she asked cheerily, "Well, what can I get for you folks?" The delicate skin around her eyes, bruised by grief, belied the cheerfulness in her voice as she ran through her litany of baked goods.

"I'll have some of that pecan pie," Dave smiled. "Can't get anything like that where I come from."

Leah had the same, while Kyle merely sipped his coffee. After serving the others, Darla joined them with a cup of tea. When the small talk had died of its own weight, Dave spoke up.

"Mike was the best pilot in our squadron." Dave decided not to speak of anything but the last three months of Mike's life. "He was also a man the rest of the flyers looked up to, a born leader. You can be very proud of your son."

Darla touched her eyes with a white lace handkerchief. "Mike was a good boy. He always was. A little high-strung, maybe. But he had a good heart."

Dave had to grope for words as he always did when speaking or writing to the families of men who had lost their lives in battle. "We're always at a loss to understand why some die and some are spared. Paul said that in this world we 'see through a glass darkly.' I guess that's the way it's meant to be. But Jesus made it possible for us to see the ones we lose again one day."

Kyle spoke slowly, staring at the table. "Mike was a different man the last time he came home before . . . He told me he was a Christian. I've never seen him so happy."

Leah felt hot tears rush from her eyes and quickly wiped them away with her hand.

Dave gazed directly at Kyle as he lifted his head, then at Darla. "Your son saved my life. I can never repay that debt, but if there's anything I can ever do for you, all you have to do is ask."

Darla reached across the table and took his hand. "That's kind of you, Dave. Mike told us that you were his best friend. I can't remember him saying that about anyone before, even with all the friends he had growing up here."

Dave found himself suddenly thrust back into the jungles of Guadalcanal. He saw again the blood as it flowed from Mike's wound into the clear waters of the river. Pain gripped his chest like an iron hand. Then he found himself speaking without any intention of doing so. "I don't fear death, but I do hate it so much! For what it robs us of! If Mike had lived, he would have been such a blessing to people. He would have been one of the treasures of Liberty." Dave shook his head slowly. "No sense going on about that though."

Leah placed her hand on Dave's shoulder. "Are you all right?"

Dave took a deep breath and smiled. "I'm fine. I tend to get carried away sometimes."

Darla looked at Dave and Leah while they smiled at each other. "You two certainly make a lovely couple."

Leah felt that Mike's mother had just given them her blessing.

* * *

"Could we make one stop before we go to the hotel?" Leah had decided to let Dave drive after she backed into a telephone pole leaving the Hardin's home.

"Sure thing," David grinned, still chuckling over her ineptness as a driver. "Where to?"

"The football stadium."

David turned toward her. "Are you kidding? It's the dead of winter. And it's freezing out there."

Leah remained silent in the knowledge that David had never refused one of her requests. Two minutes later they pulled into the gravel parking lot of the Liberty High football stadium.

"What now?" David leaned on the steering wheel with both arms. The engine purred like a big cat.

"We go inside."

David got out, walked around the car, and opened the door for her. "I hope you don't turn out to be one of those crazy writers like Hemingway."

"What do you mean?" Leah took his hand, stepping out into the heavy gravel.

"Surely you've read about his exploits. Looking for death in the streets of Pamplona when they run the bulls or on the horns of a Cape buffalo in Africa."

"What's that got to do with me?"

"Apparently you've chosen to freeze to death in a high school football stadium," David grinned. "And the sad part is I'm tagging right along with you, like Gabby Hayes after Roy Rogers."

Leah took his arm as they walked toward the stadium. "I think you've spent too much time out in that hot tropical sun without a hat, David Stone."

Her heels clicked on the wooden steps that led up into the

stadium. She walked along with David next to the railing that looked down on the sidelines. Above them, the empty benches rose toward the dark vault of the heavens. Faint light from the nearby houses and streetlights cast murky shadows about the empty and silent winter stadium, settling down to wait for September.

Leah sat down at the fifty yard line on the first row. David stepped to the rail, leaning on it with one hand as he looked out over the playing field.

"I never saw him play."

David turned to look at her.

"My parents wouldn't let me go to football games, or *any* of the after-school activities for that matter." Leah stared into his face, his eyes catching the faintest glimmer of light.

"I never did either. Meant to catch one of the Georgia Tech games, but somehow didn't make it." David began to feel an uneasy prickling at the back of his neck. *Maybe it's just the cold.* "He was a fine athlete though. Fast as a deer. If he hadn't been, I wouldn't be standing here right now."

"I've seen him play in my mind," Leah continued. "From all that people told me and from the pictures in newspapers and the school yearbook, I could see exactly what he looked like running the ball for a touchdown."

David turned back toward the field. *Even in death, she still loves him. I could never be what Mike was.*

Leah got up and stood next to him. "I just had to see where he played. I don't know why, David. This feeling just came over me after we left his parents' house. I hope you don't mind."

"Of course not." He tried to smile, but he felt that his brain would no longer carry the message to his mouth.

Leah looked down on the field. The yard lines were barely visible, the ground still torn and wounded by the cleats of the players. She knew it would heal in the springtime. *Healing comes in another season!* The words came to her like a song. "I love you very much, David Stone."

David had steeled himself for a farewell speech. Now her words were like something he had created for her to say—words he would never hear. He turned toward her, a stunned look on his face.

"You're the kindest, most gentle man I've ever known." Leah's emotions were in her smile as much as her words.

Still David was speechless.

"Let's go—wherever you want." She spoke for him, taking his arm. *Such a lovely, gentle man.*

At the end of the field, Leah stopped for a final look. She could almost see Mike standing in the end zone, helmet hanging loosely in one hand, his dark hair tousled and gleaming with sweat. The same sweet feeling stirred in her breast as she turned to walk away with David.